POTION MASTERS

THE TRANSPARENCY TONIC

POTION MASTERS SERIES

The Eternity Elixir

FRANK L. COLE

SHADOW
MOUNTAIN

For Jennifer and her story about Blip,
which may have just started it all.

Text © 2019 Frank L. Cole

Illustrations © 2019 Owen Richardson

Visit us at shadowmountain.com

Library of Congress Cataloging-in-Publication Data

Names: Cole, Frank, 1977– author. | Cole, Frank, 1977– Potion masters ; bk. 2.

Title: The transparency tonic / Frank L. Cole.

Description: Salt Lake City, Utah : Shadow Mountain, [2019] | Series: Potion masters ; book 2 | Summary: The secrets of the potion-making world are at stake when Gordy has to unravel a mystery at B.R.E.W. headquarters and defeat the threat of a powerful new group of potion masters.

Identifiers: LCCN 2018016729 | ISBN 9781629724881 (hardbound : alk. paper)

Subjects: | CYAC: Magic—Fiction. | Magicians—Fiction. | LCGFT: Fantasy fiction.

Classification: LCC PZ7.C673435 Tr 2017 | DDC [Fic]—dc23

LC record available at https://lccn.loc.gov/2018016729

Printed in the United States of America

Lake Book Manufacturing, Inc., Melrose Park, IL

10   9   8   7   6   5   4   3   2   1

1

Gordy Stitser knelt in the forest behind his house and removed a flask filled with deep-indigo liquid from a shoebox. Three other identical containers rested in the box, each separated by a thick wedge of spongy cotton. Gordy covered the remaining flasks with the cardboard lid and set the box aside.

The ground was still damp, and the trees drooped under the sag of last night's rain. Exhaust from a garbage truck driving down the street saturated the air. Gordy squinted as the noisy vehicle lumbered past the trees as it tossed and dropped garbage bins haphazardly. He saw a school bus as well and could hear the faint, chattering voices of kids as they boarded. Checking his phone, Gordy noted he had about ten minutes until he had to be in the driveway to catch his ride for his first day of eighth grade. Enough time to test out his newest concoction, if he hurried.

Gordy unscrewed the metal lid from the flask, and miniature fissures of sparkling light ignited within the potion. He held the container close to his nostrils and inhaled the fumes. The mixture smelled right. Pungent, purple, and with just a hint of Siberian salamander slime. Gordy stood and glanced toward the edge of his backyard and beyond that to the pink-bricked building that the Stitsers had called home for the past nine months—ever since their last house went up in a violent potion explosion. He saw no signs of his parents anywhere, and the fourth-grade twins had already been bussed away to school. Normally, Gordy's mom wouldn't have thrown a fit to see him testing out his potions in the forest. As a Dram, better known as an Elixirist-in-training, he had to practice, and the wooded area provided the perfect amount of privacy from prying eyes.

But this wasn't a normal potion. Gordy had brewed it the night before in the family laboratory, using several ingredients on his mother's "Only Use in an Emergency" list. The salamander slime was particularly difficult to come by. But this *was* an emergency—kind of. The Stitsers may not have been under a direct threat from an enemy at the moment, but that could change. Gordy needed to be prepared.

Gordy's leg suddenly buzzed, and he fished his phone out from his pocket.

"What's up, Max?" Gordy asked, pressing the phone to his ear.

"Dude, I can't see anything," Max said.

Gordy pulled the phone back. "You FaceTimed me?"

"Of course!" Max grinned. His round face, distorted

from being too close to the screen, resembled a freckled volleyball with bushy eyebrows.

"Why?" Gordy asked, checking the purple potion to ensure the mixture hadn't settled back to dormancy.

"Because I knew you were about to test out Trapper Keeper, and I wanted to see."

Gordy scrunched his nose. "'Trapper Keeper'? That's what you're calling it? That's a dumb name."

"It's an awesome name! Show it to me," Max demanded.

Gordy sighed and pointed the phone toward the flask. Max whooped excitedly.

Gordy started to smile, but then stopped in an instant. "Wait a minute. Are you on the bus right now?"

"Oh yeah," Max said. "Smells like death! Wish you were here." He laughed.

"You know I can't ride the bus to school anymore. I've told you that at least a hundred times. And I'm hanging up. You're breaking the most important rule. If anyone finds out what I'm doing—"

Max rolled his eyes. "Dude! I'm all the way at the back of this rolling metal prison and no one cares. It's the first day of school, and the whole bus is filled with seventh-graders." Max craned his neck. "All these minions, sitting with their heads down, fearing the day of reckoning of junior high." He cackled.

"Where's Adilene?" Gordy asked.

"How should I know? She's probably getting a ride too. But quit stalling. Let's see what our little masterpiece can do."

"*Our* little masterpiece?" Gordy considered hanging up. His best friend, Max Pinkerman, was anything but discreet. He shouldn't have been allowed to brew this potion with Gordy last night, but Gordy's dad had been preoccupied on the phone, settling some dishwasher dispute, and Gordy's mom had been working late in her office at B.R.E.W. Headquarters. At least, that's what she told everyone. Lately, Gordy's mom had been acting strange, and he wasn't sure why.

"Hey, I chopped up those . . . seeds and stuff," Max muttered. "And if you were to ride the bus with me and some dark potion lords showed up trying to mess with you, I'd have your back. You know that, right?"

Gordy groaned. Max couldn't keep talking about the potion community like that out in the open. Maybe Gordy would have to administer a heavy forgetful elixir, just in case. "You need to zip it, okay? I don't care if you think no one is paying attention. Someone might be listening."

"You're right," Max said. "And I'll zip my lip as soon as you carry on with the demonstration."

"Okay, fine."

Gordy stared down at the target, a two-foot-tall stuffed elephant, resting on a cleared-off patch of ground ten yards away beneath a towering dogwood tree. For just a moment, Gordy felt a twinge of regret about what he was about to do. He had won the elephant at a fair several years ago and had kept it in his room ever since. Gordy used to cuddle the floppy thing whenever he freaked out about some odd noise he had heard in the house, and it was one of the only toys that had survived the house fire. But he was entering the eighth grade, which meant no more stuffed animals.

Covering the mouth of the flask with his thumb, Gordy shook the bottle, agitating the liquid. More lightning bolts cut through the thick goop. A high-pitched squeal escaped Max's lips as Gordy chucked the bottle.

Glass shattered at the elephant's feet, and a dense cloud of smoke mushroomed up from the spot where the potion connected. Gordy shielded his eyes, and when he looked again, the stuffed elephant had vanished.

"That's what I'm talking about!" Max cheered.

Gordy approached the bare patch of ground where the animal once stood.

"Well, I'm not sure it will work exactly the same on a person, but it will stop them for sure. I'd call the Trapper Keeper a success." Gordy stepped on the dirt. It felt firm and solid, almost like stone.

"The name's warming up to you, isn't it?" Max asked.

The guttural roar of a car engine sounded from the driveway at the front of the house. Gordy jumped and spun around. It wasn't a normal vehicle noise by any stretch of the imagination and resembled the sound a lion might make right before it pounced on an unsuspecting gazelle, mixed in with the subtle machinery tone of a backhoe.

"I have to go," Gordy said.

"Wait, just let me see—" Max pleaded, but Gordy ended the call before he could finish.

Bolter Farina sat cross-legged on the hood of a faded orange Buick with flaking, gray racing stripes painted along the sides. Bolter had dark skin and long black hair parted evenly down the middle of his head. He riffled through the pages of an automotive magazine dated from the 1970s with the use of two fingerless nubs.

"Whoa! Where did you get this?" Gordy asked, nodding at the vehicle. Sputtering, the car filled the air with explosive bursts of white smoke from the exhaust. "Did you paint it yourself?"

Bolter raised his eyebrows and smiled, but before he could reply, the car lurched forward almost a foot, narrowly missing Gordy's leg with the bumper.

"Hey, who's driving?" Gordy asked, stepping back and laughing in surprise.

"That's not very nice!" Bolter shouted, swatting the side of the car with the rolled-up magazine. "Sorry, Gordy. She can be slightly temperamental in the morning."

"Who can be slightly temperamental?" Gordy approached the driver's side but couldn't see anyone inside.

Suddenly the Buick's horn erupted with a shrill, ear-piercing blare. Gordy leaped back from the door, hands shooting up to shield his head. The engine roared again, rumbling with a sound that almost resembled the gurgled snarl of a large cat.

"You're not going to make many friends with that behavior, Estelle." Bolter wedged the rolled-up magazine under his armpit, unfolded his long, narrow legs, and hopped down from the hood. "Gordy's just a curious boy asking curious questions, and he's our friend. He even complimented your paint job."

The car made another sound, different from before, a cacophony of buckling metal and twisting plastic.

Bolter frowned. "I'd move if I were you, Gordy." He pulled Gordy out of the way as the Buick continued to produce the unsettling noise. Then the car shuddered and vomited out an oily mass of mesh and wire from beneath the hood.

Gordy's mouth dropped open, and he gawked at the metal lump lying in the driveway.

"This is why you need to control your emotions, Estelle," Bolter said. "You get worked up over the silliest of things."

"Is your car . . . part cat?" Gordy's face contorted with confusion.

Bolter's head bobbled from side to side. "Yes, but just a very small part. The essence, really. It's a new fusion potion

I've been perfecting over the past few months. Estelle is prototype G. I won't bore you with the details of the failures of prototypes A through F, but they were disastrous."

Upon closer examination, the Buick did in fact possess feline features. The headlamps were slanted with an inquisitive expression, and two sections on either side of the roof had been crimped in a way that made it look like pointed ears poking up above the windshield. Even the interior looked oddly like cat fur.

"Where's the actual cat?" Gordy demanded, eyes widening. "You're not keeping it under the hood, are you?" He squinted, trying to see if he could identify any signs of a poor, trapped cat tied up beneath it. Perhaps one running on a large hamster wheel. Animal-rights activists would have passed out had they known about Bolter's experiment.

"Oh, my word, no, no, no! Of course not." Bolter playfully shoved Gordy's shoulder. "How absurd. *Essence*, Gordy. It's just the animal's essence. That's all."

"How do you get the animal's essence?" Gordy asked, curious, but also slightly disturbed. Bolter was an unusual Elixirist who specialized in automotive potions and had been known to imbue all manner of mixtures within his vehicles. But this latest creation was definitely his most bizarre.

Bolter waved a fingerless hand in the air dismissively. "It's simple. Just saliva and fur, and maybe a claw or two. It's nothing the cat misses, I assure you. My work has all been sanctioned by B.R.E.W., so no need to raise the alarm."

B.R.E.W., or the Board of Ruling Elixirists Worldwide, was where Bolter worked, along with Gordy's mom and hundreds of other highly skilled Elixirists. B.R.E.W. monitored the potion-making community across the continent as well as in many places overseas. And they had their fingers dabbling in almost every area of society: medical, military, and, for Bolter, machinery.

"I do believe the clock is ticking away. The first day of eighth grade waits for no one." Bolter extended his hand toward the passenger side of the Buick. "Your chariot awaits."

Gordy blinked. "You expect me to ride to school in that?"

"You can't very well walk, now can you? There's too much at risk. Oh, don't be so worried," Bolter said when he noticed Gordy's reluctance. "Where's the Gordy Stitser, young man of adventure?"

"I guess it's fine." Gordy cautiously stepped around the front of the car. "But I think I'm allergic to cats."

Bolter nodded. "Aha! Me too! But don't worry. I've brought drops." He dug into his pocket and produced a tiny, clear bottle of eye drops.

The cat car produced a low, threatening rumble, its headlamp eyes seeming to narrow even more at the prospect of allowing Gordy as a passenger. He wondered if Estelle could bite. Then he wondered how it would accomplish such a feat. Lastly, he wondered if he would even survive the trip to school.

"When she purrs, the seats vibrate." Bolter patted the dashboard enthusiastically, strapping on his seat belt.

Gordy carefully opened the door and sat down next to him. Estelle's growling continued.

"It's like a massage chair!" Bolter shouted over the escalating volume. "I daresay Estelle provides the loveliest ride you'll ever experience. Once she warms up to you, of course. You wouldn't happen to have a mechanical mouse hiding in your backpack, would you?"

Gordy's seat lurched forward a few inches underneath him, and he worried that Estelle might launch him through the windshield.

"Oh well." Bolter shrugged. "I'm sure it will be just fine. Buckle up and cross your fingers. I don't have any." He held up his hands as a reminder of the absence of any digits and laughed maniacally.

Large sheets of colored paper decorated with hand-written messages plastered the mottled green walls of Kipland Middle School.

Welcome Back to School, Kipland Knights!
Bullying Is Not Cool! Be a Knight in Shining Armor!

Gordy skimmed the messages indifferently as he filed in through the double doors along with at least a hundred other students. Folding tables lined the hallway, where several members of the faculty sat, encouraging students to sign up for a variety of programs. Gordy avoided the tables. Not that he wouldn't have minded some extracurricular activities, but he was too busy brewing potions.

Outside, Gordy heard the screech of tires as Estelle made a less-than-discreet exit from the parking lot. Gordy cringed, feeling as though a thousand pairs of eyes were suddenly looking at the back of his head.

"You ready for this, Gordy?" Adilene Rivera sidled up next to him and nudged him gently with her shoulder.

"Ready for what?" Gordy ducked beneath a low-hanging banner announcing a back-to-school dance on Friday night.

"The eighth grade," Adilene said. "We're so old. Look at all of them." Her voice took on a squealing tone as she gestured to a group of seventh-graders gathering outside the office where the assistant principal, Mr. Hapsburg, barked instructions. "They're so little!"

So little? Gordy smirked. He wished that were the case. Most of the seventh-graders looked as though they had ingested growing potions over the summer. A couple of the boys had actual facial hair. Gordy instinctively dragged his fingers over the smooth surface of his chin. Oh well. There was always next year, though if he really wanted to, he could mix up something in the lab to remedy the situation.

"I just want to go over there and put my arms around them and tell them it's going to be all right. Don't you?" Adilene asked.

Gordy snorted. "No! They're just entering the seventh grade. They're not going to war."

Adilene had done something different with her hair, and it fell about her face in round curls. And was that makeup? Gordy had never seen her wear makeup before, but he was almost certain she had applied some sort of lip gloss and eye shadow. She may have been one of Gordy's best friends, but he wouldn't dare mention the makeup. Not in a million years.

"Do you have your class schedule?" she asked.

Gordy pulled a folded piece of paper from his pocket and handed it to her. Adilene scanned the document and clicked her tongue disapprovingly. "All we have together is geometry."

"At least we have that. Max and I don't share a single class all semester."

Adilene gasped. "Whatever will you do?"

The two of them found Max rummaging through his old locker in the seventh-grade wing.

"What are you doing, Maxwell?" Adilene asked. "You have a new locker this year, remember?"

Max flicked his chin in a greeting at Gordy and then frowned at Adilene. "Yeah, but my combination still works. I'm just checking on a few of my things." The inside of the locker looked like an animal's nest, with every possible inch crammed with papers, tattered binders, and old textbooks.

"Maybe you should clean it out for the next student," Adilene suggested. "That would be a decent thing to do."

"Oh yeah. Good idea." Max pulled what he wanted from the shelf and then slammed the locker door closed, preventing the impending avalanche of last year's past-due homework assignments from escaping. He brandished a frosted fudge brownie wrapped in cellophane at Gordy. "Breakfast? I'll split it with you."

Gordy shook his head and grinned. "How old is that?"

"Don't know. Didn't ask." Max stuffed the brownie into his mouth, and Adilene groaned. "So, check it out. Word on the street is Mr. Pugmire took another job at some high school in another state."

"Mr. Pugmire's gone?" Adilene looked worriedly at Gordy, who shrugged with equal surprise.

"Yep. We have a new principal, some guy named Brexil." Max looked over his shoulder, then lowered his head secretively. "And he's got a daughter in the eighth grade. Her name's Sasha." He whispered the name mysteriously.

Adilene folded her arms. "And you discovered all this in the five minutes of time you've been here in the hallway?"

"Uh-huh." Max wadded up the cellophane wrapper and crammed it through the slot in his old locker. "Word travels fast if you know where to listen. And get this, I heard Sasha was asking about you." He pointed a fudge-coated finger at Gordy.

"Me?" Up until that point, Gordy hadn't been too interested in the conversation, his thoughts lingering on his uncomfortable ride to school, seated in the passenger seat of Estelle. Sure, Mr. Pugmire was a nice enough guy, but he was the principal. Gordy had had almost zero interaction with the man all of last year, other than at pep rallies or occasionally hearing his voice over the intercom. "Why was Sasha asking about me?"

"Not a clue. Anyways, I got to sign up for wrestling. You coming?"

Gordy raised an eyebrow. "Wrestling? You can't be serious."

"I told you I was going to. After last fall, when I tackled all those bad dudes almost by myself, I took it as a sign."

"You had a third arm from Gordy's potion," Adilene said, glaring at him. "You won't have that anymore."

Max shrugged and flexed his muscles. "Whatever. I guess I'll see you around the hallways. Catch you on the flip side." Max waggled his eyebrows, stuck his tongue out at Adilene, and huffed away down the hallway.

"He's so . . ." Adilene sighed. "What's the word? *Absurdo.*"

"Yes, he is." The first bell rang with the five-minute warning, and Gordy and Adilene walked hurriedly toward their homeroom in the eighth-grade wing.

"So, are we both still meeting you this Friday afternoon?" Adilene asked, winking.

Gordy nodded. "Yep. Training begins, and I need my lab partners."

Adilene practically hopped out of her shoes, collapsing upon Gordy with a massive hug. "This is going to be the best year ever!"

"Okay, okay, calm down," Gordy said, laughing, but staring awkwardly around at the people whispering and watching them embrace in the hallway. "People are going to get the wrong idea."

"I'm sorry! I just can't believe how lucky I am to have such a great friend like you."

Eighth grade was more than just the start of a new school year for Gordy. It was also the beginning of his formal Elixirist training at B.R.E.W. Every other Friday afternoon, directly following class, he and his two lab partners, Max and Adilene, would meet at B.R.E.W. Headquarters with Gordy's mother as his trainer. There she would teach Gordy how to do all sorts of Elixirist things. Gordy wasn't sure what else there was to learn. He felt he had mastered all the necessary skills, but according to his mom, there was still much more to discover. Gordy was eager to find out.

There were about a dozen new students in Gordy's first-period class, most of whom he didn't recognize. But out of all of them, only one girl locked eyes with Gordy and immediately claimed the desk directly behind his. She was tall, maybe an inch or two taller than Gordy, with braided black hair and dark skin. She wore a green-and-yellow checkered dress, with several jangly bracelets on her wrists, and she carried a small handbag sparkling with rhinestones.

"You're Gordy Stitser, aren't you?" she asked, dropping her purse on her desk with a light thud and leaning close enough to whisper in Gordy's ear. "You don't actually need to answer. I know who you are. My name's Sasha Brexil.

This is my first year at Kipland, but you already guessed that, didn't you?"

"Uh, yeah, I suppose." Gordy hadn't been expecting anyone to hunt him down right at the start of the eighth grade. Who was this girl, other than the principal's daughter?

"So, tell me. Do you like Kipland, or do you feel it's a waste of your time and talents?" Sasha carried an air of authority with her as she spoke. No nonsense, with a distinct chip in her voice. "Personally, I can think of at least a dozen places I'd rather be and not just because it's a lame school. What would you rather be doing, Gordy?"

"How do you know my name?" he asked. Every other student in the classroom appeared to be playing catch-up with friends, asking about summer vacations and comparing class schedules. No one paid Sasha any attention. Which was a good thing—at least, Gordy thought it was. For the moment, it meant he and Sasha were alone with their strange conversation. Maybe that wasn't a good thing.

"That's not all I know," Sasha purred. "I know you live in that pink house in the cul-de-sac, and I know where you lived before that. I know about the gas explosion that wasn't really a gas explosion at all."

Gordy's eyes narrowed. This was rapidly going downhill. How did Sasha know these things? He had never met the girl before in his life. No one, other than Adilene and Max and some important people from B.R.E.W., knew where he lived. There were Distraction and Redirection potions all over the neighborhood. When strangers drove into the cul-de-sac, they saw only an empty lot where the Stitsers' home should have been. And Gordy's mom had worked hard to cover up the disaster of their exploding house in the media, but somehow, Sasha had learned the truth.

"And I know, Gordy Stitser"—Sasha continued, lowering her voice—"that you are a Dram. And a pretty good one at that."

Gordy stiffened as the hairs on his forearms prickled with gooseflesh. It was then that his nostrils took in an odd smell. He wondered how he had missed it earlier. Most kids at Kipland smelled for a variety of reasons, but those scents had never mattered much to Gordy. Beneath the mask of perfume and hair-styling mousse, Gordy caught a whiff of ingredients on Sasha. Potion-making ingredients.

Being able to identify the faint residue of the components of a potion was just one of the many talents he possessed. Pass a bottle under his nose, and Gordy could recite a grocery list of items used to concoct it. But over the past several months, Gordy had also honed his Ciphering skill to the point of being able to recognize when someone had recently brewed. By the smell of things, Sasha Brexil had been in a potion laboratory earlier that morning. Gordy detected barberry, thorn apple seeds, and toasted kernels of a Lebanese sika plant. Someone had been brewing a Polish Fire Rocket, a dangerous potion used for battle. Which could mean only one thing.

Gordy spun around, coming face to face with the dark-eyed Sasha. He nudged his leg against his backpack and tried to remember what protective potions he had stored within the hidden compartments. There were at least two vials of Torpor Tonic for stunning, as well as a small container of Booming Balls. Gordy wasn't sure how he would get away with launching either one of those inside the classroom, but if he didn't have a choice, he would take the risk. Maybe Sasha was in cahoots with Esmeralda Faustus, the dangerous lady who not only attacked B.R.E.W. Headquarters but also destroyed Gordy's home nine months ago. Esmeralda was supposed to be in exile, but he wouldn't put anything past her. Maybe Sasha had been sent as an assassin.

Sasha eyed Gordy's fingers as he inched open the zipper on his backpack, and she puckered her lips. "Relax. You think I'm a threat? Don't be ridiculous. I'm a Dram just like you. There aren't that many of us at this school, and I'm looking for friends."

"I don't even know you." Gordy's fingers hesitated upon the zipper.

"Well, let's change that."

Lightning quick, Sasha whipped out something from her purse, and Gordy recoiled, clamping his eyes tight in case the potion might explode. When it didn't, and he heard Sasha begin to giggle, he opened one eye. She was holding out a card with glittery lettering.

"This is an invitation," she said. "I'm having a small party next Saturday night at my house. I think you should come. There will be others there as well. You know them from school. And we're going to brew all sorts of fun things. Okay?" She pressed the card against Gordy's shoulder. "Just take it, silly!"

He did, slowly, then opened the card and read the address.

487 Harper Hood Lane

He had no idea where that was, and, aside from the handful of birthday parties at Adilene's house, he had never been invited to a party before. Not by a girl. Not by anyone!

Gordy suddenly became aware of the crisp cardstock paper in his hand, and he pinched it between his thumb and forefinger, holding it out like it was a dirty tissue.

"It's not Stained," Sasha whispered. "You're not being Blotched."

"I didn't say it was," Gordy said. But it wouldn't have been the first time someone had tried to Blotch him with a piece of paper.

"You really are a jumpy guy. I can't wait to find out why. Next Saturday. Seven o'clock. Bring your supplies, if you know what I mean. You had better be there." She pushed away from the desk and gathered her things.

"Wait. Uh . . . where are you going?" Gordy asked.

"To class, of course," she responded. "All my classes are honors courses, so I don't spend any time in this hallway. I doubt we bump into each other again." She scanned the room and tossed the handbag strap over her shoulder. Then, with the same air of confidence she had shown when she entered the room, Sasha Brexil made a grand exit.

A piece of ice the size of a shopping mall broke free and plummeted into the Greenland Sea with the sound of echoing cannon fire. The brackish water lapping at the sharp edge of the glacier swelled, the caps of the waves frothy with foam as they fell upon the mainland a few miles to the west. The wind whooshed and howled, the bitter sleet fell in stinging sheets against Mont Forel, but inside his cave, Mezzarix Rook, a wizened old man well into his seventies, with a flowing mane of ratted gray hair, sat in his rocking chair. He blew across the lip of his teacup, humming a tune known only by him.

Doll, Mezzarix's servant, stood several feet away, plunging his bony fingers into a bucket of soapy water and cleaning off the bits of his master's earlier dinner with a scrub brush. Doll didn't speak as he washed the dishes— reanimated skeletons rarely did—but even if he had been an anomaly, it still would have been impossible for him to utter a single word. Doll didn't have a proper head; his original skull had been swapped out and replaced with an egg-shaped stone by Mezzarix a few years prior. So while he couldn't grunt or make any sound as he labored vigorously, he did manage to work the water into a murky lather.

"Not so rough!" Mezzarix straightened in his chair mid-sip, and some of the liquid from his cup dribbled across his suit lapel. "You wouldn't want to chip my only plate now, would you?"

Doll paused for a moment and raised his head toward Mezzarix. The face on the skeleton's once-faceless stone had been recently redrawn, giving Doll an endlessly inquis-itive stare.

Mezzarix leveled his eyes at the creature. "Just be gentle."

Doll looked back down at the dish and resumed clean-ing, but with less vigor, using long, slow strokes with the brush. When he finished, he obediently carried the bucket outside into the swirling snow to dump the dishwater.

Mezzarix carefully laid his teacup and saucer on the table beside him and moved to the counter next to the cave wall, where a chipped, fungus-covered cauldron no bigger than a common soup tureen bubbled with harsh-smelling liquids. A kerosene-fed torch burned the underside of the cauldron, and Mezzarix checked the consistency of the po-tion with a rusted metal spoon. He held the utensil at eye level and frowned as the gloppy mess plopped back into the bowl.

"This won't do," he muttered. What he wouldn't give

for some decent equipment. And he was running danger-ously low on fuel.

Mezzarix turned his attention to two small plastic bags lying next to his workstation, each containing a single strand of hair. One of the hairs was brown, while the other was chartreuse and clearly synthetic. Those two hairs represented Mezzarix's only hope of leaving the Forbidden Zone. Of course, none of it would matter if he couldn't successfully complete a potion that required far more than his rudimen-tary tools and more ingredients than he had access to. He'd been working on it for the past nine months without success.

The sound of footsteps near the mouth of the cave re-turned, and Mezzarix grumbled. "Why are you so noisy today, Doll? I'm going to sew you some shoes. A pair with thick, padded . . ." His voice trailed off as he looked over his shoulder toward the entryway.

Someone stood in the opening of the cave. An actual person with flesh and blood, wearing a warm, woolly coat with a hood.

"So this is where you've been all these years," the man said with a distinct Irish brogue. He pulled the hood back to reveal white hair, as soft and light as chick feathers. "Living the high life with someone to wait on your every need."

Mezzarix rubbed his eyes with his palms in disbelief. "Ravian McFarland? Is that really you?"

"Aye." The man kicked wet snow from his boots. "Wonderful place you've made for yourself here. Quaint and cozy. Much like my mother's old cottage on Inishmore." He moved to one of Mezzarix's bookcases and curiously plucked a leather-bound tome from the shelf and flipped it open.

"I remember your mother," Mezzarix said. "But last I recall, she had earned herself a lifelong banishment."

Ravian grazed a hand across a wispy patch of hair, tucking the strands behind his ear, but the hairs immediately fell back. "Not anymore." After examining a page, he held the book up over his shoulder. "She finally kicked the bucket. Had much use for this?"

Mezzarix narrowed his eyes. "Which one would that be? Ah, *Carditon's Seventh Law of Stone Siphoning.* Actually, that one has come in quite handy as of late. Why are you here?"

Ravian curled his lip and shrugged. "Was in the area and just happened upon your place."

Mezzarix grinned wryly. The wards protecting his Forbidden Zone were powerful, binding him to his cave and, more importantly, shielding him from all outside eyes. No one just stopped in by accident.

Ravian returned Mezzarix's leather book to its spot on the shelf. "And I say to myself, 'What's that light amid the snow?' And then I answer myself, 'Why, there's a nice dry cave over there.'" Ravian's mouth twisted into an unsettling grin. "And with it blowing a hoolie outside, I thought I might go warm myself by that roaring fire. Then, lo and behold, who do I find snoozing in his rocker but none other than Mezzarix Rook, the legendary Scourge of Nations. What are the odds of that?"

At one time, Mezzarix had found Ravian's accent pleasant to the ears, but his patience had run thin, and he was in no mood to be lied to. "Enough of this," he snapped. "You're in a Forbidden Zone. You've probably already set off an alarm, so you haven't got much time. Speak your peace or be gone."

"Did your daughters trigger an alarm when they came here a short while ago?" Ravian asked. "Surely that would've raised a few eyebrows from the higher-ups at B.R.E.W."

Mezzarix cocked his head to one side, studying his strange visitor. How did he know about his daughters' visit? "No, they did not, because they were the ones who bound me here, which gives them special privileges."

"Banished you, now did they?" Ravian clicked his tongue. "Family quarrels are the worst. Goodness knows I've had my share. My boy, Tobias, is full of resentment for me. As I recall, though, I warned you about Wanda and Priscilla's possible intentions to betray you, but did you listen to me?"

"You told me to ExSponge the both of them."

Ravian nodded. "Would've saved you thirteen years of hobbling around this hole. But you needn't worry. I bypassed all those little booby traps you set up along the way to alert you of any B.R.E.W. intruders who might try to sneak up on you, and I waltzed right up to your front door without you knowing." Ravian winked. "Now, how did I do that?"

Mezzarix dragged his dry tongue across his lower lip. "I suppose it was sheer dumb luck."

Ravian laughed heartily. "You might be righter than you know." He rolled back the woolly sleeve of his coat to reveal his bare forearm. "You've seen almost everything, old friend. Every draught and droplet." He took a step closer, and Mezzarix noticed a faint layer of substance coating Ravian's skin. "But you haven't seen this. I guarantee it."

Mezzarix's nostrils flared as he attempted to Decipher the various components of the strange substance. He took in a whiff of air but came up almost empty, only smelling Ravian's body odor and a small inventory of potions concealed within the man's satchel at his side. Those Mezzarix could identify without exerting any effort: a paper packet of Detection Powder, an ampoule of Ogon Oil, and a billfold of sundry ingredients. If the substance on Ravian's arm was a potion, it should have given off a hint of something. But he couldn't sense anything other than a vaguely oily taste on the back of his tongue.

"It's called Silt," Ravian offered. "This gives me the power to be here, for as long as needed, even after it dissolves."

"And this Silt has the ability to tell you where people are hiding as well?" There were potions that could cloak an Elixirist so they could pass beneath a ward undetected, but they were rare and difficult to make and, in most instances, not worth the hassle. Ravian never struck Mezzarix as someone with the patience to brew one of those. But a potion with a built-in tracking device? Mezzarix had never heard of such a thing.

"Oh, my lands, no. But a few months ago, I came across something particularly interesting in the Swigs." Ravian plunged his hand beneath his thick coat and pulled out a gnarled, gray rib bone. "There's no mistaking your handiwork. I sensed great potionery, and, with just the right mixture of sprig and herb, that bone acted as a fine homing device." He tossed the bone to Mezzarix. "I believe it belongs to your friend outside."

Mezzarix hadn't noticed if Doll had been missing any parts, but then again, he had never taken the time to inspect Doll in the first place. Mezzarix stared at the bone with disgust and tossed it aside. Stroking his chin beneath his bedraggled beard, he sat down in his chair as the clickety-clack sound of skeletal feet echoed through the cave.

Doll hefted the empty bucket across the room and then dropped it in the corner, all the while ignoring the stranger standing beside the bookshelves. Doll did, however, take notice of the bone—*his* bone—lying on the ground. Slowly picking it up, he tilted his head toward Mezzarix, as if to ask where it had come from.

"Don't look at me." Mezzarix jutted his chin toward Ravian, and the skeleton swiveled to face the stranger. "Doll used to be more helpful," Mezzarix said dryly. "He would bring me all sorts of wonderful things. That is until my daughters strengthened the wards of my banishment. Now he's more of a nuisance." Doll looked back at his master, his shoulders drooping slightly. "Enough of this talk. Where did you find this Silt?"

"My new friend gave it to me. Just an ampoule. Enough to lead me safely here."

"This friend of yours, did they come along for your evening jog?"

Ravian shook his head. "I'm afraid not. She has a thing against flying in airplanes, and a journey to this miserable rock would've taken ages by boat. Though she remained behind, she's anxiously awaiting my return."

"Well, then I shouldn't delay you any longer." Mezzarix leveled his eyes. "The way out is back the way you came in."

The heavier man started to chuckle. "Oh, I'll go. But I'd like you to come with me."

Mezzarix regarded Ravian with little interest. He had never been one to let anyone ruffle his feathers. "And go where?" he asked. "The weather's not fitting for a hike, and I'm afraid you'll be disappointed with the scenery."

Ravian shook his head. "I have no desire to tour your bleak mountain. I want you to take a short leave of absence from this island so I may introduce you to my friend. She has an interesting proposition—one I know you'll be keen to hear." He flashed his arm again, the Silt faintly glowing upon his skin. "This does more than just sneak you past wards and into the Forbidden Zone. It does many wondrous things. And if you agree to my friend's terms, she'll help free you—permanently."

"Why does she need me?"

"She needs the best of the best. That's why she came to me first, clearly." His eyes twinkled. "And after I ran through a list of people we could recruit for this mission—all of whom, of course, have been dead for many years—I finally remembered my old friend Mezzarix and said to myself, 'That's who we need.' You still know a thing or two about Replication, do you not?"

Mezzarix sighed with annoyance. "I dabble. But, you know, it's like riding a bike."

"Then this will be your finest Replication work of all."

Despite knowing Ravian for many years, Mezzarix had never considered him a friend. He didn't mind doing business with him, but he wasn't someone he could trust. "I take it this Silt can't lift my banishment for me, then, can it?"

Ravian shook his head. "I'm afraid the only thing that can accomplish that is the Vessel. But what if I told you my friend could help us overthrow B.R.E.W. and take the Vessel?"

"I'd say the cold has had an unfortunate side effect on your brain." Mezzarix reclined in his chair and interlocked his fingers behind his head. "How do you propose I follow you?"

"I find it hard to believe that the great Mezzarix Rook, Scourge of Nations, has been stewing in this cave all these years and hasn't come up with a temporary exit strategy.

Surely you've thought about taking a stroll beyond the boundaries."

Ravian crossed the room to the workstation, his nostrils flaring as he sniffed the chemicals in the air. "How you ever concocted a single brew in this place is a testament of your greatness," he said. "I'm sure the two of our minds, melded together, could work out a plan."

Mezzarix sighed and glanced over his shoulder at the malfunctioning potion brewing beneath the kerosene torch, his eyes flashing toward the plastic bags containing a strand of his grandson Gordy's hair and a Replicated copy. "There might be something we can do," he said, the inklings of an idea beginning to form in his mind. "But I'm going to need a lot of special ingredients."

Ravian removed a pad of paper and a pencil from beneath his coat and dabbed the lead tip to his tongue. "Shall we make a list?"

CHAPTER

5

The practice lab at B.R.E.W. Headquarters looked like a normal chemistry classroom, minus the rows of desks and students. There was a blackboard with chalk and an eraser, a bookshelf in one corner of the room with a few books leaning against each other, and a weathered Bunsen burner with a fraying fuel line resting on a center table. In preparation for Gordy's training, his mom had already laid out several ingredients, along with a mid-sized copper cauldron and a row of glass containers.

Upon entering the room, Max dropped his backpack on the floor with a thud. "So, where are all the potions and stuff? Where are all the Elixirists?"

"We passed a whole bunch of Elixirists on the way in," Gordy said, taking extra caution to lower his backpack to the ground. His bag doubled as his potion satchel and needed to be handled with care.

"Seriously?" Adilene asked, her face alight with childish glee. She'd oohed and aahed as they'd passed through the security checkpoints leading up to the enormous hexagonal building. And she'd flashed her temporary visitor's badge to anyone within shouting distance. For Adilene, she just loved being invited along for the ride.

"They have to be Elixirists to work here at B.R.E.W.," Gordy replied.

Max twirled his finger. "Sure. Right. Whatever. When do we start blowing stuff up, Gandalf?" In a way, Gordy felt bad for his best friend. He knew Max had hoped to find wizened old men with beards and robes and carrying staves, but that wasn't the case. Aside from the odd-looking Bolter, most Elixirists looked like everyday office workers. Max should have known that. Nine months ago, he had accompanied Gordy into B.R.E.W. Headquarters in order to save Adilene and her family. Not much had changed since that incident, aside from the extra guards patrolling the grounds.

"Are we ready?" Gordy's mom announced as she stepped into the room and closed the door behind her. She looked tired, but that wasn't new. As Lead Investigator, she often spent days hunting down some of the nastiest Elixirists across the country.

Mrs. Stitser had pulled her light-brown hair back into a bun, and she wore glasses. Gordy hardly ever saw her wear glasses, mostly because she preferred the specially treated contact lenses she had made in their home lab, ones that enhanced her vision and could flash over a hundred different programmed recipes in her line of sight whenever she mixed potions. She also wore dress slacks and a button-up blouse. Her name badge was clasped to a lanyard around her neck. To Gordy, his mom looked oddly professional.

"I think we're ready," Gordy answered. At least, he was as ready as he could be having not known his mom's expectations prior to this afternoon. Over the past couple of months, she had been distant, working long hours on special projects.

"And your lab partners?" She looked down at her clipboard and penciled in a few items on the page. "Are they prepared to assist you?"

"We're ready to do whatever you tell us!" Adilene volunteered enthusiastically.

Gordy grinned as Adilene removed a pad of paper from her backpack and several colored markers for taking notes. On one of the pages she had written Elixirist Training in bright purple ink.

"I still don't understand why we can't do this at your home," Max said. "You have way more ingredients in your lab."

Gordy's mom glanced up from her clipboard and cleared her throat. "Because, as Gordy already knows, a Dram is not allowed to brew questionable potions within the confines of a home laboratory. Only mixtures from B.R.E.W.-approved recipe manuals are permitted."

Gordy raised an eyebrow. Why did his mom sound as though she were reciting a prepared speech? Had that been written on her clipboard? Gordy had never seen the inside of a B.R.E.W.-approved recipe manual. Did they even have any of those in their lab?

Max grinned. "We brew questionable potions all the time, Mrs. Stits."

Gordy had a potion journal filled with semi-dangerous concoctions—most of which his mom didn't know existed. Of course, she could have found out at any time if she wanted, but Mrs. Stitser often turned a blind eye to Gordy's potion making. He liked to think she trusted him.

Gordy's mom returned her attention to the clipboard and made a mark on the page. "In order to advance beyond the level of a Dram, Gordy needs to be observed brewing these approved potions in a sanctioned laboratory." She raised her voice and pointed to the ceiling, where a small, round security camera had been angled in their direction. Then, with her eyes flashing a warning, she silenced Max from pressing the issue any further.

Adilene glanced up from taking notes to look between Max and Mrs. Stitser.

Gordy elbowed Max in the ribs. "Be quiet, dude. You're going to get us all in trouble." The camera meant they were currently under observation, which also meant someone important, probably a high-ranking officer at B.R.E.W., was watching them. If they found out Gordy wasn't following the guidelines for Drams in training, they might prevent him from advancing to the level of an Elixirist.

Max rolled his eyes. "I guess that means we're going to be brewing chicken broth the rest of the afternoon, huh?"

"I don't make the rules; I just follow them," Gordy's mom said, her tone softening. Somewhere in the back of Gordy's mind, he could almost hear his Aunt Priss laughing hysterically at that comment. "Now, Max, if you don't feel up to the task, or if this isn't going to be fun for you, I can make arrangements for someone to take you home. Gordy will do just fine with Adilene. One lab partner is usually the standard, but I've made an exception because of Gordy's insistence."

Max scoffed. "Whatever. Me and Gordy are a team. We're like Bonnie and . . ." He scrunched up his face. "That's a bad example. We're like Frodo and Sam."

"What's that make me?" Adilene asked.

Max curled his lower lip in thought. "You're Gollum."

Had she not been concentrating so intently on writing notes, Adilene might have successfully swatted Max on the back of the head, but she missed.

"Are we done with the interruptions?" Gordy's mom asked with little enthusiasm. "Let's begin."

For the first assignment, Gordy's mom had him Decipher the contents of seven different vials while blindfolded. Adilene and Max stood on either side, ready to pass the containers under his nose, and Gordy's mom pulled out a stopwatch.

Piece of cake, Gordy thought. He didn't know how fast he was supposed to complete the task, but it didn't matter. Gordy was a Cipher. One of the best at detecting any Elixirist ingredient in the vicinity. With the camera watching his every move, Gordy's nostrils expanded as he took in a whiff, and he instantly smelled the residue of at least a dozen ingredients. The average person would never be able to smell such things, but Gordy wasn't exactly average.

Adilene clapped each time Gordy successfully named off the potion and its key ingredients. Gordy's mom made several notations on the clipboard, occasionally glancing up at the camera on the ceiling.

Next, Gordy mixed three potions using only the ingredients provided: a Norwegian Vintreet Trap, a Torpor Tonic, and a container of Boiler's Balm. All standard-issue potions used by Elixirists. Gordy had brewed each of them at least a thousand times and could've mixed them blindfolded as well.

Ten minutes later, three perfectly prepared potions simmered in test tubes. Gordy's mom held up each of the vials to examine their color in the light and then made more markings on her clipboard.

"How much longer do we have?" Max asked, yawning from the other side of the prep table. "Other than sticking bottles under your nose, what good are lab partners anyway?"

Gordy's mom sighed. "When potions become more advanced, an Elixirist's lab partner will have more to do."

"Don't listen to him, Mrs. Stitser," Adilene said. "This is a lot of fun."

Gordy's mom smiled warmly at Adilene and then

nodded at Gordy. "We'll end here for the afternoon because I have more—" She stopped midsentence as a piercing alarm rang out overhead.

Gordy clamped his hands over his ears, as did Max and Adilene, and a red light flashed from a bulb just above the chalkboard. Gordy's mom, however, looked sharply at the door as it opened and a man with short black hair appeared.

"Hoffman, what's going on?" she asked.

Hoffman handed Gordy's mom an electronic tablet. "This is the live security feed. There doesn't appear to be anything on it." He fumbled his words breathlessly. "But the alarm means there might have been a breach."

"A breach?" Max shouted above the roaring alarm. "What's that?"

Hoffman blinked at Max, as though surprised to see the three children gathered behind Mrs. Stitser. He closed his mouth and swallowed, his eyes widening with hesitation. "Um, uh . . . not sure . . ."

"Hoffman!" Wanda bellowed, tapping a code onto the tablet's screen and bringing up the video feed. "Stay focused, and tell me what area was breached."

The volume of Mrs. Stitser's voice snapped Hoffman back to attention, and he gaped at her in shock. "Level Zero," he wheezed. "There was an unauthorized entry into the Vessel room."

6

S tay by the elevator. Do you understand me?" Gordy's mom instructed, glaring sternly at Gordy and Adilene, her eyes lingering on Max longer than the others. "You shouldn't even be on Level Zero, but I don't dare leave you behind."

"I could call my mom," Adilene suggested, her voice squeaking. "She could pick us up and take us home."

The alarm continued to echo through the building, loud and unyielding. Gordy felt a twinge of fear, but that also might have been adrenaline.

"It'll be fine," Gordy's mom said, patting Adilene's shoulder. "I've already spoken to the guard on duty, and nothing seems out of the ordinary. And I've seen the security footage. It's possible it was just a false alarm."

"But it's the Vessel room, Mom!" Gordy blurted.

The Vessel was a silver chalice containing a centuries-old potion that governed B.R.E.W.'s involvement all over the globe. It was the most important potion in existence, and the protective wards surrounding the Vessel room were supposed to be the strongest ever made. No one without permission should have been able to enter the elevator, let alone breach the hallway. If someone took the Vessel, everything would change. Three hundred years of advancement would topple, and the world's most hardened criminals, Scourges that his mom had banished, would suddenly be free. They would exact revenge upon Gordy's family; that much would be for certain.

"The Vessel was moved several weeks ago," his mom said. "If there was indeed an actual breach, it was a failed attempt from the start."

"Moved?" Gordy asked. "Where?"

"I don't know," she replied. "The new Chamber President determined that B.R.E.W. Headquarters was no longer the safest location for the Vessel. I suppose you and I are somewhat to blame for that belief."

"Don't forget about me," Max said, patting his chest. "I was there too!"

Gordy's mom stepped out of the elevator onto the lowest level of B.R.E.W. Headquarters. "Stay," she said, pointing a finger at the floor.

Gordy followed after her but obediently stopped to wait by the elevator doors. Max and Adilene filed out next, and Gordy had to grab Max's collar to keep him from continuing down the hallway. Red lights flashed overhead, but the shrill alarm had finally been shut off.

Gordy noticed something different immediately. Gone

was the familiar glow of the Vessel that usually filled the hallway from beyond the plexiglass windows. A security guard stood at the other end of the corridor, leaning against the wall and massaging his temple with his fingers as Mrs. Stitser approached.

"What happened?" Gordy's mom asked, folding her arms.

"Doesn't make any sense," Gordy heard the guard grumble. "One second I was eating my lunch, the next, lights started flashing and the alarm's blaring."

Gordy dropped to the ground, unzipped his bag, and pulled out a couple of vials.

"What are you doing?" Adilene asked.

"I'm just being cautious." It didn't look like anything was wrong, but Gordy thought it was better to be safe than sorry.

"Pass me Trapper Keeper," Max whispered, holding out his hand demandingly.

Gordy eyed the purple potion in his bag, but he hesitated. Max and vials of dangerous potions didn't always mix. He had a tendency to not listen to instructions, and that could be disastrous. Trapper Keeper hadn't been tested yet on humans, just a stuffed-animal elephant.

"Come on, dude! Don't hold out on me," Max insisted.

Instead of Trapper Keeper, Gordy placed a thin test tube bubbling with yellowish ooze in Max's palm.

"What's this?" Max eyed the potion curiously.

"Don't worry about it." Gordy grabbed himself a

Torpor Tonic and passed Adilene one as well. "You probably won't need it, but if you do, you'll be ready."

"Wait a minute!" Max exploded with anger. "Is this Toe-Itch Sauce? It is! I don't want this. This won't stop criminals in their tracks."

Adilene shushed him, her brow knitting with concern. "The guard just said that the door to the room was opened."

"He did?" Gordy looked up from his bag. He watched as his mom and the guard entered the Vessel room. The door closed behind them, silencing their muffled conversation. Gordy felt the urge to sneak closer so he could hear what they were saying.

"You're going to break that, Max!" Adilene hissed.

Gordy looked over to see Max casually tossing the Toe-Itch Sauce in the air while simultaneously waving his foot between the elevator doors, causing them to open and close jerkily.

Max scoffed, but then fumbled the vial in his fingers, only catching it before it fell.

"You know what? Let me have that back." Gordy had given the potion to Max as a joke, but now he regretted it. If Max broke the bottle, there was enough liquid to cause the trio plenty of discomfort.

"I'll only trade it," Max said. "For Trapper Keeper." He dangled the vial enticingly, but pulled it away when Gordy snatched for it. The elevator door rumbled, but Max stuck out his rear end, preventing it from closing.

"Why are you doing that?" Adilene asked. "What if someone needs to come down here?"

"I'm pretty sure everyone else evacuated the building," Max said. "Besides, what if we need a quick getaway? You'll thank me for not having to wait for the elevator."

And then suddenly Max was on the floor, sprawled out on his back, with a painful "oof." He lost his hold of the Toe-Itch Sauce, and the vial shattered beneath him.

It happened so fast, Gordy and Adilene only had time to look at each other and laugh in shock. Then Max started screaming.

"Why did you shove me, Rivera!" Max bellowed, tearing at his shoes and ripping out the laces. Both of his feet had turned bright pink as red dots began appearing on his toes.

"I didn't shove you," Adilene insisted, covering her mouth to hide her smile.

The elevator door closed, sending the dimly lit hallway into almost complete darkness. Gordy felt his own toes starting to itch, but it was probably just sympathy pains. He didn't think any of the potion had made contact with his skin. The entirety of the vial's liquid had landed on Max.

Max wailed and scratched and thrashed about on the floor. The door to the Vessel room opened, and Gordy's mom charged out, grasping a bottle of something frothy and scarlet.

"What happened?" she demanded, her eyes narrowing with anger.

"Nothing," Gordy said. "Max fell down."

"Shoved!" Max sulked. "Rivera wanted me to suffer."

"I did not," she said with an annoyed sigh.

"So, what's going on?" Gordy nodded toward the guard exiting the Vessel room.

"Everything's fine, just as I suspected," his mom answered. "All right, you three, it's time to go home." She pressed the call button for the elevator, but the door took almost a minute to open. So much for Max's quick getaway plan.

Max gathered up his socks and shoes from the floor and then paused to attack his toes once more with his fingernails. "It feels like there are ants building a colony under my toenails," he whined.

"Well, maybe next time you'll stop fooling around," Gordy said.

Max glared at Gordy and lowered his voice. "I'm not kidding. Someone pushed me."

"I was standing right beside Adilene the whole time. It wasn't her," Gordy said. "And you know I wouldn't push you."

Max just huffed and hugged his shoes close to his chest as he boarded the elevator, barefoot and miserable.

CHAPTER

7

A dilene Rivera stood in her kitchen, sifting flour into a mixing bowl. She sliced cubes of butter and leveled sugar and salt into various measuring containers. She had already whipped up a tantalizing batch of cream-cheese frosting to go on her favorite cupcakes. As an only child, Adilene had most of the house to herself on Saturdays, which was great if she had things to do, like baking or homework or—well, that was it. Mostly she found herself bored by the lack of activities to keep her occupied.

Now, if she were a Dram like Gordy, Adilene knew exactly where she would be for the rest of the weekend—brewing in the family lab. But she didn't have a lab, and she wasn't a Dram. At least she hadn't shown any signs of becoming one. According to Gordy's mom, the ability to concoct rarely manifested itself in someone already in their teens, and Adilene had turned thirteen two months ago. Most kids showed signs of the potion-making ability when they were still quite young. Adilene wanted badly to mix and create, and a big part of her was jealous of Gordy's exciting life.

The preheated signal chimed, and Adilene slid her cupcake pans into the warm oven and closed the door. In eighteen minutes, she would be enjoying a tasty treat.

"Now what?" she grumbled to herself. She didn't have any homework, and her mom and dad would be at the farmers market until the afternoon. They sold El Salvadorian delicacies, such as *pupusas* and *pastelitos*, and this was one of their last opportunities before the market closed for the fall.

Through the window above the kitchen sink, Adilene noticed a blue pickup truck pull into the driveway across the street. The Stitsers had lived in that house for years until a madwoman burned it down. Now, it was just a shell of blackened walls and moldering wood. There was even a large hole in the roof where smoke still poofed out on occasion. Over the past seven years, Adilene had spent quite a lot of time in Gordy's living room. They'd watched movies together and played games. It wasn't until last year that she'd finally seen the other room in the house, the most important one, when Mrs. Stitser allowed Gordy to show her the family lab, and Adilene's life had changed forever.

An older, gray-haired gentleman stepped down from the truck and walked into the yard.

Adilene pushed her palms onto the counter to hoist

her body up so she could see better through the window. "What's he doing?"

The man didn't move much. He just stood on the lawn, staring up at the charred remains of the house. Adilene supposed he could have been a construction foreman. Maybe he was checking a few things before scheduling the house for demolition, which was way past due. Then, to Adilene's utter astonishment, the man walked over and pulled on the wooden slat that boarded up the window into the Stitsers' old living room.

"Hey!" Adilene smacked the window, but the stranger couldn't hear her. Too curious to wait around wondering, Adilene wiped her hands on a towel and then hurried out the front door.

She trotted across her yard and into the street. Even though the Stitsers had moved, it seemed impolite to rummage through their previous property without an invitation. Did this man have an invitation? Adilene didn't think so.

"Hey. Did you know the people that used to live there?" Adilene asked.

The man turned abruptly and looked at her, but he didn't say anything.

Adilene shivered, but not because of the cold; it was late August, and the breeze felt warm and pleasant. But she didn't like the way he stood there, wearing a distant expression, as though looking past her at some unseen object in the road.

"They were my friends," Adilene explained. "There was

a gas explosion, but everyone's fine. That's why they had to move. Are you with a construction crew?"

The man opened his mouth and gasped, his eyes bulging, his cheeks puffing out like a goldfish.

"Are you choking?" Adilene took a couple of steps toward him, fearing that she might have to perform the Heimlich maneuver. He was so tall! How would she ever be able to help him?

"My uncle doesn't say much."

Adilene looked to her right and saw a young girl standing at the edge of the driveway. She must have been hiding, because Adilene hadn't noticed anyone else inside the truck earlier. The girl wore a yellow-striped dress, and her light-blonde hair swished and swayed in the breeze.

"He doesn't say anything, actually," the girl added. "He has a condition where he can't make words."

Embarrassed, the man looked away, back toward the house.

"He's your uncle?" Adilene felt weird standing in the center of the road, but she wasn't ready to commit to crossing over completely.

The girl nodded. "His name's Uncle Carlisle. My name's Cadence. What's your name?"

"Adilene," she answered. "What was he doing by the window?"

Where she had been politely skirting the question with odd Uncle Carlisle, Adilene felt no reservations about getting right to the point with this girl. Cadence was definitely the same age as Adilene, maybe even a year younger.

Cadence's smile faltered slightly. "Nothing, he was . . . he was just looking around."

"Well, he shouldn't." Adilene folded her arms and watched Cadence's uncle suspiciously. "That house burned. It's unsafe to go inside."

"Where are you from?" Cadence asked.

Adilene raised an eyebrow and pointed to her house behind her. She knew what this girl was doing. *Don't try to change the subject.*

"No, I didn't mean that. You have a really nice accent."

"Oh." Adilene studied Cadence for a moment and then decided it was probably safe enough to move all the way across the street. "I was born in El Salvador, but my family moved here when I was six. I still have a bit of an accent, but I speak English."

"Yeah, I can tell," Cadence replied. Along with her yellow-striped dress, Cadence also wore scuffed running shoes with Velcro straps. "I heard you say that you knew the family that lived here before the fire?"

"I still do," Adilene said. "Gordy's my best friend."

"Where did they move to?" Cadence asked.

"They moved . . . well," Adilene hesitated. Cadence watched her, patiently waiting for an answer. "Across town." She noticed something about Cadence that she hadn't before. Dangling from straps at her waist was a small leather bag. It might have been a purse, but Adilene could see what looked like the wax-filled tip of a tiny glass vial poking out of one of the pockets. She gasped and covered her mouth.

Cadence noticed her reaction and followed her gaze down to her leather bag. "Ah, that's just . . ." She tucked the vial deeper into its pocket with her thumb.

"You're an Elixirist!" Adilene whispered. "Aren't you?"

Cadence looked down one side of the street and then up the other. "No, I'm not," she whispered back, but her grin stretched wide.

"Yes, you are! That's a potion, isn't it?"

Cadence pressed her finger to her lips and shushed Adilene. "You really shouldn't talk about this out in the open, you know."

Adilene frowned. "You're right! We're not supposed to draw any unnecessary attention to the Community." She could remember the parchment posted in Gordy's lab listing the Five Rules of Potion Making. If she wasn't careful, Adilene might break rule number one. But the other girl didn't seem offended.

Adilene smiled. Another Elixirist. Just like Gordy, with potions and a satchel and a knowledge of all things mysterious.

"Do you go to school at Kipland?" Adilene didn't recognize her from the hallways, but Kipland was a big school with loads of kids. Maybe Gordy knew who she was. He knew all the other Drams.

"No, I go to school somewhere else," Cadence answered. "I'm just visiting my uncle for a little while."

Adilene suddenly heard a faint piercing sound. Looking around, trying to locate the source of the noise, Adilene's eyes suddenly widened. "My cupcakes!" she said. "I have to go."

"It was nice meeting you," Cadence said.

"Yeah, you too." Adilene turned to hurry away, but paused in the street. "Hey, do you want to come over and have a cupcake? They're strawberry with cream-cheese frosting."

After a brief pause, Cadence nodded. "Yes, that would be wonderful." She joined Adilene in the road, walking toward the house.

"Shouldn't you see if it's okay with your uncle?" Adilene asked.

Cadence looked back as Uncle Carlisle glanced in their direction, his mouth tight-lipped, his expression unreadable. "He doesn't care if I go."

Adilene had many more questions to ask, but the oven wouldn't shut itself off on its own, so she picked up her pace.

———

A centerpiece of piled cupcakes separated the two girls at the kitchen table. The slathered-on cream-cheese frosting made the cupcakes—browner than Adilene would have liked—all the more appetizing. Soon, both girls sat peeling the wrappers and giggling as they ate.

"Where do you keep your lab?" Cadence asked between gulps of her glass of milk.

"My lab?" Adilene looked down at the table, embarrassed. She hadn't told Cadence that she wasn't a Dram. "I don't have a lab."

Cadence appeared confused. "But . . ."

"I'm not an Elixirist," Adilene interjected. "I should have told you outside. I just know a lot about the Community, and I'm friends with Gordy, so, you know, if you want to leave, you can. I won't feel bad."

"Why would I leave?" Cadence selected another cupcake from the pile and prized off the wrapper with her finger.

"Well, I kind of lied to you. I made you think I was a potion master, when I'm really not."

"That doesn't bother me," Cadence said.

Adilene breathed a sigh of relief. "I really wish I could make potions like you guys. I just don't have the gift. And I guess I never will. Do you want to watch a movie or something?" Adilene asked. "We could go to my room, and I can show you my books and things."

Cadence started to nod when a low rumble rose up from beneath the table. Adilene peered beneath the tablecloth.

"What's the matter, Hercules?" she asked. Normally docile, the Riveras' beagle rarely made more than an occasional peep. In response to Adilene's question, though,

Hercules barked loudly, and both girls jumped. The dog scrambled out from beneath the table and stood at the front door, snarling. Adilene flinched. What had gotten into Hercules? She walked up next to him and peered out through the narrow side window.

Uncle Carlisle stood on the porch facing the road, his back to the door.

Adilene gasped and leaped back in surprise. "Your, um . . . It's your uncle," she said.

"I need to go," Cadence answered. "It's been really great to meet you, and these were delicious cupcakes. Maybe I could stop by some other time?"

"Yeah, sure," Adilene said.

Cadence returned to the truck with her uncle and drove away. Slightly confused, Adilene watched them leave the neighborhood. Then her eyes drifted back toward Gordy's old house—to where the front door had been left open just a crack.

CHAPTER

8

The following Wednesday, Gordy fiddled with the combination of his locker. A wave of students bustled past, hardly paying him any attention, but Gordy didn't want them to notice what he was doing, because that might make them suspicious.

Pressing his thumb to the center of the combo lock, Gordy nonchalantly looked over his shoulder as his Fingerprint Recognition Rub, a concoction he had brewed up himself, went to work. The dial spun on its own, engaging the correct combination before opening the locker with a soft click. Most of the potions he made were one-time jobbers. They had to be tossed or poured or consumed, and the results were instant. Gordy had never made a lingering potion that operated on something with moving parts like his combo lock. Maybe he had a future in Machinery working alongside Bolter.

He had enough things swimming around in his brain right now without adding a locker combination as well.

For starters, he hadn't had more than a one- or two-word conversation with his mom in several days. She had been too swamped with work. And when she was home, Mrs. Stitser spent most of her evenings reviewing the security footage on her electronic tablet from the supposed breach at B.R.E.W. She wouldn't even look up or shoo Gordy away when he entered her bedroom and watched the video over her shoulder.

"Excuse me, may I have a word?"

Gordy jumped sideways into the lockers, and a deafening clatter filled the hallways. Dozens of his classmates spun around, gawking at Gordy in shock.

"Whoa, easy. I didn't mean to startle you, son." A dark-skinned gentleman with graying hair and wearing a navy-blue blazer reached out to steady Gordy. "You're Gordy Stitser, correct? I'm Mr. Brexil," he said, nodding as if trying to coax recognition from Gordy. "I'm the principal."

Gordy opened his mouth, but other than a big mess of strange sounds, no words came out. Had he not been hugging his backpack so close to his chest, he might have dropped it. That would have been bad. Shattering all those vials together at once could possibly turn the hallway into a river of volatile chemicals.

"I'm assuming you know who I am?" Mr. Brexil's eyes seemed kind, but he expected an answer.

Gordy found his voice. "Oh, yeah, hi."

"I think you know my daughter, Sasha. At least, she

spoke highly of you." Mr. Brexil clasped Gordy's hand and shook it.

Gordy's fingers went limp. *Get a hold of yourself!* he thought. He tried to nod, but he could only blink in response.

"This is probably not the best place to have a conversation, out here in the hallway." Mr. Brexil smiled at a few students hurrying past. "Perhaps you could stop by my office this afternoon before you head home. There's something I'd like to discuss with you."

"Discuss what?" Gordy had never been to the principal's office, not counting that one time he had poured Fuzzing Foam into the drinking fountain during the fourth grade. Half his classmates had sprouted a coating of fur on their tongues and had to be picked up by their parents. The prank had been Max's idea, but Gordy had concocted the potion. But he didn't get in any trouble. The principal had just asked him whether or not he had noticed anything peculiar in the hallway that day.

"Not now," Mr. Brexil said, keeping his eyes fixed on Gordy's. "We'll talk later."

⌒

"What does he want to talk about?" Max asked, trailing behind Gordy as they wove their way through the throngs of students.

"I told you already. I don't know," Gordy answered.

What a crummy start to the eighth grade! The whole

day had flown by in a blur. Gordy had been unable to focus on any subject, which meant he had to cram several pages of homework, which he had no clue how to complete, in his already-stuffed-to-the-brim backpack. He had too many things to worry about: Mr. Brexil's topic of discussion, Sasha's party invitation—

Gordy skittered to a halt. "That's it!"

"What's it?" Max asked, plowing into his back.

"The party." He snapped his fingers. "He probably just wants to talk to me about coming over to his house."

"What are you rambling on about? What party?" Max raised his eyebrow and then gripped Gordy's shoulder for balance as he dug his heel into the top of his other foot, scratching furiously. The effects of the Toe-Itch Sauce should have faded by now, but Max didn't act that way.

"Sasha's a Dram," Gordy said, lowering his voice. "She's invited me to a brewing party this Saturday night."

"What?" Max started laughing. "She's an Elixirist?"

"Shut up!" Gordy dove forward and clamped his hand over Max's mouth.

"Why didn't you tell me?" Max's voice sounded muffled beneath Gordy's palm. When Gordy didn't remove his hand right away, Max licked him.

"Ah, come on!" Gordy wiped the spit off on his pants. "There's lots of stuff I haven't told you yet, but I was planning on it. Things just got crazy, that's all." He honestly didn't know why he had kept Sasha's party a secret. He had meant to tell Max and Adilene, but between the excitement from the incident at B.R.E.W. and the fact that Gordy rarely saw his friends at school because of their schedules, he had forgotten all about it.

"*¡Sacapuntas!*" Max exclaimed in his best Hispanic accent. It was Max's first year taking a foreign language, and he couldn't wait until he learned how to insult Adilene in her native tongue.

"Did you just swear?" Gordy asked in disbelief.

Max nodded confidently, but then shrugged. "Nah. It means 'pencil sharpener.' But it sounds bad, doesn't it?"

"You seriously have problems."

Max rubbed his hands together mischievously. "That's why Sasha was looking for you last week. She can brew. Nice. Hey! Who's all been invited to this soiree?"

Gordy ran his fingers through his hair. "Just the Drams in the school."

"Those goobers? What a boring party."

"Doesn't matter, because I'm not going." Certainly not anymore. If the principal of Kipland wanted to talk to him about going to Sasha's house, no good would come of it.

"Ah, Gordy, I was wondering if you would remember." Mr. Brexil appeared in the doorway of his office, and Gordy, sadly, jumped yet again.

"Twitchy fellow, aren't you?" the principal asked. "And who is this young man?" He squinted down at Max.

Max slid a hand across Gordy's chest and moved him out of the way. "Max Pinkerman," he said, rolling his shoulders. "State wrestling champion."

Mr. Brexil curled his lip, impressed. "I wasn't aware Kipland had a state wrestling champion." He glanced at the secretary behind the desk. Though she was on the phone, having a conversation, she looked up at the principal and shook her head.

"Well, not yet," Max explained. "But I just signed up for the team. I'm gonna bring more bling to this school than ever before."

The principal offered a curt nod. "I'm sure you will. Now, if you don't mind, Max, I need to have a talk with Gordy."

Mr. Brexil's office had a desk, a window, and a filing cabinet behind a leather chair. There were stacks of papers in neat piles on the desk, as well as two paintings resting on the floor, waiting to be hung.

"Sorry about the mess," Mr. Brexil said, gesturing to a row of chairs slid against the far wall of the office. Gordy picked the middle seat and plopped his backpack into the available spot next to him. "Typically, a new principal spends the summer preparing his office. I, on the other hand, landed this job three weeks ago. As you can imagine, I have a bit of catching up to do."

"Those are nice pictures," Gordy said, but then cringed. *Nice pictures?* What was he trying to prove? That he was the world's biggest dork?

"Thank you! I like how art brightens up dull rooms." He lifted one of the pieces and showed it to Gordy. "I prefer peaceful landscapes. Something to calm my mind when the day gets rough." Mr. Brexil returned the painting to the floor and sat down in his seat. He slid a stack of papers to one side. "I won't keep you long, Gordy. But I know what you can do. I know what you're capable of, and I must say I'm impressed. Kids with your talent at brewing are rare. My beautiful Sasha can create things that I can only dream of."

"She told me she was a Dram," Gordy said, feeling the tension ease, if only a smidge.

"Indeed. And she tells me that you might be even better."

Gordy felt his cheeks flush with heat. "I don't know about that. When did you find out Sasha could brew?"

Mr. Brexil studied Gordy for a moment and then tapped his chin with his fingers. "When she was still quite young. Her mother and I knew it was a possibility when she was born, but, as I'm certain your parents have told you, you never really know for sure until the gift manifests itself. But boy, when it did—" He laughed. "You can imagine my surprise."

Gordy smiled. "I made all my teeth disappear."

This evoked an even heartier guffaw from the older man. "That's something else! And your family? Do they all brew?"

Gordy pressed his hands on his knees. "Only me and my mom."

"I bet you have a great lab, don't you? We have an extraordinary one. Bottles and baubles and Bunsen burners galore."

Gordy nodded. "Oh, yeah, well, it's kind of nice. We used to have a much bigger lab. This is our second house." He stopped himself before revealing too much about the circumstances that had forced his family to move. Even though Sasha had mentioned knowing all about the supposed gas-leak explosion, it wasn't smart to talk about it with everyone. Especially to an adult he had just met. Still, Gordy hadn't expected to have such an easygoing conversation with the principal.

"I see. And you brew regularly, I assume?" Mr. Brexil asked.

"All the time," Gordy said. "Every night, if I can."

The principal brought his hands above the desk and pressed his fingertips together. "Do you ever bring your concoctions to school with you?"

Gordy opened his mouth to answer, but then clamped it shut. He looked embarrassedly at the backpack sitting next to him like a glaring piece of evidence.

Mr. Brexil's smile had been completely erased. "That's what I thought." He leaned forward, his expression stern. "My daughter, as stubborn as she can be, understands the rules and the consequences of breaking those rules. She doesn't bring bottles to school. Having been around potions for the entirety of my professional life, I've seen what an unchecked Dram can produce. I've witnessed, firsthand, dangerous explosions in school hallways. I've had to call an ambulance on numerous occasions for injured students because of unexplained phenomena linked to mysterious substances. I once watched a school bus float ten feet off the ground and into a neighboring orchard. All because some kid thought it would be cool to show off a potion to a buddy of his. Am I making myself clear?"

Gordy swallowed. "I think so, sir."

Mr. Brexil pointed at Gordy's backpack. "I'm giving you this one and only opportunity to walk away from my office without punishment. Consider yourself warned. Should you ever cart in just one ampoule of liquid, other than a juice box from your lunch, onto the grounds of my campus, I will expel you from my school—permanently. Understood?"

Though the principal kept his voice even and controlled, Gordy could see his jaw clenching.

"I need you to answer me, Mr. Stitser," he said.

Gordy's eyes widened. Mr. Brexil might have been the scariest person Gordy had ever met. "I . . . I understand, sir. I won't bring any potions to school."

"Not a one," Mr. Brexil added. "Now, hurry along, and have a wonderful afternoon."

9

An olive whizzed past Gordy's face while he sat at the dinner table, on its way to striking his sister, Jessica, on the chin. Jessica giggled and smiled at Isaac, the culprit who had thrown it, and then scooped up a handful of soggy pieces of pineapple. Gordy's dad looked up from his magazine before she could retaliate.

"Why are we throwing food?" Mr. Stitser asked, unperturbed.

"I wasn't throwing food," Isaac responded. "Jessica said she wanted to catch it in her mouth."

"That's still throwing," Gordy said. Eating dinner with his feral twin siblings could give anyone indigestion.

Jessica slid out of her chair for a moment and then returned with the stray olive in her fingers. After blowing away the debris it had collected from rolling around on the floor, she plopped the black orb into her mouth.

"I'm no good at catching it," she said.

Gordy shook his head. "Well, you shouldn't be practicing at the dinner table."

"He's right." Gordy's dad tossed aside his magazine and vigorously patted his chest. "This arena is for professionals only. Give me a go, Isaac!"

"Dad, are you serious?" Gordy couldn't believe what was happening.

Isaac grinned and selected a plump offering from the serving platter of vegetables at the center of the table. After winding up like a baseball pitcher, he took aim and tossed the olive. Mr. Stitser caught it like a seal snatching a fish from the air.

The twins laughed gleefully.

"Nice toss," Gordy's dad said, praising Isaac. "Your turn, Gordo."

"What? No!" Gordy looked at his father, dumbfounded. His mom was still in the kitchen, cooking rice and chicken for their Hawaiian haystacks, while the rest of the Stitser clan was busy whittling away at the toppings.

"You don't like olives? Well, we have plenty of other choices." Gordy's dad picked a cherry tomato from the platter.

"I don't want to catch food. It's childish." Gordy knew how ridiculous he must have sounded to his dad, but he wasn't in the mood for games. Not now.

"You're a child," Jessica said.

"Yeah, a big goofy one," Isaac added.

Gordy glared at his younger brother. "Keep it up and

tonight, while you're asleep, I'll spray you with a potion that covers your face in makeup. It doesn't wipe off for at least a week."

Isaac's mouth dropped open in shock, but Jessica squealed excitedly. "Oh, yes! You can spray me with that right now, if you want to."

Gordy whirled on his sister. "Nah, yours will be something that gives you a permanent unibrow."

Her smile vanished. "Dad, make him stop!"

"Okay, someone's being a grump," Mr. Stitser said. "Do you want to talk about what has you all worked up?"

Gordy flinched at the question. "I just don't like being pestered by these little dorks."

"You know better than that. We don't call each other names," he scolded, his voice sterner than before.

"Isaac just called me a big goofy kid!" Gordy protested, feeling the heat rising in his throat. Why was he suddenly the enemy? All he had been doing was patiently waiting for dinner when his bratty siblings started the trouble, and now his dad was taking their side.

"Enough!" His dad stomped his foot, shaking the dinner table. "Spill it already. You've been distant all evening. What's got your dishwasher churning, Gordo?"

Gordy's shoulders slumped. "Nothing," he muttered, staring down at his empty plate and silverware. The scolding Mr. Brexil had handed out to him earlier that day was still fresh in his mind. Plus, there was also Sasha's party. Gordy had been fighting with himself on whether or not he should go. On the one hand, it was a chance to make potions with other Drams, but on the other, it was at the principal's house. And apparently the principal didn't like him.

"You sure you don't want to talk about it?" Mr. Stitser pressed. Gordy shook his head. "That's perfectly fine. I understand there are things going on in your life that you'd rather keep to yourself. I've been there myself. Okay?"

Gordy nodded somberly.

"Good. Now open up."

"Huh?" Confused, Gordy glanced at his dad, who held a cherry tomato between his fingertips, poised to toss.

Gordy knew he wouldn't take no for an answer. Exhaling through his nose, Gordy surrendered and opened his mouth. The tomato soared through the air at the perfect angle, and Gordy would have easily caught it had Jessica not splattered him with a handful of pineapple at exactly the same time. Everyone held their breath, waiting for Gordy to explode as tart juice dripped from the tip of his nose.

But instead of raging with anger, Gordy burst out laughing.

Then food flew.

Gordy chucked shredded cheese and green onion. Jessica dropped below the table, shrieking hysterically as pieces of ham—Isaac's ammo of choice—peppered the walls. Mr. Stitser rolled up his magazine and batted the bombardment of flung food like a seasoned slugger in the World Series.

When Gordy's mom finally emerged from the kitchen, toting a steaming container of rice, only a few veggies remained on the platter. Debris littered the floor.

"Oh, boy," she said, whistling. She looked at her husband, who smiled brazenly back at her as if to suggest this had been the planned outcome from the beginning. "Who cares about vegetables anyways, am I right?"

"You are the coolest family in the world." Max stood in the opening between the dining room and the foyer, surveying the aftermath and grinning. The front door had been pushed open, and Adilene cowered behind the barrier, unsure of what to do.

"What are you guys doing here?" Gordy stood, a dollop of sour cream dropping from his forehead.

"It's Wednesday," Max said, stooping over to rescue a clump of cheese from the floor. "We always brew on Wednesdays."

"Since when?" That was news to Gordy.

"Since now," his mom said. She placed the container of rice on the disheveled table. "The pressures of being a teenager can get anyone down, especially in junior high. So I invited your lab partners over for a brewing session."

Pressure was right. Gordy needed a break, for sure, and he couldn't wait to get a Bunsen burner ignited beneath a cauldron.

Like a skittish deer, Adilene crept through the front

door, shuffling up next to Max and trying her best to conceal the backpack behind her. The bag bulged at odd angles.

"Can we go now?" Gordy asked, hunger the farthest feeling in his stomach.

"I suppose you'd better," his mom said. "With dinner ruined, I guess we'll order pizza."

Gordy's dad frowned, looking as though he regretted having destroyed the evening meal. "Pizza again? How about we go out for hoagies?" The twins cheered, and Gordy's mom didn't object. "We'll bring you home a meatball, Gordo," his dad said, pushing back from the table and flicking away several cucumber slices stuck to the front of his shirt.

"Be careful about what you brew," Gordy's mom instructed. "Nothing volatile or complicated."

"Don't worry, Mrs. Stits," Max said, his cupped hands full of cheese. "We're strictly brewing Dismemberment Potions tonight."

10

Y our family's really fun." Adilene hefted her backpack onto the table, and Gordy could hear what
sounded like aluminum clinking within. "If I
threw even a single pea at the dinner table, my mom would
swat me with her oven mitt."

Gordy grinned. They *were* fun, Isaac and Jessica included. He heard the family van pull out of the garage and
onto the road, leaving the trio alone to brew. "What did
you bring?" he asked her.

"Uh, well . . ." She fretted with the zipper. "*Esto es em-
barazoso.* I thought maybe you could give us a lesson." She
opened her backpack and several containers toppled out.
Adilene had brought two metal cauldrons, an electric hot
plate, and a small assortment of vials and bottles. "I have
my own supplies so you don't have to use any of yours."
Adilene looked away awkwardly, but then scowled at Max,
who was making faces at her. "Quiet, Maxwell! Don't tell
me you're not interested to try it yourself."

"I've already brewed hundreds of potions with Gordy," Max said smugly.

"Whatever," she snapped. "It's just that Gordy's always the one making things, and I thought it would be neat if I tried to do it myself, while you watch."

Gordy didn't think it would work. Mixing potions wasn't exactly like following a recipe for brownies. If you messed up the ingredients a little, the brownies might not end up the way they were intended, but they'd still be food, more or less. With potion making, there were actions and sounds and ambiance in addition to the ingredients. Certain mixtures required a good scolding while adding ingredients, while others needed the cauldron to be tipped on its side and tickled on its underbelly to produce the desired results. But even following the specific instructions wasn't enough. There was no good way to describe it, but Elixirists and Drams, such as Gordy, had something else about them that made the potion work. Maybe it was magic, or maybe it was just the necessary skill inherent within them. Just as Gordy lacked the natural balance to walk a tightrope, he suspected Max and Adilene lacked the knack for concocting. But how could he ever say that to his friends?

"Okay," Gordy agreed. There seemed to be no harm in trying, and he walked to the bookcase to select a recipe manual.

He dragged his finger along the spines of his mother's tomes. Some were leather-bound and smelled ancient, while others were spiral-bound notebooks with multicolored tabs protruding from the edges. Gordy considered going to his room to grab his personal potion journal from beneath his mattress, but as he started to turn away from the shelf, a small, weathered book caught his eye. It had been wedged between two three-ring binders with plastic sheet protectors, but Gordy recognized it at once. It was his Grandpa Mezzarix's potion journal, the one he had given Gordy as a gift when he and his mom had visited Greenland several months ago. Directly after arriving home from the trip, Gordy's mom had confiscated the journal for safekeeping. Nothing his grandpa had concocted over the past twelve years would have been suitable for a Dram to brew, she'd told Gordy.

He carefully untucked the book from its hiding place and removed the elastic band from off the edges.

Gordy flipped the journal open to the first page and began to read.

Steeped lily of the valley, heated to a simmer on smoked wormwood.

Seven durian seeds caterwauled upon by an arctic wolf dropped into settling mixture.

Slime from a zombie snail brushed around the lip of a limestone cauldron.

Stir with the severed horn of a rhinoceros beetle.

While keeping thoughts only upon the throat of your

intended victim, bring to a staggering boil and add monks-hood petals.

Allow to percolate before smothering with the tanned hide of an ibex.

Such weird instructions. Weird even for an Elixirist. The recipe had no title or explanation at the top of the page, but near the bottom, written with almost unreadable penmanship, were two words.

Throttling Agony

"Did you forget about us?" Max hollered, and Gordy snapped the book shut.

The journal was a stark reminder of how dangerous his grandfather was, even while safely exiled thousands of miles away. There was no chance Gordy would be brewing anything from those pages anytime soon.

Half an hour later, Adilene's aluminum cauldron drummed its legs angrily against the countertop. She had clamped it tight with Gordy's brass holder, but the heat from the electric hot plate had stirred the metal bowl into a frenzy.

"You're absolutely one hundred percent sure I'm doing this correctly?" Adilene's voice carried the same rhythm as her dancing cauldron. "I'm not missing any ingredients?"

"As far as I can tell," Gordy said, but her potion didn't look correct. At this point during the mixing phase, the liquid should've settled to a gentle slosh in the cauldron, with the distinct color and consistency of cotton candy. Adilene was trying to make a Slovenian Sottusopra Serum that would make everything look right-side up while standing on one's head. She had recently taken up gymnastics and struggled to keep from getting dizzy during all her required tumbling.

"What about mine?" Max was having even less success than Adilene. The contents of his cauldron, a bubbling mass of brownish goop, recoiled as each drop of liquid from the test tube made contact.

Suddenly, Max's cauldron leaped across the table, gobbling up an empty test tube like a greedy bullfrog. Every bit of his potion sizzled against the countertop, and Gordy patted his friend on the shoulder consolingly and handed him a roll of paper towels.

"You rotten, no good . . ." Max snarled. His potion was supposed to have been a Decurdler. "I'll never win a milk-guzzling challenge with this worthless slop!"

It was what Gordy had expected. Max had followed the directions to the letter, but it hadn't worked. Adilene's brew, however, had started to simmer, which was promising.

Gordy turned his attention fully onto Adilene's mixture. "Not bad. Keep stirring slowly."

Max had already moved on from his failed brewing attempt and crouched close to a container holding a mammoth tarantula. He tapped something against the glass.

The arachnid tucked its legs in more and more tightly with each annoying tap.

"What is that?" Gordy asked, glancing distractedly at Max.

"It's my lucky rock," Max explained, holding up some sort of circular stone. "Touch it! It feels different, doesn't it?"

Gordy touched the onyx-colored stone with his finger. It had a smooth texture, light and airy. He felt if he pressed hard enough, his finger might pass through it. Yet the stone made a sharp sound as Max continually whacked it against the glass terrarium.

"Where did you find it?" Adilene asked, keeping her eyes glued to her constant stirring.

Max grinned. "Under my shoes last Friday when we were at B.R.E.W. Headquarters. I think it's an Elixirist artifact."

Gordy blinked and turned away from Adilene. "You found that on the ground at B.R.E.W.? You have to give it back."

"No way, man. It's my souvenir." Max squeezed the rock in his fist. "It's no different than taking rocks from a National Park."

"That's actually illegal," Adilene said. "You can get fined for that."

Max frowned at Adilene and slipped the stone back into his pocket. "Let them try. Besides, Rivera, it's your fault I found it to begin with. If you hadn't—"

"I didn't push you, Maxwell," she interjected, her voice

even. Adilene's eyes flickered up momentarily from her mixing. "I wish you'd stop saying that." Max opened his mouth to protest, but Adilene quieted him with a threatening finger. "I think it's ready." She pulled back from the cauldron to allow Gordy a clear line of sight.

"Wow!" It actually looked right. Perfect color and consistency.

"How do we know for sure?" she asked eagerly. "Without, you know, drinking it, of course."

Gordy crossed the room and opened a cabinet. He removed a bottle of Detection Spray and brought it back to the workstation. He hadn't expected to use it, and he could tell by Adilene's giddiness that she was thrilled with her accomplishment.

"Maybe everyone should back away from the counter while I spray it," Gordy instructed. "Just in case."

"Beginner's luck," Max grumbled, turning up his nose at Adilene's cauldron.

"Don't be a poor sport, Maxwell," Adilene chided. "I worked really hard on this."

"And what did I do?" he asked. "Pick my nose the whole time?"

"Maybe." She playfully kicked Max's shoe.

Gordy applied a generous dose of the Detection Spray across the surface of the cauldron. If it worked, it would crackle like rice cereal. He stepped back and felt Adilene's trembling hands squeeze around his arm. He could hear her breathing, both hopeful and nervous, and he glanced at Max, who looked bummed.

Then they waited. A few seconds ticked away, then several more, then a full minute slipped past. No popping or fizzing. No indicators that Adilene had brewed a successful Sottusopra Serum. When two minutes had elapsed and Gordy had resprayed the potion to no avail, Adilene released a disappointed sigh.

"Oh well," she said, crestfallen. "At least I came close, right?"

"That's right," Gordy agreed. "It was almost perfect."

"If you look at it that way, then so was mine," Max said.

Adilene smiled at Max. "I think yours was perfect too. We just need to practice more." Despite her failed attempt, Adilene was as chipper as ever as she cleaned her workstation. She returned her containers and flasks to her bag, as well as several pages of scribbled notes she had taken that evening.

"I'm so excited!" Adilene said as Gordy walked her to the door. "Do you think there's a chance I could become an actual Dram like you?"

"I guess it's possible." But from everything Gordy had been taught, Adilene was too old to show the signs of a potion master. Judging by her potion, she seemed more skilled than most second-year Drams, even though she wasn't one herself and would likely never become one. Then again, after tonight's near triumph in the lab, maybe one day she would.

CHAPTER 6

The wards surrounding the opulent hotel were some of the strongest Mezzarix had ever felt outside of his cave in Greenland. He could sense a bending in the air, as if the protective potions were made of a solid substance, shielding the outside world from peeking through a crystalline window or striding into the immaculate lobby unannounced.

"Good morning! Welcome to the Maestoso, Mr. Rook," said a woman behind the receptionist counter, smartly dressed in a velvety blazer.

Morning? Mezzarix glanced back through the lobby door. The sky had a pinkish hue to it, as if it couldn't decide what time it wanted to be. Mezzarix supposed it *was* morning now, though. The long flight had messed with his internal clock.

"Your room is all prepared for you. May we assist you with your luggage?" The woman gestured to a bellhop in a tasseled hat, who stood at the ready beside the counter.

Mezzarix frowned at her and pulled his knapsack closer to his chest. It had been more than a decade since he had seen the inside of any building, let alone one with bellhops and sumptuously baked cookies steaming on the counter. Out in the open, he felt exposed. Chilly air nipped at his neck from an overhead vent. Almost thirteen years in the frigid temperatures of upper Greenland, yet this was the first instance he could recall actually shivering.

"Don't be so stiff, friend," Ravian McFarland whispered from behind Mezzarix. "The staff have all been Blotched. Every last one of them." He reached across the counter and snatched several cookies from the plate, shoving one into his mouth. Ravian licked each of his fingers directly in the receptionist's face, though she did nothing but smile in response. "Should you request it, this woman would personally taste-test every one of your vials in that ridiculous bag of yours."

Mezzarix scowled and looked down at his vinyl knapsack. Aside from a few potions he had brewed aboard the flight, it contained two jars of a special murky, gray liquid mixed with pieces of stone taken from his cave back in Greenland. Mezzarix didn't care if every member of the hotel's staff had been placed under the mind control of Ravian's Blotching potions. No one would be relieving him of his bag.

"Can we get on with this?" Mezzarix asked. It had been a long flight from Sermersooq, and with his thread-bare tuxedo, bare feet, and ratted mane of hair, Mezzarix looked more out of place than a six-foot-tall toad. They were in B.R.E.W. territory now, and he suspected there were hundreds, if not thousands, of Elixirists residing in the bustling town.

"Of course!" Ravian crammed another cookie into his mouth, dribbling crumbs. "My dear, would you mind telling us where the meeting will be held this evening?"

The woman smiled. "It would be my pleasure. Ms. Bimini is waiting with the rest of your associates in the Beekman conference room."

Ravian nodded and led Mezzarix to the elevators.

A banquet table laden with desserts awaited them beyond the door of the Beekman Room. Mezzarix couldn't help but wistfully eyeball the spread of cream-topped delicacies, a far cry from his usual meals of cave crickets and fricasseed bat. But unlike Ravian, who fell upon the table like a ravenous wolf, scarfing down pastries three at a time, Mezzarix wasn't about to let his guard down. He clutched his bag and focused his attention to the circle of chairs at the center of the room—chairs occupied by a couple of familiar faces.

"Where did you dredge up such an awful sight, Ravian?" a middle-aged woman bellowed in a resonating voice. She was both portly and tall, with stout legs that she extended into the center of the circle. She wore a blue jumpsuit adorned by several gold necklaces, which matched her gold-capped front teeth. Her hair, a mess of tightly wound curls, bounced when she spoke, and upon seeing Mezzarix, she folded her arms at her chest and spat an orangish wad onto the floor next to her seat. The woman was just as Mezzarix had remembered her from the last time he had seen her, thirteen years ago. Right down to the laceless white sneakers.

"Lolly Gittens," Mezzarix said. He hadn't planned on showing any emotion during this meeting. Keeping his expressions unreadable would make it easier to negotiate his terms. But one didn't simply lay eyes upon Lolly Gittens and avoid a scowl. "I see that you've managed to avoid capture despite looking like a member of an eighties rap group."

"I know how to blend in." Lolly cracked her knuckles, and it sounded like a strand of exploding firecrackers. "You remember my husband, Walsh, don't you?" She nodded to the man seated across from her.

"How could I forget?" Mezzarix asked.

Though not as tall or as thick as his wife, Walsh was still massive in his own way, and he had several gold chains as well, sparkling against his white tank top. Gray-haired with sunken cheeks and bulging eyes, Walsh had the unfortunate appearance of someone who had just swallowed a carton of rotten eggs. Mezzarix had worked with the Gittens before, and they were difficult to control, often preferring brutish methods as opposed to using their limited wit in battle.

"I have heard wonderful things about you, sir," said an elderly woman seated in one of the remaining chairs, staring up at Mezzarix with wonder. Her face was pinched with deep wrinkles, but her eyes twinkled with an almost lavender glow. "Your friends have told me about how you were once the most esteemed Elixirist in all the world." The woman's gentle voice held an odd accent, one Mezzarix couldn't readily place. "But then you disappeared."

"You must be Ms. Bimini." Mezzarix offered a slight bow. "Ravian has told me very little about you, but that has always been his way. Pointlessly secretive."

"Secrecy is all I have left in my ancient years." Ms. Bimini steepled her fingers, fixing Mezzarix with a piercing gaze. "Tell me, what are your desires? To become greatest amongst Elixirists? Powerful beyond comprehension?"

Mezzarix gazed around the room. Aside from the dessert table, there were also several brewing workstations with heating elements, cauldrons, and an expansive display of ingredients. The sight of it almost made him salivate.

"I have little on my wish list," he said, returning his attention to her. "A quiet place to brew and to be at peace."

Ms. Bimini clicked her tongue in disbelief. "But Ravian assures me that you have lofty aspirations to rid the world of order and thrust it into chaos." Her lips curled into a smile.

Mezzarix's eyes darkened. "Well, there is that. I do struggle when the corrupted oppress the innocent."

"The noble goals of a misunderstood master! What about treasure?" she asked. "I can provide you with all the treasure you could ever desire. Is it your wish to hoard valuables?"

"Do I look like someone who needs treasure?" Mezzarix considered living above one's means as a sign of weakness. Even before his banishment, the Rooks had always resided in meager conditions. Money meant nothing.

Ms. Bimini clapped her hands and filled the room with rich laughter. "I like you, and I can see us prospering together in a wonderful partnership."

"Partnership?" Mezzarix raised an eyebrow. "I haven't agreed to anything. I'm not even clear on what you want, nor am I convinced you have the means to deliver on any of your promises. And since I don't have much time to stand here and banter with you, perhaps we should cut the casual niceties and get to the point of this meeting."

Ms. Bimini puckered her lips. And then she vanished. It happened so suddenly, Mezzarix could only suck in a breath. He saw nothing that would have caused such an abrupt disappearance. Her chair never moved, and from what he could tell, she hadn't swallowed any concoction. Mezzarix tried not to look awestruck, but he was afraid it was obvious as he searched the room for the disappearing woman.

After a few seconds, Ms. Bimini reappeared, regarding Mezzarix with a serious expression.

"Silt," she said. "Wondrous Silt. It allows me to become invisible whenever I choose. I can go anywhere I please and remain hidden for as long as I desire. Mr. Rook, we both want the same thing. We both have been banished from our true homes." She pressed her hand against her chest. "I wish to resume my rightful place on my island, but I can't do that without your assistance. If you help me, I shall help you, and perhaps together we can achieve our hearts' desires."

"What did you have in mind?" He hadn't been out of Greenland long, but he could already feel the effects of his temporary departure from the cave starting to wear off. He had maybe a couple of days before the Link would force him back. Should he resist it, Mezzarix would die. He needed to find a way to increase his stock of potions, and the sooner he could do that the better.

"I will supply you with whatever tools and ingredients you require." Ms. Bimini gestured toward the brewing workstation behind her. "You will then Replicate my supply of Silt. Ravian has explained to me that though your ability to Replicate is unmatched, the effects of the Replication process will be temporary. I believe the risk will be worth it." She opened a black case that had been resting next to her chair and pulled out seven small vials, each one partially filled with inky liquid. "This is all I have left of the Silt I took from my people when they banished me several years ago. Though I tried to go back, I never had the means or the support I needed to do so. Until recently, just when I thought all was lost, I discovered a new world. Your world, Mezzarix. The world of the potion master. This Silt is not much, but with your skill, we could perhaps gather a small group to overthrow B.R.E.W. and grant you the Vessel—and your freedom."

"We have already started recruiting Scourges for our uprising," Lolly said, leaning forward in her seat. "Walsh, myself, and Ravian could have a formidable army at our disposal in less than a week."

Mezzarix didn't doubt Lolly's ability to stir up trouble, and he knew once word spread of his involvement, there would be plenty of others who would rally to his cause.

Mezzarix narrowed his eyes. "You would just give us the Vessel?"

"What would I do with such a thing?" Ms. Bimini asked. "I'm no Elixirist."

"Then how did you make this Silt?"

"Make it?" She smiled as if Mezzarix had said something absurd. "There is much you need to learn, dear sir. Silt flows freely from a fountain on my island. My ancestors scoured the ocean in search of it centuries ago. It's the only one of its kind." She cleared her throat. "After you seize the Vessel and free yourself permanently from your exile, you will help me take back my island. You shall force my people to release my banishment, and then I'll show you the way to the fountain, where you can fill your vials and bottles with as much Silt as you can carry. After that, I'd say you'll be well on your way toward your goal of global domination." She sat back in her cushioned chair, watching Mezzarix closely.

Mezzarix sat down, stretching his legs and wiggling his

toes as he processed her proposal. It all sounded favorable. Freedom. Power. And unless Mezzarix captured the Vessel, which would break him from his banishment, he would have no obligation to deliver on his end of the bargain.

"What if I say no and we"—he nodded at Ravian and the Gittens—"eliminate you from the equation? We find this island of yours and take the Silt for ourselves."

Ms. Bimini raised her eyebrows. "The oceans are wide and wondrous, and the route to my island is invisible to any but those who are from there. I'm the only one who knows the way back. And, if I'm not mistaken, your hours are limited. By the time you've procured yourself a boat and charted your futile voyage to wander the seven seas, you'll be left with nothing."

"Then maybe we should take your supply of Silt right now. That looks sufficient to achieve our goals. Why would we need you, if we have that?"

Ms. Bimini nodded knowingly. "I see what you're trying to do. You're testing the strength of my resolve. But, my dear sir, you didn't really think I'd travel all this way alone, did you?"

Mezzarix felt an invisible hand grip his shoulder, and something wrenched his bag free from his arms and carried it across the room.

"That's mine!" he gasped, panic flooding through his chest.

The bag unzipped, and the two glass jars containing

the grayish liquid emerged, drifting haphazardly over to float beside Ms. Bimini.

"What are these?" she asked, gazing upon them inquisitively. "I don't recognize them."

Mezzarix stepped forward, holding up a desperate hand. "Be careful with those!"

"And should I drop them?" she asked. "What then becomes of the great Mezzarix Rook?"

The jars hovered for a moment before gently being returned to the pocket. The zipper closed, and the bag floated back across the room and into Mezzarix's arms. Mezzarix felt the blood pounding in his temples.

"I'm sorry I had to tease you like that," Ms. Bimini said, pouting. "But I wanted you to see what I'm capable of, and I don't think highly of threats. Now, are there any further inquiries? I do believe we have a revolution to plan."

12

A hulking man with a grizzled silver beard hunched in the driver's seat of a sputtering gray pickup truck parked one block east of Kipland Middle School. He gripped the steering wheel, calloused knuckles jutting up from beefy, bent fingers. Next to him, equally crammed in the tight quarters of the pickup's cab, sat one of the man's associates.

The second man had a black beard spanning the width of his chest, save for one thinning section on his left cheek, where a patch had been burned and only recently started filling back in. The man's lips puckered around the end of a foul-smelling cigar, and he carried a test tube filled with a roiling, smoky liquid. It was a Friday afternoon, and the weather was warm and sunny, not a cloud in the sky, but the two lumberjack-like men, in their thick, fleece-lined coats, looked ready to explore the upper regions of the Klondike.

"Keep your head about you and wait for my command,"

the driver instructed, plunging his hand into a paper sack at his side. His fingers emerged, closed around a mound of mashed french fries, a dusting of salt glittering upon his skin. The whole operation had him on edge. After so many months of hiding out, planning for the right moment to strike, he couldn't wait for it to be over. "The moment Bolter arrives in the parking lot, we make our move."

"How will we know when he arrives?" the other asked, expelling a puff of smoke. The cloud lingered above his head before escaping through a crack in the window. He flicked the gray vial in his lap, and the contents unleashed a staticky crackle. "The parking lot's full of vehicles."

"He'll be the only one driving car that looks like cat," the first answered. The other man nodded but then screwed his face up in confusion. Before he could question further, the driver cut him off. "I don't need to explain everything to you, Burke. You're not in charge."

"Neither are you, Yeltzin!" Burke spat, the two sounding more like a pair of toddlers fighting over a toy.

"Aye, but I outrank you. So keep your mouth shut and your eyes peeled."

The school bell had rung, class had been dismissed, and a flock of children, boys and girls carrying backpacks, emerged from around the corner. Yeltzin nearly choked on his fries when he caught sight of someone at the end of the road. Several someones. As they approached the vehicle, all but one of them veered off across the road at the crosswalk, heading into a subdivision. Lingering back at the rear, timidly casting wary looks in every direction, was Gordy Stitser.

Yeltzin's wooly eyebrows nearly folded in upon themselves as he scanned the parking lot and the road, looking for signs of Bolter's vehicle roaring up the block. But it was nowhere to be seen. Perhaps the nuisance Elixirist had changed cars, but Yeltzin didn't believe that to be true. He just wasn't there. Why was the boy walking? He never walked!

"Looks like there has been change in plans." Yeltzin gripped the gearshift, plunking it down into drive, but kept his foot on the brake. He shot a warning glare toward Burke. "Take your hand off that handle. I gave no command."

Burke chomped down on his cigar, nearly rending it into two pieces, but he complied, easing his fingers away from the door handle.

"Stay calm and cool like cuticle," Yeltzin said.

"The correct saying is 'calm and cool like a cucumber,'" Burke corrected.

"Not in Russia it isn't."

As Gordy passed by the truck, he came to a sudden halt. Yeltzin's fingers tensed upon the wheel as the boy faced the vehicle, his eyes widening. Then, without warning, Gordy broke into a run. Yeltzin jerked the steering wheel, taking the turn sharply, and causing Burke's head to smack his window, which would have likely shattered the glass had he not been wearing such a thick stocking cap.

"Watch those turns!" Burke shouted. "You're going to lose it!"

"I know what I'm doing." Yeltzin tossed his cell phone into Burke's lap. "Tell the others where we're headed."

The boy ran with incredible speed, cutting across several yards and momentarily disappearing behind a tall brick house.

"Did you see where he went?" Yeltzin demanded.

"I've got eyes on him," Burke replied a few moments later, as the boy resurfaced down a side street, running in an all-out sprint. Yeltzin nearly slammed the gas pedal through the floor. Gordy reached a park at the end of the road and dashed between a pair of empty swings, heading for the woods beyond, just as the truck roared onto the lawn. Yeltzin never took his foot off the accelerator, barreling through the swing set and sending sand and woodchips flying. The moment he arrived at the edge of the forest, he slammed on the brakes. Both burly Elixirists hurriedly exited the vehicle and took to the trees on foot, hands gripping their liquid weapons.

Up ahead, Gordy continued to distance himself from the attackers, looking over his shoulder as he ran. The boy maneuvered through the woods with ease, but he wasn't paying attention. A smile broke through Yeltzin's hardened scowl when Dieter and Ridley, two of Yeltzin's companions, emerged from their hiding places, cutting off Gordy's escape just as the back end of a subdivision appeared through the fragmented space between the trees.

As Gordy skidded to a stop, his eyes darted between the new threat hedging his way and Yeltzin and Burke

closing in from the rear. Without any hesitation, he thrust his hand into his backpack and pulled out a bottle, which he threw at Dieter's feet. The glass shattered, and Dieter's hands went up, shielding his face from the fumes. He spat and coughed, and then, in an instant, he was gone.

Yeltzin blinked in surprise. What had just happened? What potion could vaporize someone so quickly? But then he realized that Dieter hadn't truly vanished; rather he had just melded into a nearby tree. Dieter's arms and legs flailed about, jutting out from the trunk, while the rest of his torso, chest, and shoulders were buried in the wood. A knothole made it possible for him to breathe, but the amber-colored potion had rendered him fully incapacitated.

Gordy turned to face Yeltzin, hand closed around another bottle, ready to fire, but Burke acted first. His vial erupted above Gordy, showering him with a smoky fluid, which instantly formed a gray sack covering Gordy's head. Gordy's hands shot up, desperately pawing at the taut fabric cinched around his face, but it was no use. Burke's Sessizlik Serum had completely silenced the boy. Yeltzin tossed his bottle, and Gordy collapsed on the forest floor, wrapped up in the writhing vines of a Vintreet Trap.

"Hello, little Stitser," Yeltzin said, elbowing Burke in the ribs. "I give you highest praise on your mighty concoctions, but we take you with us now without another peep."

13

Gordy never peeped once as Yeltzin and his gang transported him across town to their hideout. Garbage littered the sidewalk alongside the row of mostly abandoned stores with boarded-up windows and padlocked, galvanized, rollup doors. With the others trailing behind, Yeltzin carried Gordy from the back of the vehicle down a side street, past a stretch of dilapidated buildings plastered with graffiti, and through a door. He plopped the boy into a folding chair at the center of an office and worked a length of rope around his arms before removing the bag covering Gordy's face. Only then did Yeltzin relax. After more than half a year of plotting revenge, he had finally caught Gordy Stitser.

"Didn't think you'd see me again, did you?" Yeltzin asked. "The satisfaction of having you here, helpless and scared, feels so good."

But the boy didn't look scared, which gave Yeltzin a moment's pause. He should've been at least worried, but

Gordy remained silent, his teeth clenching tight enough to expose the muscles in his jaw.

"Well, what are you thinking?" Yeltzin dropped his massive hands onto Gordy's shoulders. "That your mommy will magically appear and batter down the door?" He shook his head grimly. "We covered our tracks. Not a soul saw us enter here, and no one's coming in that we don't want."

Gordy stared at him, eyes unblinking.

"Say something!" Yeltzin demanded. "Beg for mercy!"

Gordy remained rigid and silent. It annoyed Yeltzin. He leaned over to mutter in Burke's ear, "How long until your serum wears off? I want to hear him speak."

"It should have already worn off," Burke grunted.

Yeltzin puckered his lips and snarled at Gordy. "Your bravery is admirable, I'll give you that. But, my boy, what we have in store for you will shatter bravery like candied glass." A soft padding sound at the door announced a new visitor, and Yeltzin's smile widened. "We have brought special guest for you, Stitser. Old friend has been dying to see you."

Yeltzin moved to open the door. A cloud of noxious, rotting chemicals flooded in, and the boy flinched, his nose scrunching from the sour scent, as Bawdry, the mummy, lumbered into the room.

Gooey bandages dangled limply from Bawdry's shoulders, and a trail of elongated footprints stamped the floor behind him. Not wanting to touch any part of Bawdry's decomposing flesh, Yeltzin buried his mouth in the pit of his elbow and gave the mummy a wide berth.

Bawdry's crooked jaw drooped to one side as if having recently come unhinged from its socket. "Well done, I say," he said with a velvety voice unbefitting his bent and crooked stature. "You took a lot longer to snatch him than I would have hoped, but I must admit it was worth the wait."

Gordy's eyes narrowed as he finally spoke. "Esmeralda Faustus?"

"You were expecting someone else?"

"Well, yes, actually. You're the one in charge?"

Bawdry folded his arms, a length of bandage swooping out and nearly swatting Yeltzin in the chin. "I'm the only one who could be."

Gordy scowled at Yeltzin. "Why are you still following her? You could've vanished. There are plenty of Scourges you could have begged to welcome you into their care, yet you hung around to take orders from a corpse?" He shook his head in disappointment.

"You have a lot of cheek for someone snagged in our trap." Esmeralda took a stumbling step toward Gordy.

"Have you been living inside Bawdry all this time?" Gordy asked.

Bawdry cocked his head to one side, unleashing a barrage of gurgling pops. "Only when I needed to give instruction." Bawdry's thumb shot out toward Yeltzin. "Do you really think I'd remain in this body any longer than I had to?"

Gordy's scowl turned into a grin. "Wow, Esmeralda, here I thought you had a shred of dignity. I would've never believed you could have stooped so low."

"Don't you dare insult me! You'd be wise to watch your mouth, if you don't want me filling it up with all sorts of vile potions. Your mother should've been more thorough in her search. Leaving me this gateway creature has been most helpful in our capture of you. That was her worst mistake!"

An earsplitting crash shook the building. All pairs of eyes, including Bawdry's, which were really nothing more than hollow sockets, snapped toward the door. Crumbling drywall fell from the ceiling as a suctioning sound suddenly rose from outside of the office.

"Find out what that is!" Esmeralda jabbed an odd-angled finger at Yeltzin, who reached for the doorknob to wrench it open.

"I wouldn't do that if I were you," Gordy warned.

Yeltzin's hand faltered as the suctioning sound grew louder until it sounded like plungers unclogging a thousand toilets all at once.

"Who followed you here?" Esmeralda demanded.

"No one," Yeltzin said. He had been so careful. There had been no suspicious vehicles tailing them and certainly no signs of Wanda and her little nuisances from B.R.E.W.

"Not who—*what*," Gordy clarified. "I think you'll be familiar with our work."

Yeltzin eyed the boy, wondering if his Vintreet Trap had addled Gordy's brain.

Then the door burst open, and a swarm of buzzing mosquitoes the size of hummingbirds flooded the room. Burke and Dieter screamed; Ridley swatted at the swarm with her leather satchel. The mosquitoes hovered in the room, hundreds of them, pulsating, and then they dropped dead to the floor.

Yeltzin squealed, leaping back as a puddle of soupy potion pooled beneath the insects.

"The wards," Esmeralda muttered through Bawdry's slack jaw and stared over the morbid pile of bug corpses.

"That's right," Gordy said. "Do you want to know what your worst mistake was?" Esmeralda didn't answer. "You should've never brought me to your hideout." Gordy suddenly stood up. The bindings trapping him to the chair fluttered to the floor like discarded snakeskins.

Burke growled and reached for the boy, but before he could lay his hands upon him, Gordy doused him in the face with an orange syrup from a plastic pipette. Then Burke started spinning. He resembled a ballerina at first, whirling, twirling, hands daintily raised above his head, but then the spinning transformed into a cyclone, and the dead pile of mosquitoes were sucked up into the human tornado. Burke retched, and all around him, the others stared in horror as his body blurred and his feet rose from the ground, taking flight. He crashed through the brick wall like a rogue top sent on its destructive path.

Mercifully, the spinning halted abruptly, but Burke could do nothing but lie on the floor, covered in insect carcasses, and groan.

Bawdry swatted a clawed finger at Gordy, but the boy dispatched him with a blue bauble of frosty liquid. The mummy froze in place, enveloped in a thick layer of ice.

"Ice ball!" Bawdry screamed. The whole scene had taken on a familiar tone.

Priscilla Rook and Zelda Morphata suddenly appeared in the doorway, flinging vials in every direction. It took less than thirty seconds to subdue everyone in the room. The rabble of Scourges lay in heaps of vines and spider-webs. Only Bawdry seemed capable of talking, ice covering all but his gnarled lips.

"Oh, how I hate you, Gordy!" Bawdry hissed in Esmeralda's voice.

"You see, that was your second mistake," Gordy said, clasping a vial of tonic in one hand, as he circled the room. "You keep calling me Gordy." Then the effects of the Disfarcar Gel finally wore off, and Wanda Stitser stood in the room.

14

The real Gordy Stitser was several miles away, standing in the family lab. Bolter had picked him up early from school, long before Yeltzin and Burke had even arrived.

Irene the guinea pig squawked in discomfort and leaped from the counter onto the back of the swivel chair, a distance of about two feet. Gordy swallowed in surprise, his eyes narrowing with suspicion as the rodent chattered angrily, and several polka-dotted feathers started sprouting from its pale pink skin.

"That wasn't supposed to happen," Gordy muttered, craning his neck to look over Adilene's shoulder at the recipe.

Adilene worriedly gnawed her thumbnail. "I didn't think so, but I wasn't sure because you said there might be a mild explosion." Adilene's tone grew anxious. "Are those feathers? *¡Ay ay ay!* Why are there feathers? She's not hurt, is she?"

Gordy crinkled his eyebrows. "They're not real feathers."

At least, he hoped they weren't real. His lips moved silently as he read off the ingredients.

> *1 pint of alpaca milk poured into a cobalt cauldron on low heat.*
>
> *2 sprigs ginseng ground into powder and sprinkled haphazardly into mixture.*
>
> *1 acorn cap placed upside down in cauldron so it resembles a storm-swept boat caught at sea.*
>
> *Heat to a sweltering boil, then remove while imagining a set of toothless gums grinning in an elderly person's mouth.*
>
> *Amber Wick lit for 3 seconds then blown out into the cauldron.*

The potion wasn't a difficult one to perform; Gordy had mixed the recipe at least a dozen times before.

Adilene gasped. "There are seventeen feathers!" Her voice lowered to an excited whisper. "I think they're still growing!"

A knock pounded against the laboratory door. "Why did you lock it?" Max's muffled voice sounded from the other side. "I was coming back. I just had to go to the bathroom." He jiggled the knob and then bumped his shoulder against the sturdy oak door. The door didn't budge, and Gordy heard Max grunt in pain.

"Hold on for a second," Gordy said. "I'll let you in as soon as I figure out what happened."

"What do you mean what happened?" Max asked. "What did I miss?"

Adilene's eyes glistened in the glow of the dimly lit Bunsen burner. "Will she always look like that?"

The disgruntled guinea pig snorted and then attacked a cluster of feathers on her shoulder. They looked pretty real to Gordy, which could be a big problem.

Max thudded against the door again. "Come on! Open up. I don't like standing out here in the hallway all by myself. I keep remembering when Bawdry was walking around your old house. Creeps me out."

Adilene frowned. "All I wanted was for Irene to stop biting everyone. She thinks everything's a carrot, but it's not worth it if she has feathers! You need to fix her."

"I will," Gordy insisted.

It was supposed to be a mild form of Peruvian Dentadura Draught, which kept teething babies from biting. If performed correctly, the mixture would turn silver and smooth. Gordy peered down at the agitated coppery concoction. At some point while brewing, he must have added something else. Something not part of the original recipe.

Gordy opened the door, and Max tramped in. "What did you make?" He grabbed for the cobalt cauldron.

Adilene slapped his hand away. "Don't touch anything! Gordy needs everything in order to reverse what he's done."

Max caught sight of Irene and instantly doubled over with laughter, his freckled face turning maroon. "She looks like a mix between a parrot and Coach Garabaldi!"

"How do we fix it?" Adilene whispered.

"We can't," Gordy said, trying to ignore Max's guffaws. Adilene squealed in despair, but Gordy held up a hand to calm her. "I meant we can't make Dentadura Draught out of this mixture, but I think I can reverse the effects."

He immediately went to work, bringing the contents to a boil and grabbing a tube with a rubber bauble at one end. It always reminded him of a turkey baster.

"Can we talk about tomorrow night?" Max sat with one fist crammed under his chin, balancing on a teal-colored exercise ball.

Gordy remained at the workstation but offered Max a sideways glance. "There's nothing to talk about," he said. "I'm not going."

"Why wouldn't you go?" Adilene asked. "Sasha's a Dram, right? And it's a potion-making party. I'd want to go. I've seen the houses on Harper Hood Lane. They're so beautiful."

"I don't trust Sasha yet," Gordy said. "Plus, her dad's the principal."

"It doesn't matter," Max said. "You're going, and so am I."

Gordy sighed. "You weren't invited, so you won't be able to come. Sasha's home will be filled with so many protective wards, the moment you try to enter her house without permission, you'll wake up miles away without a clue how you got there."

Max chuckled. "That would be awesome."

At precisely the right moment, Gordy sprinkled in several graphite-colored flakes from a container marked "Cannonball Lead." He had seen his mom do this before on a number of occasions, and just as he had hoped, the potion slowed its tumbling motion, coppery bubbles filling with air but refusing to pop. He turned down the heat from the Bunsen burner, and the mixture began to steam. Gordy directed the oscillating fan toward the cauldron, and the low flow of air sent the wispy fumes out of harm's way. He then placed the end of the turkey baster on top of the gloppy potion and gently squeezed the bauble, filling the tube with the extracted fluid.

"Irene," he whispered, holding out his hand as if he were a doctor asking for a scalpel. Adilene carefully placed the agitated guinea pig into his palm. As Gordy pressed the tube to her back, Irene produced a tittering sound and then went as still as a statue, her black eyes narrowing. Adilene clenched her hands into fists, and out of the corner of his eye, Gordy could see Max's face stretching into a gleeful, almost hopeful, smile.

When he finished, Gordy removed the baster and stepped back. One by one, each of Irene's seventeen feathers dissolved and vanished. As her color changed back to normal, the guinea pig promptly charged across the table and bit Max's thumb.

"Stupid rat!" Max shouted.

From downstairs the garage door opened, followed by several voices talking in the kitchen. They were carrying on about something, and though Gordy couldn't make out the conversation, they sounded as though they were having a riotous time. Silverware clattered on the counter, and Gordy heard the sound of several chairs scooching across the hardwood floors.

"Is your mom having a dinner party?" Adilene whispered, cradling Irene close to her chest.

"Did she invite over some of her"—Max's eyes grew large—"Elixirist friends?" He started for the exit, but Gordy snagged his arm and pulled him back.

"Let me check it out first." Gordy opened the lab door and stuck his head through the opening, listening.

There had been a few instances in the past when Gordy's mom had invited guests over for dinner, but it wasn't a common event. The group downstairs suddenly erupted with laughter. Gordy heard the buttons of the microwave beep, the refrigerator door open and close, and then what sounded like a jar full of marbles being dropped on the floor.

"What in the world?" Gordy stepped into the hallway and pulled the door to the lab closed.

As he tiptoed toward the stairs, he heard a floorboard squeak behind him and felt his heart leap into his throat. Before he could turn around to face the intruder, a hand clamped over his mouth.

15

"Don't scream," a familiar voice instructed him. The intruder released Gordy, and his shoulders relaxed.

Standing behind him was Gordy's Aunt Priss. He blinked once, just to make sure his eyes hadn't deceived him, and then hugged her. Aunt Priss squeezed him back.

"I fooled you good this time, didn't I?" she asked.

"I thought Esmeralda had come back to finish us off," he admitted, his heart still beating at a rapid rate.

Aunt Priss clicked her tongue. "Well, she definitely tried."

"What do you mean 'tried'?" Gordy had meant it as a joke. "What are you doing here?" He was thrilled to see Priss—she'd been away for several months—but the mystery of her sudden appearance made him suspicious. "Where have you been?"

"On a secret mission." She smiled and whipped a sharp glare at the door leading into the Stitsers' lab. "I've told your mother at least a hundred times, a potion laboratory has no business above ground. There are too many ways for things to go wrong up here."

"It's not that bad. And I like being so close." Gordy's own bedroom was at the end of the hall. In their previous home, the Stitsers had brewed all of their potions downstairs. Most ingredients preferred the cold, damp temperatures often found within the confines of a basement.

"There's a window in there, is there not?" Priss probed.

"Yeah, but Mom boarded it up."

"Just give the whole army of Scourges access to your potion inventory, why don't you?" Her words might have come across as venomous had Aunt Priss not softened their impact with her most pleasant smile. "Oh, Gordy, I'm not mad at you, of course. Though Wanda needs to listen—to you especially now that you've proven your worth in the Community. There are still dangers out there."

"Something bad happened, didn't it?" Gordy asked.

Priss straightened. "Hush now. I'm not at liberty to discuss business while prying ears listen in." Her eyes flashed back to the door, where the muffled sound of a whispered argument carried on between Max and Adilene.

"You can come out now, guys," Gordy said.

The door dragged against the carpet, and Adilene's timid face appeared in the opening. "Hello, Ms. Rook," she said. "How are things?"

"Not well, if you insist on calling me by my dead mother's name," Priss responded.

Max squeezed passed Adilene and into the hallway. "What's up, Aunt Priss? What's all this talk about secret missions? You can tell me, you know. I'm practically a member of B.R.E.W."

Aunt Priss's nose twitched, and she winked at Gordy. "Well, *I* am not a member of B.R.E.W. Therefore, my mission doesn't pertain to them or, unfortunately, to you. Now, don't the two of you have somewhere to go? Gordy and I need to chat before his mother gets home from her meeting."

"Gets back?" Max smirked. "Isn't she already downstairs?"

"Yeah, with all those people?" Gordy added.

Priss narrowed her eyes in confusion. "Whatever do you mean?"

"All your friends." Gordy nodded toward the stairs.

She lowered her head and strained to listen. "What friends?"

"Those . . ." Gordy paused, frowning. The sounds from downstairs—the voices and the heavy footfalls on the kitchen floor—had mysteriously vanished. An eerie silence had filled the house.

Aunt Priss lightly pinched Gordy's cheek. From the satchel dangling below her shoulder, she pulled out a glass jar filled with a substance that looked like strawberry jam.

"It's my new Cacophonous Compound," she said, pursing her lips and grunting as she twisted off the red lid.

All at once the sounds returned, echoing downstairs. The sudden noise forced Gordy to cover his ears in surprise, as once again the slew of voices began clambering over each other, though never quite forming any coherent words. Gordy could hear the distinct sloshing of a dishwasher, as well as what might have been the hiss of an air compressor and who knew what other appliances whirring to life.

Priss's eyes twinkled, and she suppressed a giggle as she glanced at Gordy, Max, and Adilene before returning the lid to the container, which immediately silenced the commotion.

Gordy gawked at the jar in awe. "That's my new favorite potion."

"Mine too!" Priss agreed. "It's the perfect way to cause just enough distraction to sneak by enemies unnoticed. Took me weeks to perfect the recipe."

"Have you had to sneak by a lot of enemies lately?" Gordy asked.

She curled her lip and glanced away. "Perhaps."

"May I?" Gordy held out his hand, and Aunt Priss plopped the jam jar into his palm.

"Don't I always come bearing gifts?" she asked. "Though, I recommend you let it settle for a good hour or so. I have found that after opening the jar a few times, it agitates the mixture to a level that can make the sounds a tad inappropriate. I'd hate for your mom to come home to hear a profanity-laced tirade in her kitchen."

Max rubbed his hands together and grinned mischievously at Gordy. "You *have* to bring that to school on Monday!"

Gordy sat at the kitchen table, a bowl of chips and salsa lying between him and Aunt Priss. Max and Adilene had gone home for the afternoon, and Priss had just filled Gordy in on the successful raid that had taken down Yeltzin and his gang.

"I can't believe Bawdry's still around," Gordy said. He felt severely let down for not being involved. "So, is he buried now?" What could you do with the mummified remains of a dead king once they were no longer being used as a proxy body?

"Not exactly," Aunt Priss answered. "Your Ice Ball potion worked a little too well. Not only did it freeze Bawdry, but it temporarily trapped Esmeralda inside. Your mother thought it best to turn everything over to B.R.E.W. That's where Wanda's at now."

Gordy shook his head in disbelief. "How did you know Esmeralda and Yeltzin were going to try to kidnap me?"

"We'll get to that," she said. "But first, we don't have

much time before your mother comes home and our cover's blown. What do you have to offer me?"

Gordy cocked his head and shrugged. Offer her? He didn't know she was expecting payment.

"Oh, come on, don't play daft! You know what I'm talking about. As much as I enjoy a good salsa, I have better things to do with my time." She slapped the table, and Gordy shrunk in his seat, still confused. "I gave you a brand-new jar of Cacophonous Compound. Don't tell me you didn't make a single potion while I've been gone all these months. I granted you permission to concoct, and I want to trade!"

The light went on in Gordy's brain, and he bolted up the stairs. After tearing into his closet where he stored the good stuff, he raced back to the kitchen with a carton of clinking vials.

When they had finished trading, Gordy had another new potion for his collection to go along with Aunt Priss's Cacophonous Compound.

"It's not to be carried in your satchel," Priss explained. "This is a special potion with a special container. It's to be worn." She handed him a thin-banded silver ring.

"Worn?" Gordy looked confused. He didn't think he was cool enough to pull off wearing jewelry at school, but he changed his tune when Priss described how the potion worked. When the Sloop Solution was dropped directly into a body of water, the ring transformed into a malleable syrup that expanded and solidified into a durable surfboard. The Sloop could then be used as a small raft for a short period of time. Gordy didn't have a clue when he would ever need such a potion, but he nevertheless slipped the ring onto his pinkie finger. And though it would take some getting used to, the ring seemed hardly noticeable.

"What if I get it wet, like in the shower?" Gordy asked. He could just imagine suddenly being ejected from the bathtub by a spongy piece of board.

"As long as it stays on your finger, the ring remains intact," Aunt Priss said. She held up the potion Gordy had exchanged with her. "This—what did you call it?—Trapper Keeper? I'm not so sure why you call it that."

"I don't really like the name either, but Max came up with it."

"I figured as much. You say it will make actual quicksand?" She held the glass container close to the kitchen chandelier, examining the vibrant purple liquid in the light.

Gordy nodded enthusiastically. "Fast-moving quicksand. Your target has less than a second before they sink and then the ground becomes solid around them."

"Perfect!" Aunt Priss tossed the flask into the air and caught it in her hand before tucking it away for safekeeping. "I want the recipe too. You can't imagine how handy this potion will be in the Swigs."

"The Swigs?" Gordy asked.

Priss scooped a chip filled with salsa into her mouth

and munched noisily, crumbs falling from her lips. "Swigs are areas where B.R.E.W. has zero jurisdiction."

"What do you mean? I thought B.R.E.W. had control everywhere."

She laughed. "Your mother and other Investigators do their best to take down the nastiest Scourges when possible, but B.R.E.W. is understaffed, which allows a whole slew of sludge to slip through the cracks. 'Swigs' is just the term we use to indicate a gap within B.R.E.W.'s governing borders."

"So it's like the Wild West." Gordy imagined a saloon with robed criminals ordering drinks and tossing Vintreet Traps at each other's feet.

"Not exactly," she said. "More like several shady trading posts. Most of the B.R.E.W. elite will go their whole careers without stepping foot in them."

"How's that possible?" Gordy asked. "If they wanted, couldn't a Lead Investigator just walk right in and start arresting people?"

Priss nodded. "If they wanted to spend all their time and energy hunting them down. But the location changes randomly, and an alarm is triggered when anyone bloodlinked to the Vessel, like your mom, for instance, comes within a mile of the entryway. What Wanda wouldn't give to gain access to the Swigs."

Gordy narrowed his eyes suspiciously, finding it hard to believe his mom had yet to discover their location.

Priss smiled. "Besides, not all who do business there are

considered high-level threats. Many of them just choose not to be governed by B.R.E.W. Take me, for example. You wouldn't want to see me go out of business, would you?"

"So what we just did right now—me and you potion swapping? Is that what happens in the Swigs?"

Priss crinkled her nose. "Better watch yourself, Gordy Stitser. You'll end up like me before you know it." She opened a can of soda, sending a light spray of carbonation into the air before she took a sip. "Trading, I'm afraid, is not all that takes place there. There are quite a few unsavory dealings as well. My most recent purpose was to get information. I was listening to the chatter. Seeing if your name would get brought up by anyone on my watch list."

Gordy brought a chip up to his mouth but paused before biting. Aunt Priss's watch list was undoubtedly made up of menacing characters. Scourges who stirred up plenty of trouble for B.R.E.W. "I guess, judging by what happened today with Esmeralda, it did."

Priss opened another can of soda and handed it to him. Instead of taking a drink, Gordy held the cold container in his hand, rubbing the condensation off with his thumb.

"But I'm okay, right?" he asked. "You caught Yeltzin and Bawdry. Does that mean I don't have to drive to school with Bolter every morning?" Estelle was seriously starting Gordy's eighth-grade year off on a sour note.

"We need to make sure before we decide anything. There could be others who rally to Esmeralda's cause, and your name is now at the forefront of every discussion."

"Why me?"

"Why do you think?" Aunt Priss cracked a smile. "You're the troublemaker who foiled their grand plans. But you're also the grandson of the legendary Mezzarix Rook. That carries weight in all sorts of nasty circles, for better or for worse."

Gordy couldn't understand how it could be for the better. Gordy liked his grandfather, though the only conversation they'd had occurred several months ago. Still, Gordy knew his Grandpa Mezzarix was possibly the most dangerous Elixirist alive.

"Who tells you these things?" Gordy asked.

"I have a reliable source. Someone I trust who can get information for a cost. Believe me, I've paid a pretty penny to stay informed on matters that involve you." She reached over and tousled Gordy's hair.

For the second time that afternoon, Gordy's mom came home from work. Only this time, she wasn't just a figment of Gordy's imagination. He barely had time to hide his carton of potions beneath his chair before she stormed into the kitchen. Aunt Priss casually spun around in her seat, watching Gordy's mom as she moved about the appliances. Her footsteps were heavy, and she rattled the cupboards, her breathing labored and erratic, as though she had raced all the way home from work on foot.

"Hi, Mom." Gordy smiled at her as innocently as he could. "Aunt Priss and I were just—"

"Swapping. Yes, I know." His mom began moving several dirty dishes into the sink. They clattered noisily.

"I can wash those," Gordy offered.

"No, I'll do them." His mom closed her eyes and smiled, but it looked strained.

"Are you okay?" Gordy asked.

"I'm fine. Now, up the stairs you go, and take your box of contraband with you. Priscilla and I have important matters to discuss."

"Do we now?" Aunt Priss asked. "Here I thought we had done everything of importance already."

After sliding his carton of vials out from under the chair, Gordy began walking slowly toward the hallway, hoping to hear a morsel of the conversation.

"I had a meeting after depositing the convicted," his mom said to Priss. "I thought it was just a standard one-on-one, but . . . Gordy, please don't try to listen in!" she snapped. Gordy froze in the doorway, his shoulders creeping up toward his ears. "I have a million things to do before our guests arrive, and I don't need you distracting me right now."

Gordy turned around and cast a sideways glance at Priss. "Who's coming over?"

His mom dug her fist into her side and ran her fingers through her hair. It was then that Gordy noticed her smudged makeup and the faint streak of mascara trailing down from the corners of her eyes.

"You've seen better days, sis," Aunt Priss said, breaking

the silence. "And you might as well spill the beans. Gordy's a smart kid. He'll find out soon enough when people start knocking on the door."

"Bolter and Zelda are coming," Gordy's mom said, controlling her voice. "They'll be here in less than an hour. Your father's already on his way."

"What's going on?" Gordy could sense the tension. Bolter and Zelda were two of his mother's most trusted friends at B.R.E.W., and they had been over a number of times. What made this meeting so different?

Gordy's mom pulled a chair out from the kitchen table and dropped into the seat. "I had to attend a disciplinary hearing this afternoon."

"A disciplinary hearing?" Aunt Priss asked. "For whom?"

"For me," she answered, massaging the crease between her eyebrows with her fingers. "The new Chamber President asked for my resignation. As of this moment, I no longer work for B.R.E.W."

She can't just fire you," Bolter said later that evening when he was seated on the living room couch. His satchel, a handmade bag of pieced-together automotive upholstery, rested in his lap. Normally in good spirits, Bolter's demeanor was somber, his brow furrowed, his voice steady and deep.

"You are a decorated Investigator with countless arrests to your name," Bolter reasoned. "Half the exiled world owes their imprisonments to the great Wanda Stitser!"

"That's not making me feel better." Gordy's mom sat next to him with her elbows resting on her knees, her face buried in her hands. She wasn't crying, but the conversation seemed to be sapping the energy from her body.

Gordy sat in the recliner across from the couch and had been quiet for most of the evening. All he had been told was that his mom had been in a lot of hot water recently because she and the new Chamber President, the senior member of the B.R.E.W. Chamber of Directors, did not see eye to eye. Gordy couldn't imagine a life where his mom wasn't B.R.E.W.'s Lead Investigator anymore. What would she do now?

Bolter flashed an embarrassed smile. "All I'm saying is that no one in their right mind will go through with this."

"It has already happened, Bolter," she said.

"Then you'll file an appeal," Bolter said. "I will testify in your behalf. That should be sufficient to clear you of this bogus verdict."

A chirping hiccup rose from the floor. "You act as though your opinion matters, dear," squeaked Zelda, her natural voice sounding as though touched by helium. A squat woman with bright-green hair and white eyelashes, Zelda couldn't have been more than four and a half feet tall. She sat cross-legged next to the couch, her nimble fingers weaving two crochet hooks through a purple-threaded tea cozy.

"My opinion carries some weight." Bolter puffed out his chest with purpose.

"Yes, in Machinery." Zelda nodded.

Bolter slapped his knee. "Precisely!"

Zelda giggled, which sounded like a baby goat being tickled. "You're the only one who works in Machinery anymore." She never looked up from her crocheting.

"You don't understand," Gordy's mom said. "If I hadn't hidden the Eternity Elixir in Chixculub or involved my father in this whole ordeal, perhaps I wouldn't have faced these charges."

"Oh please, Wanda," Aunt Priss said from her spot by the fireplace. "You act as though B.R.E.W. deserves to know everything. You risk your life protecting them, and what do you get in return? There's a reason you kept the Eternity Elixir hidden for all those years, remember?"

Gordy's mom glanced tiredly at her sister. "At the time, I didn't trust the Chamber President would take care of it."

"And you trust the current president?" Priss asked.

Wanda exhaled forcefully in exasperation. "I don't know her well enough to condemn her."

Priss sighed in disappointment. "Head wrongfully placed in the stocks, with the axe barreling down, and you take the side of the executioner! Pardon me if I don't go boohooing along with the rest of you. From what I hear, the Chamber of Directors has started ExSponging criminals. Did you know that?"

"That's just a rumor," Bolter said. "We don't know that for sure."

"I do," Priss said. "My source has kept me plenty informed."

"Let's discuss that source, shall we?" Zelda asked. "Can we trust him?"

Priss stiffened. "Why wouldn't you be able to?"

Zelda licked her lips. "We can't very well launch a full-scale investigation into Chamber matters without verified information. That might be how business gets handled in the Swigs, but not within B.R.E.W.-governed boundaries."

"What does ExSponge mean?" Gordy asked.

Zelda cleared her throat. "It's the process of removing an Elixirist's ability to brew—permanently."

Gordy flinched in surprise. "Isn't that considered cruel?"

"Precisely!" Priss snapped her fingers and pointed at Gordy. "The youngest one of us can see the sadistic nature of the practice. Why can't the rest of you?"

"It's not against the law to ExSponge a dangerous criminal," Gordy's mom said. "The new president is just trying to maintain a measure of order."

Priss threw her hands up in disgust. "I need some fresh air!" Snatching up her satchel, she stormed out the front door.

"Refreshments are ready!" Gordy's dad entered the living room, carrying a tray of glasses that swirled with a variety of colors. He raised an eyebrow, smiling awkwardly. "What did I miss?"

"Nothing, dear," Gordy's mom replied. "It's what we've already discussed."

"Well, then, here's a root beer for you and one for Bolter." He carefully plucked two glasses from the center. The tray wobbled, but he managed to keep the rest of the beverages from falling.

"Lovely, Gordon!" Bolter accepted the drink. Gordy didn't know how Bolter had lost his fingers, but by the way he held his glass without spilling a single drop, he would've never guessed they were missing.

Gordy's dad puffed out his cheeks as he handed Gordy

a lemonade. Then he turned to Zelda. "And last but not least"—he furrowed his brow—"a cup of hot-and-sour soup and a glass of milkweed nectar for Ms. Morphata. I'm assuming I added everything correctly, because I just tossed in whatever Wanda had left in the Tupperware dish on the counter."

Zelda's eyes twinkled, and she carefully cradled the porcelain teacup in her hands before dipping a pinkie in and tasting the steaming liquid. The green-haired woman was momentarily subdued with satisfaction, her eyes drifting wistfully closed. "Hope it wasn't any trouble," she said.

"Not at all," Gordy's dad replied. "I've been wanting to try out my new beverage dispenser. It's one of the many perks in my line of work, you know?"

Zelda's mouth fell open slightly. "Your beverage dispenser has hot-and-sour soup on tap?"

The corners of Mr. Stitser's eyes crinkled. "No, it doesn't actually."

"Well, this is quite delicious." She flicked the side of her cup with one sparkly fingernail.

"I guess Gordo and I will head upstairs and watch a movie," Gordy's dad said. "I picked up a rental. Lots of blood. Lots of gore." He waggled his eyebrows and made his voice sound angry and British. "At least as much blood and gore as to be expected in a PG-13 horror movie." He grinned sheepishly at Gordy's mom. "We'll leave you all to your meeting."

Mrs. Stitser reached out and squeezed her husband's forearm. "Actually, I'd like Gordy to stay."

"You would?" Gordy leaned forward in the recliner. He had been wondering if there'd be more to discuss that evening but knew better than to ask too many questions.

"This subject deals with you directly, Gordy," his mom answered, and she looked up at her husband. "You should probably be a part of this too." She slid to one side of the sofa, giving Mr. Stitser a place to sit in the middle. After a sip of her root beer, she placed the drink on the end table next to the couch. "I'll get right to it," she said. "Because of my termination, I will no longer be allowed to continue Gordy's training at headquarters."

Gordy slumped back in his chair. He hadn't thought about that, but it made sense. If his mom didn't work for B.R.E.W. anymore, there was no way they would allow her to train him.

"What happens to me?" he asked.

"I wasn't given an opportunity to press the issue while I was being escorted from the building," his mom answered. "Having said that, I believe it's safe to assume your testing will continue, but under the watchful eye of someone else."

"Who?" Gordy wondered.

"Someone appointed by the Chamber President," Bolter suggested. "Someone she deems a fitting trainer."

"That's good, then," Gordy's dad said. "Gordo will still be able to advance."

Gordy's mom took in a deep breath and held it. "There's

something we need to consider. Gordy was very much in-volved during the attack on B.R.E.W. Headquarters. I had been able to keep his abilities somewhat hidden from the Chamber's knowledge up until that point, but now that has changed. They know that Gordy is . . . unique."

Gordy didn't like being talked about as if he were some sort of lab animal in the living room. In a way, it was cool having a reputation for being unique among the upper echelon of the B.R.E.W. elite, but then again, lab animals tended to be dissected from time to time.

"The Chamber will want to see if Gordy poses a threat to their way of governing. His testing will certainly be ex-tensive," his mom said. "The good news is that they should see the potential in him that we already know exists, Gordy will most certainly graduate to the level of an Elixirist."

Gordy liked the sound of that. He already felt as though he were operating at an Elixirist level. He just needed the training to become full-fledged. "Sounds good to me."

Zelda clicked her tongue. "I, myself, wouldn't want all that attention."

Gordy stared down at the small woman who sat twirl-ing one of her crochet hooks with a tiny finger. "Why not?"

"What if they *don't* see the potential in you?" she asked. "What if they see you as a hazard? I'd say you have a fifty-fifty chance of either impressing them or confirming their fears."

Gordy's mom nodded. "That's what I'm worried about. With me being fired for nearly causing the downfall of

B.R.E.W., I suspect they'll wonder if Gordy is in danger of ending up like his mother."

"What's wrong with that?" Gordy's mom was his hero. He'd be lucky to end up just like her.

Zelda giggled. "Oh my, this could be disastrous."

"I don't understand," Gordy's dad chimed in. "What exactly will they have him do during these training sessions?"

"Nothing," Gordy answered. "Last time, I just Deciphered ingredients and brewed a handful of easy potions." He could have done that all night without breaking a sweat.

"That's because you had your mother there controlling the session," Bolter said.

Gordy looked at his mom and saw her deeply concerned expression, and something clicked in his mind. That first training, when she had been so strange, had all been an act. His mom had purposely made Gordy perform easy brewing techniques because she didn't want the people watching on the other end of the camera feed to know what he could actually do.

"Can I just skip my training?" Gordy asked.

Zelda giggled again, which was becoming quite annoying. "If you want to delay becoming an Elixirist for many years, or never become one at all, sure! Why not?"

"That's just the way the new Chamber President works, I'm afraid," Gordy's mom said. "She has a passion for older methods. Stronger and more-lasting punishments. She won't tolerate anyone deviating from the Chamber's orders."

Gordy folded his arms and stared at his untouched lemonade. "What do I do?"

"For now, you'll continue on as normal," his mom said. "We'll keep our fingers crossed that the Chamber President assigns you a solid trainer, someone we can trust to give you a fair shot, and then we'll take it one step at a time. But, Gordy, do you know how to keep a low profile?"

Gordy thought about the question for a moment and nodded. "I think so."

"That means you have to play by the rules from now on," his mom said. "No more taking risks. No more breaking procedures. Don't do anything that will draw unnecessary attention to yourself. Not at school. Not in the neighborhood. Not with your friends. Do you understand?"

"I understand," he answered.

That should be easy enough. Gordy could keep a low profile. He would just do what he did every day at Kipland Middle School. He would blend in. Fade into the background. Become invisible. Then, during his next training session, Gordy would show B.R.E.W. that he could play by the rules.

18

Gordy woke up to a buzzing vibration.

"What is that?" he called out, bleary-eyed and confused. When he saw his cell phone trembling on his bedside table, he snatched it up and checked the screen. He didn't recognize the number. Plus, it was 12:14 a.m. He'd barely been asleep for two hours, only to be rudely awakened. With an agitated growl, Gordy attempted to toss the phone back on the table, but it broke free from its charging cord and toppled into a pile of laundry, where it nestled down deep enough that he could no longer see the brilliant light from the screen cutting through the darkness.

Gordy collapsed on his pillow. His head felt fuzzy, and the whole room had fallen completely black. Palming his eyes, he dragged his fingers down his cheeks.

Bizz, bizz, bizzzzzzzz!

The cell phone started up again, buzzing angrily amid his crumpled clothing. Gordy considered ignoring it, but the caller persisted. Plunging his hand into the pile, he pulled the phone free and brushed away a sock stuck to the back.

"Who is this?" he grumbled.

"Rude," a female voice answered. "Do you always answer your phone like that?"

Gordy pulled the phone away from his ear and checked the number again, trying to place the voice. "I do when people call me after midnight," he said.

"And that happens a bunch, I bet. Of course it does," the girl replied, without any attempt to mask her sarcasm. "You're the great Gordy Stitser. I'm sure loads of fans call you at all hours of the night."

"Sasha?" he asked, not entirely certain.

"Obviously."

"It . . . uh, what are you calling for?" He sat up in bed, now fully alert, and reached over to turn on his lamp, illuminating the room. Sasha Brexil had called him. How did she get his number? And why was she calling so early in the morning?

"I was just brewing in my lab, as I do, and it dawned on me that maybe I forgot to tell you a few of the rules for my party."

There definitely hadn't been any mention of rules. Gordy's whole interaction with Sasha had happened more than a week ago and had lasted less than five minutes, and she had dominated the conversation.

"Nothing major," she continued. "You just need to bring your own satchel. I'm assuming you have one."

Gordy looked over at his backpack leaning against his closet door. It was the closest thing to a satchel he owned. Most official potion-makers' satchels came specially equipped with compartments and leather straps to secure test tubes and prevent vials from spilling. His backpack had a decent amount of webbing woven on the inside pocket, but that was about it.

"You'll also need to bring your own ingredients," Sasha continued, not giving Gordy any time to respond. "This is a sharing party, so bring a recipe or two to try out in the group, and come prepared with empty containers to take home new findings. And don't forget the invitation. That, along with my approval, will get you past our wards. They're quite strong. I helped brew them myself."

"Really?" Gordy asked, trying to sound interested. He wanted to say he hadn't decided yet if he was actually going to attend her party, but for some reason, Gordy didn't have the guts to say anything that might trigger an angry outburst. Plus, he felt jealous of Sasha's late-night concocting, as if she might somehow gain the upper hand on Gordy. Which was ridiculous. Upper hand to what?

"Oh, and don't bring anything volatile or my parents will flip," Sasha said.

Gordy cleared his throat. "Your dad's going to be there?"

"Why wouldn't he be?" Sasha's withering laughter

poured from the phone. "Don't tell me he got into your head the other day when he yelled at you."

Gordy frowned. "He told you about that?"

"My dad tells me everything. He just likes to mess with everyone. Every Dram, that is."

It sure hadn't sounded like he was just messing with Gordy. The expectations had been laid out plain and clear. Gordy could imagine Mr. Brexil hovering over his shoulder while he did his best to brew safe and friendly potions. Ones that made flowers bloom or produced soap bubbles.

"Does he know how to brew?" Gordy asked.

"He's the principal of Kipland, remember?"

"Yeah, but lots of Elixirists have a day job."

"No, my dad's not an Elixirist. He can barely brew coffee," Sasha said. "But my mom? She's the best potion master in the country."

Gordy imagined Sasha arrogantly staring at her fingernails while sprinkling herbs into a cauldron.

"I doubt that," he muttered.

"Oh, a challenge. Throwing down the gauntlet, eh?" Gordy could hear what sounded like thick, bubbling liquid being poured into a container. He could have been mistaken, but he had brewed enough potions over the years to recognize the sound. "One second," she said. "Let me just stopper these."

More bubbling, along with the gaseous whistle of a Bunsen burner torching a cauldron. Then Gordy heard the plunk of several corks being wedged into test tubes.

"That should be what we do tomorrow," Sasha said. "Let's have a game to see who can concoct the most difficult potion."

"How's that a game?" Gordy asked.

"If I win, then my mom is the more skilled Elixirist, because she taught me everything I know. And if you win, your mom can hold that title."

Gordy wanted to tell her to go bob for apples in a vat of Balding Booze, but he didn't. Sasha Brexil didn't seem like the type of person he could easily insult without facing consequences.

"I think that's everything," Sasha said. "Own satchel, own ingredients, own recipes. No volatile potions—but something definitely difficult. Bring your invitation. And . . . oh, I remembered! Don't tell your parents."

Gordy started nodding before realizing what Sasha had said. "Why not?"

"Because." She paused and sighed. "That's the other rule."

"That's a strange rule."

"Maybe, but it's the most important one."

"And yet you forgot to say it until the end." Gordy swung his legs over the side of the bed and slid his feet into his slippers.

Sasha snickered. "No, I was pausing for dramatic effect. I wanted to plant that rule in your head, and I knew if I waited until the end, you'd honestly hear me."

"You can count me out, then." Gordy quietly moved to the closet and picked up his backpack.

"You're not coming because you can't tell your mom about my little get-together? Aw, Gordy, I didn't know you were so sensitive."

"I'm not sensitive. I just don't like lying to my parents."

"It's not lying. They can know about the party, just not the details. Besides, both my parents will be there, along with me and Dez Mumphrey, Brianna Washburn, and Pedro Rodriguez. Now you know everyone who is attending. All the mystery's gone. Besides, it was my mother's idea to keep the potion part of the party a secret."

"Your mom said that?" Sasha's snooty behavior now had an origin. Mrs. Brexil sounded shady.

"Uh-huh. My mom doesn't want any other adults bothering us during our brewing time. She knows how important it is for young Drams to have privacy and freedom to concoct. Don't you agree?"

"I guess," he said.

"Good. Keep it tight-lipped until tomorrow night. *Au revoir.*"

The line went dead.

What responsible parent set a rule that no other adult could know about some brewing party? He knew for a fact his mom would never allow him to go to Sasha's under false pretenses, especially since she had just instructed Gordy earlier that evening to keep a low profile. And yet, now more than ever, Gordy felt as though he needed to go. Sasha's party had sparked his curiosity. Beyond that, he needed to prove his superiority over Sasha. His mom's reputation was at stake!

Most Saturday nights, Gordy's parents went out on a date, and they were usually out until late. That meant Gordy would have no problem sneaking out of his house to go to the Brexils. He'd be back before his parents even knew he had left. Yes, Gordy would need to babysit his brother and sister, but he could leave them watching movies all night until he returned.

No longer tired, Gordy clutched his backpack in his arms and crept to his door. He opened it and checked the hallway. All the lights were out, including the ones downstairs. Everyone was sleeping.

Gordy dragged a knuckle across the bottom of his nose. No doubt about it, he would be at that party, and he would show Sasha's little gathering a thing or two. But for now, Gordy needed to brew.

19

Maintaining focus throughout a brewing session had always been one of the most important rules of potion making. Gordy knew that rule well. His mom had pounded it into his brain throughout his training. But he had also developed a knack for fudging it when it came to basic brewing. Some potions were just a cinch. Six simple ingredients, a lightly heated brass cauldron, and a few actions while sprinkling in items were all it took to make a batch of Torpor Tonic, a knockout agent regularly used by Elixirists. Over the course of Gordy's lifetime, he had probably made enough Torpor Tonic to fill a kiddie pool.

While his cauldron simmered, Gordy tossed in pieces of magnolia bark with a garden trowel, and he gazed at the rows of multicolored recipe books lining one of his mother's bookshelves. He barely paid any attention to the potion in front of him, routinely adding several fluffs of dandelion, snapping the gossamer seeds into the mixture with his fingers. The potion sputtered, forming lazy bubbles at the surface.

Gordy blew out his cheeks and cranked the knob on the Bunsen burner to the maximum level. The flames intensified, coloring the cauldron with an orange glow. He moved to the apothecary table and selected two separate containers of ingredients, their labels unreadable. He added both to the potion without glancing down at the now-roiling liquid spitting out of the bowl. On the countertop, he diced a stalk of pokeweed and squished the spine of a dried caterpillar with the dull edge of a scalpel. He rolled the pieces together and dropped them into the potion.

The potion produced a squealing sound, like a tea-kettle demanding release from the heat, and Gordy turned off the Bunsen burner. He plucked a test tube from the rack and was about to dip it into the cauldron when the light to the laboratory snapped on.

Wearing her bathrobe and pink slippers, Gordy's mother stood in the doorway, leaning into the jamb with her shoulder.

"Hey, Mom," Gordy said, startled. He squinted in the sudden brightness.

"It's late, pal." She glanced at the clock.

"I know. I—" Gordy yawned. "I just couldn't sleep."

His mom's eyes looked droopy, but she exhaled and smiled. "What are you making?"

"Torpor Tonic," he answered.

The fumes from Gordy's potion wafted across the

room, and his mom inhaled briefly. Her smile faltered, and she crossed the lab, arms folded, brow furrowed as she peered into the cauldron. "You sure about that?"

"Yeah, why?"

Gordy's mom opened her mouth and laughed in disbelief. "What have I told you about brewing volatile potions when I'm not around? It's a big rule to break."

"Okay." Why was she looking at him as though he had done something bad? "Why are you telling me this?"

Gordy's mom picked up an oven mitt and slid the brass cauldron off the wrought-iron holder, being careful not to slosh the potion over the edge. "Is that why you chose to brew at this hour? So I wouldn't accidentally stumble in?" She pointed to the squished remains of the insect lying a few inches from the cauldron. "That's a Lonomia caterpillar husk. Am I wrong?"

Gordy shrugged. "I think you must have left it out earlier."

She glared at him. "Nice try, bub." She sniffed the fumes coiling up from the potion. "Hemlock. Oleander. Pokeberry stalks. Were you trying to brew a Mangle potion?"

"A what?" Gordy's mom had been stressed out lately, but she wasn't making any sense. Gordy didn't have a clue what she was talking about.

"This mixture is designed to cause permanent bodily harm. Who did you plan to give this to?"

"It's a Torpor Tonic, Mom!" Gordy glanced down at the cauldron as his mom probed the surface of the potion with a long wooden spoon. The brownish liquid promptly snapped the spoon in half. He reached for the bowl, but she pulled his arm back and pushed him away from the counter.

"I understand you know your way around a lab, but that doesn't give you the right to brew things beyond your grade level. This is dark stuff, Gordy. Scourge material!"

Scourge material? Gordy opened his mouth in shock. "That's not what I was doing—honest! I wasn't trying to brew anything bad. See?" He held up a sprig of lavender still clutched in his fingers and pointed to the evidence of Torpor Tonic ingredients scattered on the counter.

"Then what happened?"

Gordy couldn't remember. His head felt foggy as though he had just woken up after an afternoon nap. He must have zoned out while he had been mixing the potion.

"Am I supposed to believe that you don't remember making this?" his mom asked.

Gordy nodded. "Don't you believe me?"

She chewed on the inside of her cheek and looked around the workstation at the opened drawers near the base of the table—drawers that were strictly off-limits to anyone other than herself. Her eyes snapped back on Gordy. "You didn't get any of it on your skin, did you?"

"Would I be mangled if I had?"

"Maybe." She grinned weakly. "And you just blacked out and this happened?"

Gordy felt his heart pounding in his chest. "Mom, what's wrong with me?"

Her stern gaze softened, and she pulled him into her arms. "Nothing's wrong with you, I don't think," she said into his ear. "I don't know the methods of Blind Batching, so I'm not sure how that works. This could just be a side effect of that skill. Let's be done with lab work for the night, okay?"

Gordy didn't protest. After helping his mother clean the countertop and watching her carefully stopper the Mangle potion into several small vials that she tucked away in the bottom drawer, he followed her out of the lab. But Gordy doubted sleep would come easy to him that night.

20

For the second time in as many weeks, the blue pickup truck rolled into Adilene's neighborhood. Adilene was out in the yard with her dad, pulling weeds, when the vehicle stopped in the road and Cadence climbed down from the passenger side. Her uncle Carlisle hunched in the driver's seat, staring glumly through the windshield. The girl waggled a scolding finger at him, and though Adilene might have been mistaken, the older man cringed away from her, offering his niece an imperceptible nod.

"Hello, Adilene," Cadence said, crossing the road and waving cheerily. "Would you like to play?"

Play? They weren't in elementary school anymore. No one in the eighth grade used the word "play" when they wanted to hang out together. She started to laugh but then realized Cadence wasn't telling a joke. Adilene felt embarrassed for the girl.

"Ah, I suppose." Adilene looked at her father for

confirmation. They had only just begun their Saturday chores, which normally took until lunch to finish.

Adilene's dad shrugged. "You'll have to work later," he grunted and went back to yanking deep-rooted weeds from the flower bed.

"Great!" Cadence said, marching up to the porch and waiting by the door. "I really enjoyed those cupcakes we had the other day. They were so good. Should we go inside?"

Adilene hurriedly dusted off her knees and shot a wary look at Carlisle, who had yet to drive away, the truck idling in the middle of the street.

"What's he doing?" Adilene asked.

Cadence followed her gaze. "Just one moment, please," she said, stepping down from the porch and glaring at her uncle. Without saying another word, she swatted a hand in the air and pointed aggressively down the road. Though Uncle Carlisle never looked in her direction, the blue truck lurched forward and sputtered away.

Odd family, Adilene thought. She glanced at her dad, who raised his eyebrows as if he had been thinking the same thing.

"If you like baking, we could make brownies," Adilene suggested, leading the way into the kitchen. She had planned to make a treat later that afternoon anyway.

Cadence scrunched her nose. "Maybe, but I thought we could go to your room first."

"And do what?"

Cadence shrugged. "Whatever you want."

Adilene scratched the back of her neck, her eyes drifting down to the bag dangling at Cadence's hip. "I know what we could do!" She checked around the corner to make sure her mother wasn't nearby and lowered her voice. "We could make potions together." Why hadn't she thought of that before? Cadence curled her lip into a smile and nodded. Adilene almost cheered. "My room's upstairs, third door on the right," she said. "I'll gather my things and meet you there."

~

Adilene balanced a cauldron on her portable hot plate in her bedroom. It wasn't really a cauldron, but a stainless-steel pot was better than nothing. Nervous about heating anything up on the carpet, she had placed the hot plate on a TV tray and had opened her window to prevent any exhaust from setting off the smoke alarm. Several sheets of her handwritten notes she had taken during the many brewing sessions with Gordy lay strewn about her on the floor.

Cadence sat cross-legged, perusing Adilene's seventh-grade yearbook in her lap. "Is this him?" she asked, pointing to a small picture midway up the page.

Adilene glanced over. The picture was of a boy with dark hair, dark eyes, and wearing a Gryffindor T-shirt with a small rip underneath the collar. Adilene remembered that day; one of his potions had exploded, and a piece of shattered test tube had sliced through the air and his shirt. "Yeah, that's Gordy."

"Funny—you wouldn't be able to tell he was a potion master just by looking at him," Cadence said.

Gordy wasn't really a potion master. Not yet, at least. Still, Adilene couldn't help but smile about her best friend's amazing talent. "Isn't that how it works, though?" she asked. "You're all just regular people, but with a special gift."

"His mom's an Elixirist, right?" Cadence asked, staring at the picture.

Adilene nodded. "Yes, she's great."

"What does she do for B.R.E.W.?"

The coils on the hot plate glowed red. The cauldron was ready for ingredients, but so far, the two of them had yet to decide what to make.

"She catches people."

"Catches people?" Cadence looked up from the page, frowning. "Why do they need catching?"

Adilene couldn't remember the name Gordy had called them, but it started with an *S*—savages or scavengers, or something like that. "They brew bad things and harm people, and she's someone that goes out and stops them."

Cadence closed the yearbook and ran her hand over the cover. "Where do they put these bad people once they catch them?"

Adilene shrugged. Shouldn't Cadence, a Dram, already know the answer? "I guess in prison." She gestured to the cauldron. "This is getting hot, and we need to start putting in ingredients, I think."

Cadence rubbed her hands together. "What are you going to make?"

"I don't know. Um, Gordy has a potion that can make plants play music from your phone." Adilene pored over her notes, no longer certain. "It creates a Bluetooth signal through photosynthesis, or something like that."

"Let's see that one," Cadence said eagerly.

Adilene's grin faltered. "You're going to have to look at the recipe, and then I can hand you the ingredients."

"Why?"

Why? Adilene flinched. "I told you I can't brew. Oh, here's one that Gordy made last year that makes the paint on your wall see-through." She held out the paper to Cadence. "It's good for spying on your neighbor, I suppose. But it's an easier one, I think. Not too many ingredients. Shouldn't be too difficult."

Cadence refused to take the page. "They both sound great. Whatever one you want. Go ahead."

Adilene's shoulders dropped. "Is this how you're going to be?" She didn't want to sound agitated. She hardly knew Cadence, and she didn't want to seem rude to her new friend. "I'm not a Dram, remember?"

"Neither am I."

Adilene lowered her recipes and scratched the side of her nose. "What do you mean?"

"I never said I was a Dram," Cadence answered. "You just assumed it."

Adilene could have sworn Cadence had told her that

she was a Dram, but now that she thought about it, that conversation hadn't ended the way she had imagined. "Then what are we doing?" she wondered aloud, turning down the knob of the hot plate and killing the heat beneath the cooking pot.

"Maybe we can't brew together, but we could try something else." Cadence pulled open her bag and removed a vial that Adilene had seen on two separate occasions. The contents had an inky, bluish hue to it.

Adilene dropped the page of notes and rested her chin on her hands. "If you're not a Dram, where did you get that potion?"

Cadence held the vial up to the light. The substance remained murky, despite the glow from above. "It's a gift."

"From your uncle?" Adilene asked, confused.

Cadence shook her head. "No, from me. To you."

Adilene narrowed her eyes, studying the strange liquid, watching it bubble as Cadence rolled the vial between her fingers. "What can it do?" she asked.

"Rub some on your skin and you can go wherever you want, whenever you want, and no one can keep you out."

Adilene leaned forward, and to her surprise, Cadence handed her the vial. Clasping the glass container in her fingers, she swirled the liquid round and round. As she took hold of the wax stopper, she paused to see what Cadence would do.

"Go on," Cadence urged. "Open it."

"What if I spill it?" She didn't want it to stain the carpet if she dropped some on the floor.

"You won't."

Adilene pulled out the wax and held the vial up to her nose. The dark blue liquid smelled metallic and oily. "You don't drink it?" she asked.

"You can, but it might make you sick the first time. Drinking it will make you disappear."

Adilene's eyes widened. A disappearing potion? Gordy had never shown her one of those. "Like really disappear?"

Cadence wiggled her fingers. "Poof," she said. "Gone."

"Why are you giving this to me?" Adilene asked.

"Because I would like to be your friend."

"You *are* my friend. You don't have to give me anything." She held out the vial, but Cadence shook her head.

"Try it. But just a drop the first time to see what happens," Cadence said. "Rub some on your arm."

Adilene hesitated. "What does it do again?"

"Here." Cadence took the vial from Adilene and placed her index finger over the opening. "The skin on your fingers and hands is too tough for this to penetrate," she explained, removing her finger, which now had a light-blue coating. She rubbed the liquid on her forearm.

The inky substance glistened on Cadence's skin. As it dried, it became nearly invisible. Adilene waited for something to happen. Several seconds passed while Cadence held her arm perfectly still, and then . . .

"Boo!" Cadence tapped Adilene on the back of her shoulder, and Adilene screamed.

"How did you get over there?" Adilene demanded, clutching her chest and whirling around. Cadence knelt on the ground behind her, giggling gleefully. "You were just in front of me a moment ago!"

"Was I?" Cadence gave Adilene a mischievous look. "Are you sure?"

"Well, no. I'm not sure anymore." It felt as though some time had passed. Was that how the potion worked? Did it confuse Adilene into thinking that Cadence had stayed seated the whole time? "So what do you do with it, besides sneak up on people and scare them?"

"You can fool people into thinking you're someone you're not," Cadence explained. "You can go anywhere. Into Gordy's home. Or his lab. Or into B.R.E.W. Head-quarters, if you wanted it. You could walk right past the wards, and if you don't want them to, no one will see you enter."

Adilene felt a prickle on the back of her neck as tiny hairs stood on end. "Why would I go there?"

Cadence smiled innocently. "No reason. But if you wanted to, you could. And once you're past the wards, you won't be turned away even after the effects wear off."

"Cadence," Adilene whispered, staring at the floor. "You're scaring me a little."

"Oh!" Cadence stiffened. "I didn't mean to. That was

just an example. It's actually really fun. Do you want to try it?"

Adilene looked at the vial again and thought she might want to. Would she feel different? Would she still be the same girl? Maybe she should talk to Gordy and ask his opinion. If Cadence wasn't a Dram, where had she found such an unusual potion? She seemed like an ordinary girl, but perhaps she had stumbled upon the vial by accident.

"I don't think so." Adilene pursed her lips. "I want to wait for now."

"Suit yourself. Why don't you keep it, and then, when you're ready, we'll try it together."

Adilene looked down at the mess of glass containers and the still-warm cauldron balancing on the hot plate. "What do we do now?" she asked. "Should we bake brownies?"

"I should go." Cadence stoppered the vial with a soft piece of wax and gently laid it on Adilene's upturned palm. "Carlisle will be expecting me."

"Oh, okay," Adilene said uncertainly, but she followed Cadence out of the room regardless.

Sure enough, Uncle Carlisle had returned, the truck rumbling in the driveway.

"I had a wonderful time!" Cadence hugged Adilene.

"You did?" Adilene asked.

And then Cadence joined her uncle in the vehicle, and they backed out of the driveway. Cadence waved goodbye, and Adilene returned the gesture.

Someone needed to explain to Cadence that when you came over to "play," you generally stayed longer than thirty minutes.

"Why did your friend have to go?" Adilene's dad asked from where he knelt in the flower bed.

"I guess she had some place to be," she said.

Her dad tapped two garden trowels together and motioned for her to join him. Adilene started for the steps but realized she was still holding something in her hand. She looked down at the vial of inky liquid and felt a shiver travel up her spine.

"Just one second, Papa," she said, hurrying back to her room. She placed the bottle into the top drawer of her dresser and nestled it beneath her socks. Eventually, she would gather her courage and test out Cadence's mysterious concoction. But for now, Adilene would tend to her chores and daydream about potions.

The Beekman Room of the Maestoso Grande Hotel had been transformed into an assembly hall of Scourges. Lolly and Walsh Gittens had been working around the clock, sending word throughout the country about Mezzarix's return and their impending attack on B.R.E.W. Headquarters. At least a dozen new recruits arrived each day, filling the hall with a volatile mass of chemicals as they all brought their own eclectic mixes of potions and rare ingredients. Not to mention the smell. Scourges had never been known to bathe much, and the noxious cloud floating above the immaculate hotel may not have been the by-product of so much potion making as it was the lack of personal hygiene.

"Where did you find these people?" Mezzarix asked Ravian. He nodded toward a group of about fifteen individuals who looked as though they were wearing animal skins covered in mud. Several members of the group were laughing boisterously at a woman who was pouring a corrosive, acid-like potion onto the center of the ballroom, reducing the marble floor to slush. After several moments, the liquidized floor began to bubble, and a cephalopod-like creature emerged, blinking one enormous yellow eye at the group.

"Charming," Mezzarix said as the mud-covered woman tried coaxing the squid from the hole with her finger. "Is this how far we've fallen? These people are savages, and most of them I don't even recognize. They're practically babies."

"That's because they are babies," Ravian answered. "Sons and daughters of those once faithful to you, but who have since been banished or ExSponged. Lolly's telling everyone that once you regain control of the Vessel, you'll right the wrongs carried out against their families over the years."

"I wouldn't get their hopes up." Chaos was one thing. Mass hysteria was something entirely different. Once he took over B.R.E.W., Mezzarix intended to be selective of whom he freed from banishment and whom he invited into his close-knit circle. These newbie Scourges would be at the bottom of that list, if they were lucky enough to make it at all.

Mezzarix returned his concentration to his workstation, where he had constructed an elaborate contraption of Bunsen burners and cauldrons. A single vial containing a few ounces of Silt had been clamped beneath an evaporator. Glass tubing snaked across two banquet tables, eventually reaching the other end, where a dropper dispensed a turquoise liquid into a beaker. The beaker was nearly filled to the brim, and Mezzarix removed it from under the dropper and placed it next to a row of six other containers, each identically filled with a bluish-green potion.

"How's it coming?" Ravian selected one of the beakers and examined the contents with one squinty eye.

"It works," Mezzarix said dryly. "But the effects wear off within ten to fifteen minutes, depending on the mixture."

"That should do just wonderfully."

"It doesn't give us much time to storm the castle." Mezzarix increased the heat on one of the burners and tossed several Portuguese man-of-war tentacles into the center cast-iron cauldron. He slid another beaker under the dropper as it once again began dispensing liquid.

"We don't need much time, remember?" Ravian studied Mezzarix's face. "Are you feeling all right?"

"I'm fine," Mezzarix replied. "I just—" He felt something jerk within his stomach, a painful tugging sensation that dropped him to his knees.

While Ravian scrambled for help, Mezzarix curled into a ball on the floor, his fists digging into his abdomen. Lolly and Walsh, who had been arm wrestling in the corner of the hall, rushed over, pulling out potions from their satchels. Ones for healing and ones that numbed pain and several that could turn a patient bright yellow and give off heat like a radiator. Mezzarix swatted away their offerings.

"Take something for it, will you?" Ravian begged. "It's

not natural seeing you squirm like a maggot baking in the hot sun. How long is this going to last?"

"I need my space," Mezzarix managed to whisper.

Such episodes had transpired sporadically since Mezzarix's departure from the Forbidden Zone in Greenland, but they had become more intense as time progressed, now often happening two to three times a day. They gave no warning, and Mezzarix always ended up in the same fetal position, gasping for breath.

"How about I break his legs?" Lolly offered. "Take his mind off the stomach pain for a while?" She looked at her husband as though wondering if he'd like to help carry out her suggestion.

"And how will that help if he can't walk into B.R.E.W. on his own?" Ravian scowled at Lolly. "Are you going to carry him?"

"I could carry him," she grunted, swiveling her neck in a way that produced a series of pops from somewhere buried in her spine. "Piggyback. He can't weigh more than a buck twenty-five." She elbowed Walsh in the ribs, a goofy grin stretching across her wide face.

"Touch me and I'll brew a potion that makes that curly wig of yours float above your head for the rest of your life," Mezzarix wheezed. "It'll follow you around like a conscience, reminding you of how it was to once have hair."

Lolly's smile rapidly fizzled.

"There has to be a better way," said a voice near Mezzarix's workstation, but seemingly coming from thin air. Ms. Bimini appeared, her frail body materializing next to Ravian, deep concern apparent in her eyes. "What can we do for this poor soul?"

"Bring him the boy. Don't look at me like that, old friend," Ravian said when Mezzarix glared up at him. "It's the only way you'll be able to see this carried through to the end."

Mezzarix gritted his teeth, fighting back the urge to scream as another painful thrust attacked his gut. "Gordy is not to be involved. That wasn't part of the arrangement. I will approach him when it is necessary, but no one else."

"Always the soft one when it comes to family." Ravian knelt down and squeezed Mezzarix's shoulder. "You don't take anyone's potions. You don't take advice. If it's all the same to you, I'd rather not stay any longer than I have to in this cursed town and watch you shrivel and die."

"Tell us what to do to help you," Ms. Bimini said.

Finally, the pain subsided, and Mezzarix sat up. He glared at the group of Scourges congregating behind the Gittens, and they returned to their mischief on the other side of the Beekman Room. Above him, on the banquet tables, Mezzarix's potions bubbled in their cauldrons. He needed to get back to work. Six beakers of Replicated Silt would not be enough to overthrow B.R.E.W. These stomach pains were a distraction and a hindrance, but Mezzarix refused to bend on his rules. Having Gordy there could end his suffering immediately, but without the proper protections in place, Gordy's life would be in danger. And while Mezzarix sought for a chaotic end to B.R.E.W., he would never be able to live with himself should something happen to his grandson.

Dusting off the lapels of his suit coat, Mezzarix turned his back to the others and stared at his Replicating workstation. Lolly harrumphed as she and her husband wandered away.

"Are we going to have to endure many more of these disruptions?" Ms. Bimini asked, sidling up next to Mezzarix. "And what if the next bout sends you into a coma?"

"Wouldn't that be pleasant?" Mezzarix muttered, not looking the old woman in the eyes.

"Don't take this the wrong way," she said. "But I don't have time to waste watching you writhe. I care not about your life or your suffering. I only care about our arrangement. An arrangement that, so far, has only accomplished in gathering you an army to meet your needs. I need you to be able to keep your end of the bargain. Should these episodes become worse, I'll send for the boy myself. I know how to find him."

Mezzarix turned and gazed upon her with a venomous gleam in his eye. "That would be the biggest mistake you've ever made."

Ms. Bimini clicked her tongue. "You're good, Mezzarix, but I've heard whisperings that there are others who might be able to do what you can do. This grandson of yours has already developed a reputation as being someone who shares your skills. Should I grow too bored, perhaps I'll re-cruit him to my cause."

At that moment, Mezzarix felt invisible hands press-ing on his shoulders. He sucked in a breath as the hands moved to his throat.

"Can you keep your wits about you long enough to finish your work?" Ms. Bimini asked.

Mezzarix remained silent, and the hands fell away from his throat.

Ms. Bimini casually bowed and strolled away.

"What have I gotten myself into?" Mezzarix muttered as Ravian drew near.

"It's a revolution," Ravian replied. "They are never easy. And you may not like our new partner, but she's right. These fits you keep having are going to muddle your mind. And when that happens, you could ruin an entire batch of potion. This won't work if half our group triggers the alarms at B.R.E.W."

"You do know that once this goes down, there will be casualties. Anyone caught at the headquarters will be pun-ished severely." Mezzarix shifted his gaze toward Ravian. "You've lived quite a charmed life. I doubt you've seen the punishment B.R.E.W. can dish out."

"The reward is worth the risk," he replied. "I'm in it for the glory—and the gold, of course."

Mezzarix leaned forward and whirled a glass wand through one of the thickening mixtures. "There's no gold in Greenland."

"Let me approach Gordy," Ravian pressed. "Together, we can perform the proper ceremony to free you."

"I've taken steps to protect myself." Mezzarix clenched his jaw, fighting off the urge to jump down Ravian's throat. His constant pain had broken his ability to keep calm and stay in control.

"What sort of steps?"

"I've called in a favor from an old family friend. They'll make sure to put pieces into play soon enough." Mezzarix glanced over to where his open satchel rested next to the workstation. He could see where only one of the gray glass jars remained, peeking out from the pocket of the bag.

22

Gordy steered his bicycle off the sidewalk and laid it down in the yard of 487 Harper Hood Lane, its wheels still spinning. It had been a six-mile trek across several neighborhoods, but he had made excellent time. Mostly because he had doused one of Bolter's Burning Rubber Reductions on his tires before pushing off from his house. Gordy almost hadn't needed to pedal.

Gordy recognized Dez Mumphrey at once, stumbling up the steps leading to the massive oak door, sneezing and wiping his nose with a handkerchief. Almost everything triggered a reaction either on Dez's skin or in his lungs or in his hair. To be a Dram with his allergies was unfortunate and often resulted in catastrophe.

A large cluster of bushes, recently pruned, towered over Gordy's head, shielding him from the entryway of Sasha's massive home as he knelt down and checked the inventory of his backpack. He had brought a few vials of his most recent creations, his favorite brass cauldron, and several sheets of baseball card protectors, each small pocket crammed with ingredients.

For a moment, Gordy thought he heard something heavy snapping twigs in the bushes, and he peered through the branches, searching for the source of the sound. Despite the late-evening sun barely touching the treetops, the shadows in the bushes made it too dark to see, and whatever had made the noise had stopped. Gordy's skin prickled. He was having serious second thoughts about going into the Brexils' house. Even though he had left the twins snuggled on the couch where they would be set for hours watching their favorite YouTube channel, Gordy still felt bad about not telling his parents where he was going.

After checking once more for what might have been a dog rummaging around in the bushes, Gordy took a deep breath and walked to the front porch.

When Sasha opened the door and laid eyes on Gordy, she announced, "The guest of honor is here!"

Gordy smiled out of courtesy, but he didn't think she was being serious. Guest of honor? More like the next victim.

"I hope you brought your invitation like I told you." She extended a palm, blocking his entry into the house. "Can't get in without it."

Gordy fumbled in the front zipper pocket of his backpack and pulled out the creased invitation. Snatching it from his fingers, Sasha dropped it into a glass bowl resting on a table in the entryway. There were already three other cards floating in what looked like pink Detection potion.

"Our wards are the most powerful in the whole city," Sasha said, biting her lip and grinning as Gordy's invitation suddenly crackled with electricity. "Even more powerful than the ones at B.R.E.W."

Gordy hoped Sasha hadn't seen him roll his eyes. *What a crock!* He was starting to wish he hadn't made the six-mile bike ride to her party. He didn't know how much of Sasha's gloating he could handle.

The entryway expanded into a wide room with a spiral staircase that led to the second floor and a golden chandelier that, upon closer examination, was made up of cauldrons of various shapes and sizes and sprinkled with gemstones.

"The kitchen's this way," Sasha said. "That's where we'll be brewing."

Gordy frowned. "Why not in the lab?"

She rolled her eyes. "We're not allowed downstairs in my mom's lab. She keeps too many dangerous things there. And there are extra wards around the lab that won't even let me in. The kitchen will be fine. Trust me."

Sasha led Gordy through an immense hallway plastered with family portraits. Each one showcased a gradually aging Sasha, from infant to one that could have been taken yesterday. In every pose, a smiling Sasha stood between her father, who wore a stern expression, and her mother, who possessed a pleasant smile. Like Sasha, Mrs. Brexil had dark, perfect skin and large brown eyes with long eye-lashes. But unlike her daughter, Mrs. Brexil didn't seem to age. She looked identical from the first portrait to the thirteenth. Gordy thought she looked nice, even friendly, but he knew pictures didn't tell the whole story.

As they neared the kitchen, Gordy heard glass con-tainers clinking, along with hushed voices chatting to each other. Gordy followed Sasha through the opening and was almost greeted with a face full of snot. Luckily, his reflexes kicked in just in time to save him from one of Dez Mumphrey's sneezing eruptions, and he ducked out of harm's way.

"Sorry, Gordy!" Dez apologized, wiping his nose. Gordy noticed a few splotchy welts pocking the back of Dez's hands. Already, the poor kid had started reacting to what-ever it was the rest of the Drams were brewing.

"That was close." Sasha glared at Dez. "How about you use a tissue next time and give us a warning?"

Dez looked mortified as he pushed past Gordy into the hallway, sneezing several more times into the crook of his elbow. Brianna Washburn and Pedro Rodriguez, the other two Drams invited to the party, crowded around a medium-sized cauldron resting atop the gas-powered stove.

"Pedro says he knows how to brew a potion that will make the paint on any wall cycle through every color in the rainbow when you clap your hands," Sasha whispered to Gordy, though it was still loud enough that the other two could easily hear her. "I told him to prove it, because that sounds fake to me."

"I call it Cambio Compote, and trust me, it'll work," Pedro said, looking up from the cauldron. "What's up, Gordy?"

"What's up, Pedro?" Gordy replied.

Pedro was a nice enough guy, but he played soccer and ran cross-country and was like a black belt in some form of martial arts, which meant he didn't have a lot of time to hang out with Gordy. Max swore he could take Pedro one on one in a wrestling match, but Gordy knew that was all talk.

Brianna smiled at Gordy and chirped a hello, which was hard to do with the amount of hardware tightened around her teeth. It was a wonder she could even open her mouth. Just looking at Brianna's headgear made Gordy's jaw hurt.

Gordy rose up on his tiptoes to see into Pedro's cauldron. Tangerine-colored liquid shimmered in the metal bowl.

"Snacks are on the table, and sodas are in the refrigerator," Sasha announced. "Help yourself to whatever you want."

Behind Brianna and Pedro was a banquet table with several platters of sticky deliciousness. There were brownies with chocolate frosting and chopped nuts, a bowl of marshmallow-coated popcorn, and a spiral plate of caramel apple slices. A New York–style cheesecake was missing a wedge; it was resting on a plate next to Pedro. Gordy's mouth watered. Maybe he would make a pit stop at the snack table before getting down to business.

A hand dropped heavily onto Gordy's shoulder, and he looked up into Mr. Brexil's smiling face. Immediately, the air fizzled out of Gordy's lungs.

"Hello there," the principal said. "I was wondering when you would show. Hope you didn't have any trouble finding our house."

"Ah . . ." Seeing Principal Brexil in a T-shirt and blue jeans made Gordy want to throw up. It wasn't natural. Like a wolf wearing a tuxedo. Though Mr. Brexil's voice sounded soothing and inviting, Gordy didn't buy it. Not for one second. "I just rode my bike," he said, his voice trembling slightly.

"A bike rider, eh?" Mr. Brexil asked. "Any aspirations of joining a race?"

Gordy, bewildered, managed to shake his head.

"I've done a few myself," Mr. Brexil continued, taking no notice of Gordy's baffled expression. "I've never medaled, but we put together a team of teachers from my last school and took sixth place overall in a city cup. Not too shabby. I'll show you my gear later on, if you're interested."

Bike gear?

"Dad, stop bothering my guests." Sasha shoved her father in the arm, pushing him away from the kitchen.

"I know when I'm not wanted." Principal Brexil pointed at Gordy. "Later, Gordy. I'll show you my trophies too."

Oh, yeah, sign me up for that! Gordy thought to himself. *Right after I sear all my nose hairs off with a Bunsen burner.*

"I made Pedro and Brianna use the cooktop for their potions. You and I can use the two Bunsen burners on the kitchen table. They're brand-new Copen Warners," Sasha said proudly. "That way you won't be able to complain that you had faulty equipment when I beat you fair and square." She snapped her fingers close to Gordy's ear. "Hello? Are you listening?"

"What?" Gordy had been looking down the hallway, where he could see the lights from a television flashing from a tucked-away room. How was he expected to brew when Principal Brexil was within earshot of the kitchen?

"I'm going to make a Hungarian Ragaszto Ragout. Do you know what that is?" Sasha asked.

Gordy did. His mom had several flasks of the restraining potion in her cupboards back in her lab. A Ragaszto Ragout could glue an enemy's hands to any surface, keeping them immobile. Gordy's mom used it often when she needed to frisk a captured Scourge for dangerous vials. It was a tricky potion, and one that required multiple tedious steps and rare ingredients.

"What are you going to make? It had better be good or this will be the easiest competition I've ever won." Sasha wore a self-assured grin, which might have been meant as playful, but it made something inside Gordy snap.

Gnawing on his lip, Gordy dug deep into his memory for something extraordinary. There were dozens of potions he could whip up in no time. But those wouldn't be good enough.

"Oh, I don't know." He gave one final peek down the hallway toward Mr. Brexil's bedroom. "I think I'll Blind Batch something for fun."

Sasha rolled her eyes. "Don't be stupid. This is serious."

"I am being serious." Gordy leveled his gaze upon her.

Blind Batching was an incredibly rare practice that only a handful of Elixirists could do—Gordy being one of them, as well as his grandfather, Mezzarix Rook. Without following a specific recipe or knowing beforehand the ingredients needed for the desired potion, Gordy couldn't honestly predict what might transpire. He could almost hear Adilene's voice in his ears, saying he should brew something simple and safe with a recipe. But he wanted more than anything to wipe that mocking smirk off Sasha's face, and if it took Blind Batching to do that, so be it.

Sasha's eyes narrowed as she looked at the Drams who had lost interest in Pedro's Cambio Compote. The showdown between Gordy and Sasha was shaping up to be far more intriguing.

Sasha's mouth twitched, and Gordy noticed evidence of doubt wavering behind her eyes. "You can't really Blind Batch," she said. "Can you?"

Gordy's Copen Warner Bunsen burner, still gleaming from the original packaging, evenly heated his brass cauldron with a steady blast of bluish-orange flame. He had never used such high-quality equipment before, and it made brewing so much easier.

With her decent batch of Ragaszto Ragout already cooling in a corked glass flask, Sasha stood next to Pedro, Brianna, and Dez, who had finally emerged from the bathroom. The group watched Gordy add ingredients to his cauldron. Occasionally, Sasha would whisper something to Brianna and shake her head, as if to imply Gordy didn't have a chance of making a viable concoction. But Gordy kept his focus on his potion and ignored the rest of the distractions. He had already used most of the ingredients in his supply, as well as some from Pedro's personal stash.

Gordy blew out his Amber Wick across the top of the cauldron and killed the flame of the Bunsen burner. The potion, an almond-colored liquid with four-leaf-clover splotches scattered throughout, instantly cooled and hardened. With his knife, Gordy broke the surface, slicing through his mixture as though it were an elegant piece of cheese.

"What is that?" Sasha asked, scrunching her nose at Gordy's creation.

"It doesn't have a name yet," Gordy said, his tone almost reverent. He gently laid the section on a paper plate and stepped back. "But if swallowed, this will make you temporarily weigh as much as a car."

"Get out!" Pedro laughed. He elbowed Dez in the ribs, and the sickly boy expelled a wheezing *oof.* "Are you for real?"

Gordy nodded, hesitantly at first, but then with confidence. "I think so." No, he knew it would work. He had used all the right ingredients, performed each step accurately.

Hefty Cheese. The name popped into Gordy's head, but he immediately shook it away. That was something Max would have suggested. Gordy needed to be more original. *Massive Muenster.* Or . . . *Gravity Gouda*! That was the one.

Sasha remained unimpressed. "Prove it," she said. "Show us what it can do, if you're so confident."

Gordy licked his lips in concentration and then broke off a piece of the cheese no bigger than his pinkie fingernail. It was large enough to prove it worked but small enough that the effect would last just a few minutes. He held the Gravity Gouda at eye level, inspecting it one final time before he popped it into his mouth and chewed. It tasted like stinky cheese, pungent and crumbly, but he swallowed the piece down anyway.

The change happened instantly, and Gordy became rooted to the kitchen floor. It wasn't a crushing feeling—more like his entire body had been filled with cement. Gordy's arms hung at his sides, two wrecking balls for hands swaying like pendulums. He shifted his eyes toward Sasha, and she pushed him squarely in the chest. Gordy didn't move, but she stumbled backwards. Pedro, Brianna, and Dez each took a turn trying to move him. They joined forces, but even with Dez swinging all his weight on Gordy's arm, not one of them could make him step even an inch in either direction.

"How did you do that?" Pedro asked, exhausted from his effort.

As the effects of the cheese wore off, Gordy felt a sensation like sandpaper being rubbed over his skin. Then he heard the sound of clapping hands from the doorway. Gordy turned to see Sasha's mom standing there, applauding.

"Well done, Mr. Stitser," Mrs. Brexil said. "I wouldn't have believed it had I not seen it with my own eyes."

How could she have watched him? She'd only just now shown up in the kitchen. As if sensing Gordy's puzzlement, Mrs. Brexil pointed to the corner of the ceiling, where a tiny camera was perched with its lens angled toward the table.

"Had to observe to make sure all was well in my home," she said. "I believe Drams need to be closely monitored when not brewing within a sanctioned laboratory. It keeps our world safer, don't you agree?" The woman's eyes narrowed as the corner of her mouth twitched toward the beginnings of a smile. "I must say, you definitely live up to the hype."

After cleaning up their workstations, the four Drams and Mrs. Brexil sat at the table, devouring plates of sugary sweets.

"When did you know you could Blind Batch?" Mrs. Brexil asked Gordy. She had poured herself some sparkling lemonade and lounged in a chair, one leg draped over the other, swirling the pale-yellow liquid in her glass.

Sasha's mom looked as though she could've modeled for toothpaste ads with her sparkling white teeth. Gordy did notice, however, a few crow's-feet by the older woman's eyes as she smiled, showing her age, if only slightly. She wore a suit and high heels and looked as though she were about to attend an important meeting. Where did she have to go so late on a Saturday evening?

Gordy glanced at the Gravity Gouda resting as the centerpiece on the table and wanted to shrivel up. Mrs. Brexil was an Elixirist, which meant she understood the dangers of Blind Batching, even if she couldn't do it herself. The memory of Gordy's mom panicking when she'd caught

Gordy in the act of mixing the Mangle potion popped into his mind.

"No need to be modest," Mrs. Brexil said. "It wouldn't be right to turn up your nose to our discussion. Besides, you should be proud of your accomplishment."

Gordy swallowed a bite of cheesecake and wiped his mouth with his sleeve. "I guess I discovered it a few years ago."

"He's lying, Mom," Sasha announced, prodding the Gravity Gouda with a plastic fork. The solid mixture quivered like Jell-O. "He must have a recipe somewhere. He didn't just make that up."

"You shouldn't be upset, my dear," Mrs. Brexil said. "My daughter is a tad competitive, in case you hadn't noticed."

"We noticed," Pedro said, waggling his eyebrows at Gordy.

Dez, Brianna, and Pedro left on their own bikes shortly after, each with a bag of goodies generously offered by the Brexils. As Gordy knelt in the kitchen, gathering his belongings into his backpack, Mrs. Brexil cleared her throat and nodded at her daughter.

"Sasha has a gift for you," she said.

Though she acted as if she didn't care whether Gordy accepted the present or not, Sasha handed him a large gift bag stuffed with crinkly pink paper.

"Oh," Gordy said in surprise, taking the bag and

looking awkwardly away from Sasha. He hadn't brought her a gift.

"Don't let her snippy mood fool you. It was her idea to get it for you." Mrs. Brexil took a sip of her lemonade.

"Mom!" Sasha glared at her mother. "Well, open it," she said to Gordy.

Gordy felt stupid kneeling on the floor, holding the brightly colored gift, while Sasha glowered down at him. He removed the paper and peered inside to discover a medium-sized bag folded over at the bottom. Gordy's eyes widened. It was an Elixirist's satchel! One with several clasped compartments as well as durable straps to latch test tubes and vials in easy-to-reach pockets. The outside material was soft, supple leather, while the inside lining was cushiony satin.

Gordy stood, turning the satchel over in his hands. He knew it must have carried an expensive price tag and may have been even fancier than his mother's. "I don't know what to say." None of the other Drams had walked away with nice parting gifts. What made Gordy so special? "Seriously, thank you!"

Mrs. Brexil snatched up the discarded wrappings. "Shall we give you a ride home?"

Mesmerized, Gordy looked up from fawning over his new satchel. "That's okay. I rode my bike here."

"Nonsense. It's after nine o'clock, and it's quite dark. My husband will put your bike in the bed of his truck and drive you home."

That brought Gordy rapidly back to reality. A six-mile journey alone in a truck with Principal Brexil? Not a chance. He backed away from the kitchen toward the front door. "It's no big deal. I like to ride my bike."

He turned and opened the door, only to see his mother standing beside the family Subaru down by the curb, headlights cutting through the darkness like two death rays.

"Howdy, bub," his mom called out.

"Mom!" Gordy gasped. "What are you doing here?"

"Huh. That was going to be my question." She moved to one side of the car. "Let's go. Now!"

"Good evening, Wanda," Mrs. Brexil said, moving up next to Gordy in the doorway. "You may approach the house if you'd like. I'll keep the wards at bay."

Gordy glanced at Sasha's mom and then understood. The wards were too powerful for his mom to just waltz right up to the door. She needed to be officially invited in order to bypass them.

Mrs. Stitser's expression immediately faltered. "Hello, Talia," she replied, and then she walked up the length of the driveway. "I'm here to take Gordy home."

"I can see that," Mrs. Brexil said. "You have a very talented son. Full of surprises."

Gordy watched his mom purse her lips, jaw clenching, as if she were about to square off with an archenemy.

"You guys know each other?" Gordy asked.

Mrs. Brexil nodded. "Yes, we do. We work together. Or we did, at least."

"Really?" Seeing that the two women were both powerful Elixirists, it made it highly probable that they would have bumped into each other on occasion. But Gordy hadn't put that together until now.

His mom forced a smile. "Gordy, Mrs. Brexil is the new Chamber President of B.R.E.W."

CHAPTER

24

ordy opened the back door of the Subaru to discover Max sprawled in the opposite seat. Max had his feet propped up on the center console, earbuds dangling from each ear.

"For someone who didn't really want to go, you sure spent a long time at that party," Max said, yanking out one of the earbuds and sliding over an inch to give Gordy room to sit down.

"How are you here?" Gordy slammed the door and peered out the window as his mom and Mrs. Brexil, the Chamber President of B.R.E.W., had a conversation outside of the house.

"Your mom picked me up," Max said.

"Why?"

Max shrugged. "Because I was walking all by myself down Granger Avenue."

This was all Gordy's fault. If only he had told his mom about the party, he would have discovered the true identity of the Brexils and would have never gone, and his mom wouldn't have been forced to make an unwanted visit to her ex-boss's house. Through the window, both women appeared to be discussing something, but Gordy didn't like the way Mrs. Brexil stood two steps higher on the porch, talking down to his mom as though she were the parent scolding an unruly child. This was the same Chamber President who had fired her! Gordy stared down at the expensive satchel in his lap, feeling like a traitor.

Gordy whirled on Max. "Wait—Granger Avenue? What were you doing walking around over there?" Granger Avenue was at least five miles away from Max's neighborhood. "And why are you soaking wet?"

Max looked at his pants and grinned. His legs from his knees down were darker than the rest of his clothing. "Oh, you know, I was just fishing in Swinton Lake."

Was this a bad joke? Max didn't do anything outdoors if he could help it. He often referred to himself as "indoorsy."

Max suddenly hooted with laughter. "I tried to sneak into Sasha's party!" He pumped his fist triumphantly. "I followed you on my bike and then stashed it two blocks from her house."

How had Gordy not noticed Max huffing behind him on his bicycle? "Wait a minute! Was that you in the bushes earlier, crawling around?"

Max nodded. "I almost blew my cover when my shirt got snagged on some thorns." He showed Gordy the rip in his sleeve. "I swear you looked right at me, but I just laid there like a log, and you moved past. Then you went inside, and I tried to get a peek through the kitchen window when all of sudden I woke up down at Swinton Lake."

"The wards," Gordy said knowingly.

"Yep." Max didn't look the least bit perturbed by his unexpected detour. If anything, clearly Max had loved every minute of being hoodwinked by the Brexils' powerful deterrent potions. "Strong suckers. I spent the next thirty minutes fishing. I hate fishing! And I didn't even have a pole. It wasn't until I was up to my knees in that mucky lake that I finally realized what I was doing, and I headed for home. Lucky for me, your mom showed up and gave me a ride."

"What was she doing down there?" Gordy asked.

"Looking for you, I think." Max shrank in the corner of the car, holding up both hands as if protecting himself. "You can't blame me for this, but you're in hot water. I didn't even try to lie to your mom. Probably because I was still loopy from the wards."

Gordy's parents must have come home early from their date, only to find him missing. Gordy could feel the mass of sugary treats he'd eaten sloshing around in his stomach. If only he had a shrinking potion handy. He would've downed it right then and crawled under the floor mat.

Mrs. Stitser didn't say anything as she got into the car, buckled her seat belt, and pulled away from the curb.

"I'm sorry, Mom," Gordy muttered. An apology didn't

feel like enough, but what else could he have said? *I'm worthless? I'm a moron? Max would be a better son?* "I had no idea who she was. If I had known it was the Chamber President's house, I wouldn't have gone. I promise!"

Gordy's mom glared at him through the rearview mirror. Her eyes were red and puffy. Had they been that way before her conversation with Mrs. Brexil, or only after?

"I won't do anything after school, and I'll break off my friendship with Sasha first thing on Monday. I'll even give this back to her." Punishment would be an easy fix, and Gordy was ready to accept anything his mom wanted to dish out.

"What is that?" his mom asked.

"It's a satchel," Gordy answered. "It was like a gift."

"She gave you a bag?" Max asked, unimpressed. "Wow. That's awesome."

"It *is* awesome," Gordy insisted. "I mean, not really." He caught his mom's eyes in the rearview mirror. "I don't even want it."

"We'll discuss this at home," she answered, her voice trembling.

"Yeah, man, be quiet," Max added. "Now's not the time. Not with me in the car." He leaned toward Gordy and mumbled, "I don't want to witness your murder. Oh, hey, Mrs. Stits, do you think you could turn around and pick up my bike?"

Gordy's mom exhaled loudly, and her head bobbled. "Where did you leave it?"

"In the bushes behind the Brexils'. It probably won't get stolen, but still, I don't want to leave it out all night."

Gordy hadn't expected to be having this conversation with his mom with his best friend in the car. It made it all the more awkward. "What can I do to make this right?"

"You Blind Batched in the Chamber President's home!" Gordy's mom said as she flipped a U-turn and headed back in the opposite direction. "I told you to keep a low profile. I told you to blend in, but you had to go show off. And you put her daughter and those other three Drams at risk while Talia Brexil watched."

Gordy dug his fists into the sides of his head and drummed his feet on the floor mat. "It was so stupid! I shouldn't have done that." It sounded so much worse hearing what he'd done from his mom's weary voice. "Ground me from brewing, Mom. I won't go into the lab for a week—two weeks! I promise! Whatever you want."

"Whatever I want?" She scoffed. "Believe me. This is not what I wanted." She held up something in her hand that Gordy had never seen before. It was a long blue strap, almost like a belt but without a buckle. The strap's material emitted a mysterious sparkle despite the almost utter darkness inside the car.

"Dude!" Max gasped. "She's going to beat you!"

"I'm not going to beat him." Gordy's mom glared at Max. "This is a Sequester Strap. The Chamber President has issued it for Gordy."

A Sequester Strap? "What does that mean?" Gordy

asked, anxiety burning in his chest. And then Gordy saw tears dropping from his mom's eyes.

"It means you are not allowed to set foot in our family lab anymore."

25

A continuous stream of goop pooled beneath Bawdry's foldout cot in his solitary prison cell.

"Disgusting!" Bawdry said, only it wasn't the mummy's voice that emerged from his gnarled lips. Esmeralda Faustus was going to lose her mind if she spent much longer imprisoned in Bawdry's body. The mummy had an endless reserve of goop. Where it came from and what it consisted of, she didn't have a clue, but she couldn't tolerate the sight of it. To make matters worse, no one would be able to mop up the mess until the next morning, when the guards changed shifts.

Esmeralda collapsed onto the cot, the pillow squishing beneath the weight of the decomposing corpse, as she interlocked her thin, fleshy fingers behind her skull. She stared up at the mildew-covered ceiling and stewed over what she would do to the Stitsers if she ever escaped her banishment. B.R.E.W. had taken things too far. Sure, Esmeralda had been exiled to a hut on an uninhabited island in the South

Pacific, but at least there she had the freedom to move around and forage for ingredients. She could even watch the rolling waves of the ocean, though her banishment prevented her from ever touching the water. There were worse places in the world to be exiled.

But this was beyond cruel and unusual punishment. It had been more than twenty-four hours since her capture. How long would B.R.E.W. keep this up? Somewhere, at that very moment, Wanda Stitser and her intolerable son Gordy were laughing themselves cross-eyed!

Beside Bawdry, lying virtually untouched on the floor, was a meal of a crusty roll, a cold piece of cooked chicken, and a dollop of instant mashed potatoes. The Elixirist officer on duty was new to the force and had followed protocol to the letter. As a mummy, Bawdry had no need for food, and as long as Esmeralda inhabited him, her actual body remained frozen in a wicker chair inside her hut, practically in a vegetative state. She would never grow hungry or thirsty or need to sleep. She could remain like this for quite some time. Years even. It was absolute torture!

"I demand to speak to a lawyer!" Bawdry sat up as Esmeralda screamed at the top of her lungs.

"What good would a lawyer do for an old, rotting king?" someone asked from beyond the iron bars.

Bawdry's neck produced an elastic sound like a balloon being twisted into a shape as he turned to see whom the voice belonged to. The door to the cell suddenly unlocked and slid open, and a familiar woman walked in.

"Well, well, well, if it isn't Madame Brexil," Esmeralda said. "The Chamber President gracing me with her presence on a Saturday night? You're the last person I expected to see."

"I trust your stay has been pleasant," Mrs. Brexil said.

"It has," Esmeralda replied with a fake, sophisticated tone. "My quarters have been acceptable, although that dummy over there keeps bringing me meals." She pointed Bawdry's finger toward the guard's desk several feet beyond her cell. "It's a waste of good food."

Madame Brexil raised an eyebrow and smiled. "I suppose old habits die hard."

Two other Elixirists, dressed in suits and neckties, followed Madame Brexil into the crowded room.

"So, tell me, is the Chamber President going to finally let me go home? You know you can't keep me like this. It's inhumane. It's indecent. It's—" Esmeralda stopped short when she noticed what the two men held between them. A silver cup, much like a golfing trophy, with a pearly liquid roiling below the lip. "What is that?" she demanded. "Is that the—"

"The Vessel?" Madame Brexil answered. "Yes, it is."

"You carry it around with you now?" Esmeralda slid back on the cot, pulling her gnarled feet from the floor. She flicked her chin toward the two goons standing behind the Chamber President. "What are they here for?"

"We're here to grant you your wish to be sent home," Madame Brexil said.

"Well, let's get on with it. What do you have to do? Philter me out of the mummy?" Esmeralda thought it odd to see the powerful Vessel away from its usual hiding place. If only she had known it could be moved so easily. Maybe instead of going after Gordy, Esmeralda should have orchestrated another attack on B.R.E.W.

"Philtering is part of the ceremony, but first—" Madame Brexil pulled a long glass cylinder from an inside pocket.

Bawdry's eye sockets narrowed as Esmeralda peered at the strange instrument. That was no ordinary eyedropper. Chemically enhanced runes had been etched into the glass cylinder, and on one end there appeared to be a piece of porous yellow sponge.

Madame Brexil dipped the spongy end of the cylinder into the Vessel. The two men steadied their grip on the handles as the Chamber President extracted about an ounce of liquid. "Esmeralda Lilian Faustus . . ."

"Ooh, my full name," Esmeralda interjected, slouching against the wall. "Had I known this would be such a formal ceremony, I would've worn something more appropriate."

Madame Brexil smiled genially at first, but that changed into a grim expression of seriousness. "Your recent attack on B.R.E.W. and your use of a highly illegal Enfetterment Extract on a corpse have left us little choice," she began with an authoritative voice. "You have shown no sign of remorse, and you continue to endanger the lives of others as you seek for personal gain. Therefore, by the power vested in me as Chamber President of B.R.E.W., and in front of these court-appointed witnesses, I hereby declare you ExSponged."

"As if I . . ." Esmeralda started, but then Bawdry's arms suddenly dropped, his head snapping between the Chamber President and the bubbling Vessel. "ExSponged? You can't!" Her feet scrambled against the rickety cot as she tried to get away. But there was no escape. The cell door was blocked by the two men gripping the Vessel.

Madame Brexil approached, holding the cylinder of pearly liquid in her hand like a poisonous dagger. Now it all made sense to Esmeralda. The reason for the Vessel. The appearance of the Chamber President with her two witnesses.

"I demand to speak with other members of the Chamber. They won't stand for this barbaric act," Esmeralda shouted.

"They have already signed a Writ of ExSpongement. My judgment will stand."

"Please!" Esmeralda begged. "I'll just go back to my island. I'll stay there forever, if you wish. I won't cause any trouble ever again!"

Madame Brexil stood over Bawdry's panicked body. "You are correct, Esmeralda. From now on, you will pose no threat to anyone from B.R.E.W. henceforth and forever." She jabbed the end of the cylinder down upon Bawdry. The mummy instantly crumpled into a heap of dried flesh and brittle bones.

Several thousand miles away, Esmeralda opened her eyes as tears flooded down her cheeks. She sat in her wicker chair in a ramshackle hut on an island in the South Pacific. She could hear gulls cawing from above the trees and the surf tumbling against the beach.

Her beach.

Her exile.

Esmeralda sniffled as she looked over at the small pewter cauldron resting upon the dark ash of her fire pit, the flames having no doubt extinguished shortly after she inhabited Bawdry's body. Already, the cauldron and the rack of ingredients resting on the wooden counter seemed foreign to her. She opened her hands, stared at her fingers, and knew she had changed. Esmeralda Faustus had been ExSponged.

She would never be able to brew again.

Gordy sat in the cafeteria, his chin resting on his fist. His cheeseburger and fries lay untouched on his tray.

"How does it keep you out of the lab?" Adilene asked from across the table. She had only nibbled on her meal as well. A baggie of neatly stacked carrots and celery sticks rested in front of her, as did a bottle of water.

"It's like a personal ward," Gordy muttered. "It won't let me in."

Gordy's mom had tied the Sequester Strap to the outside doorknob of the family lab the previous morning. The sparkling blue material had only been attached with a simple knot and looked easy enough to remove, but Gordy soon discovered that it was impossible for him to open the door. No matter how hard he tried, the door wouldn't budge. Mrs. Brexil had coded the strap to Gordy's DNA, which meant until she or another member of the Chamber lifted his ban, he would not be permitted into the lab.

"I didn't think your mom would actually go through with it," Adilene said.

"She didn't have a choice." This was the worst thing that had ever happened to Gordy. Worse than Esmeralda Faustus. Worse than the Eternity Elixir. Not being able to brew at home was like having his legs cut off.

"But you can still make stuff, right?" Max asked, slurping pink yogurt through a plastic tube. He had brought his lunch as well, and plenty of it. The paper sack bulged with an assortment of processed snack cakes, cheese puffs, and pudding packs. "You just can't do it at home."

Gordy sighed but nodded. "I'm not supposed to make any potions outside of my B.R.E.W. training sessions. If I do, and get caught, they'll never get rid of that stupid strap."

"See? It's fine." Max shrugged. "It could be worse."

"How could it be any worse?" Adilene demanded. She was taking the news almost as bad as Gordy. When she had heard that he was no longer allowed inside the lab, which meant *she* was no longer allowed inside either, Adilene had almost broken down in tears.

Max rolled his eyes. "He could be dead!" he said, though hardly coherent through the fistful of cheese puffs crammed into his mouth. Max labored to swallow the puffs and then washed them down with his soda before wiping his chin with the back of his hand. "And we can still go with him to B.R.E.W. because we're his lab partners."

In his own way, Max was right. It could've been worse. Gordy's Blind Batching at the Brexils' house could have caused a major accident.

Adilene fidgeted with her celery sticks. "I've been meaning to tell you. I've made a new friend. She doesn't go to school here, but she's come to my house a couple of times now."

"Where does she go to school?" Gordy asked.

Adilene opened her mouth but frowned. "She never told me. But she has potions."

At the mention of potions, Gordy's ears perked up. "What kind of potions?" How had Adilene made friends with a Dram who didn't go to the school?

Adilene dropped her hands below the table and pulled her backpack into her lap. "I need you to see something." She started to unzip the pocket.

A bright, vinyl shopping bag dropped onto the table with a thud. Gordy looked up to see Sasha Brexil squeezing into the seat next to Adilene.

Adilene hurriedly lowered her backpack and stared at Sasha in shock.

Sasha wore a gold headband in her hair and large hoop earrings. "I hate eating in the cafeteria. It's so filthy." She pulled a container of salad out of her bag and a bottle of vinaigrette, which she set out in front of her on the table. She drizzled dressing over her salad and speared a few leaves of lettuce with her fork. Then she noticed Gordy gawking at her in disbelief. "What?"

"What are you doing?" Gordy demanded, no longer feeling the need to treat Sasha like royalty. Because of her hideous mother, Gordy's life had been ruined.

"I'm eating lunch," Sasha said. "Like you and your"—she glanced sideways at Adilene—"friends."

"Don't you have somewhere else you could sit?" Max asked.

"I usually go to my father's office for lunch, but he's having meetings, so I thought I'd join you."

Gordy suddenly felt the need to stand up. "I'm no longer hungry." He wanted to throw his cheeseburger in Sasha's face, but knowing the identity of her mother, he might end up banished for such an act.

"Sit down!" Sasha jabbed her index finger onto the table. "We need to talk."

"I don't have anything to say to you," Gordy said. "Not anything nice, at least."

"Yeah," Max agreed, standing next to Gordy. "There's a lot of other places to sit."

Adilene scrambled out of her seat and gathered up her meager baggies of vegetables. Gordy watched her zip up her backpack and slide her arms through the straps. What had she been so eager to show them?

"You two can go wherever you want," Sasha said. "But Gordy's going to sit down and talk with me or there's going to be a lot of problems for him."

"You don't scare me." But Gordy felt his fingers shaking.

It was probably just adrenaline, but he squeezed his hands into fists.

Sasha narrowed her eyes, pursing her lips in what had to be annoyance, but then she spoke, and her tone softened. "I'm sorry, Gordy." She forced out a breath. "I didn't know your mom had gotten herself fired."

"Gotten herself fired?" Adilene blurted out.

Sasha waved a dismissive hand. "You know what I mean. I didn't know you were going to get in trouble. I was just having a party, and we had fun. We became friends, I think."

"I'm not your friend," Gordy said.

"Yeah, not now, but we were," Sasha replied. "We were on our way to becoming best friends. Until this mess happened."

Max snarled. "You know, your mouth makes me want to punch it. And I don't punch girls. Not even Adilene." He nodded at Adilene for encouragement. She started to nod back, but then sighed and rolled her eyes.

Gordy had listened long enough. He turned to leave but felt a hand on his arm as Sasha stood and grabbed him before he could go.

"Wait," she said, almost pleadingly. She looked down the table at the faces of several other students eating their lunches and watching their discussion as though witnessing some kung fu match. "Mind your own business, losers!" Instantly, the students all found something better to occupy their time.

The four of them sat back down at the table.

"I can fix this." Sasha lowered her voice. "My mom listens to me, and she'll warm up to the idea of removing the Sequester Strap from your lab if I can convince her."

"She told you about that, huh?" Oh, how Gordy hated that woman!

"My parents tell me everything. I'm their princess, and they worship me."

"How are you going to convince her?" Gordy asked, wary but interested.

"I've been invited by the Chamber to come to your training sessions. I'll become your lab partner, and together we'll show all of B.R.E.W. how important you are to the Community."

Gordy stared at Sasha, unable to form a reply. Sasha as his lab partner? That was not the answer he had been expecting.

"Yeah, right!" Adilene said, laughing. "You'd love that, wouldn't you? But you don't want to help Gordy. You just want to help yourself. And Gordy already has lab partners." This time she did nod at Max, but he was too busy licking cheese dust from his fingers.

Sasha fixed Adilene with a withering gaze. "Who are you again? Oh, that's right. Adilene something-or-other. Please don't tell me you are referring to yourself and Max as lab partners. You have to be actual Drams in order to do that."

"Nuh-uh," Max grunted. "We were there at Gordy's first session."

"And look where that got his mom," Sasha said.

Gordy didn't want to explode in the cafeteria. Sasha was the daughter of both the school principal and the Chamber President. She could make his life miserable. Worse, she could cause more problems for Gordy's mom.

"Thanks for the offer," Gordy said. "But Adilene's right. I already have lab partners."

"Oh, did I forget to mention that my mom says that you'll have to pick just *one* lab partner? And I'm still going to be there at your training session, so . . ." Sasha jabbed another section of salad and stuck the fork into her mouth, chewing with an arrogant grace.

"Why are you so horrible?" Adilene demanded.

Sasha swallowed. "You don't even know me. I'd like to ask you something—why do you want to stunt Gordy's growth?"

"What is that supposed to mean?" Gordy asked.

"Without actual, qualified lab partners, you're never going to be properly trained. And from what I hear, it's important for you to do well at these training sessions. I'd hate for something bad to happen to you because Adilene lacked the skills to assist you."

Adilene folded her arms and leaned across the table. "I can almost brew," she said, her voice steady. "Tell her, Gordy. Tell her how close I've come to making a potion."

"It's true." Gordy remembered how Adilene had almost

successfully concocted a Sottusopra Serum in his lab. "She's actually really good."

"But she's not a Dram, right?" Sasha asked.

"No, not yet," Adilene answered.

Sasha sneered. "You're too old to suddenly become one. Surely Gordy told you that."

"Then how do you explain how I almost brewed a potion by myself?"

Sasha scratched her cheek with her fingernail. "Was Gordy always in the room with you when you mixed? I thought so," she answered before anyone else could. "I believe the correct term for that is Projecting. Which means that the Dram can use their ability through someone else. You were just the instrument, Adilene. No different than a cauldron or a spoon or any other lifeless utensil in Gordy's lab. A dog could almost brew a potion with someone like Gordy watching him. Was Max there too?"

Max's mouth dropped open. "Did you just call me a dog?"

Adilene's smile faltered. She caught her breath and looked at Gordy worriedly. "Were you just Projecting through me?"

Gordy shook his head. "I've never heard of that before."

"Look it up," Sasha suggested. She pressed her hand to her chest. "I could help you, of course. With my expertise and connections at B.R.E.W., along with your natural skill, you'll be an Elixirist in no time." She pointed her fork at Adilene and Max. "Or you could waste these precious training sessions with two fake Drams who won't offer any true assistance when your sessions require Dual Mixing. You know what that is, right?"

Gordy did know about that. Many difficult potions required two or more qualified Elixirists to mix together. If Max and Adilene truly never became Drams, those types of potions would be impossible for him to brew.

"If you're not careful, you'll end up banned from B.R.E.W. for life," Sasha continued. "The choice is yours."

"Well, I don't choose you," Gordy said. He stood and stalked away from the table.

Max caught up to him a few steps later. "Nice one!" Max elbowed him in the ribs. "But five bucks says you have an appointment with her dad later this afternoon. He'll probably give you detention for hurting his princess's feelings."

For some reason, Gordy doubted that would happen. Sasha didn't want him to think he had gotten the better of her. Punishment from the principal would prove otherwise. Gordy looked over his shoulder to where Sasha sat, still eating her salad and smiling at something on her phone. Gordy doubted their conversation had bothered her at all.

"Where's Adilene?" he asked, looking around.

But Adilene was no longer in the cafeteria.

CHAPTER

27

Adilene blew her nose into a paper towel and stared at her reflection in the girls' bathroom mirror. After hearing Sasha describe Projecting, she couldn't keep herself from running from the cafeteria and leaving Gordy and Max behind. How could she have been so foolish? What made her any more special than the thousands of other girls her age who were born without the potion-making gift? Nothing was going to change. Adilene knew that, but it didn't make Sasha's words any less painful. She swallowed as more tears threatened to spill down her cheeks.

"Why are you crying?" someone asked from behind her.

Adilene wiped her eyes and whirled around in embarrassment. She flinched in surprise when she saw Cadence sitting on the radiator beneath the bathroom window.

Covering her mouth with a paper towel, Adilene peered around to see if anyone else had followed Cadence into the room. "Where did you come from?"

Cadence pointed at the door. "I wanted to come and see you again."

"In the bathroom?" Adilene scrunched her nose.

"Well, no, but I can't really walk into your classroom. It's not my school, you know? I saw you run in here, and you looked sad. Why are you sad?"

"I'm not sad," Adilene lied. "I just have a cold."

Cadence squinted and shook her head. "You don't have to be ashamed. I heard what that girl told you in the lunchroom."

"You heard that?" Adilene wiped her nose with a paper towel and tossed it into the trash can.

"I was there, but you didn't see me." Cadence held up a vial of inky-blue liquid identical to the one Adilene had in her backpack. The one she had almost showed Gordy before Sasha had arrived.

"You were invisible?" Adilene asked.

Cadence nodded. "Why didn't Gordy stick up for you? Why did he listen to that girl?"

"He did stick up for me," Adilene protested. "Why aren't you in school?"

Cadence's smile faltered, but then she composed herself. "It's like I told you," she said. "I'm homeschooled."

Homeschooled? Had she told her that? Adilene tried to remember the conversation the two of them had shared on Saturday. "But you're not at home right now."

"I know. I took a break to come see you." Cadence looked sympathetic. "And I'm glad I did."

"I have to go back. My lunch is almost over, and then I have class. You should probably go too. Is your Uncle Carlisle somewhere?"

Cadence nodded. "He's outside the bathroom waiting for me."

Adilene looked at the bathroom door and shuddered. She hoped Cadence hadn't noticed, but the thought of her creepy uncle loitering in the hallway gave her the heebie-jeebies.

"Here's what you should do." Cadence climbed down from the radiator. "You should try that potion I gave you. You brought the bottle, right?"

Adilene glanced at her backpack. "I did, but I wanted to show it to Gordy first."

Cadence nodded. "Don't you think you should try it first, before you show him?"

"I don't know."

"You don't trust me, do you?" Cadence asked.

"It's not that," Adilene answered, folding her arms. "I just . . ." Why was she being so cautious? How many times had Gordy concocted something new and exciting and immediately tried it out? Sure, he was good at potions, but that didn't make it any less dangerous. Gordy took risks. Drams took risks.

"Okay, I'll do it." Adilene dropped to her knees and fished out the vial from her bag. "You'll just need to show me how again."

Cadence grinned. "This will be so much fun!"

The atmosphere inside Gordy's house felt oddly eerie. Silence engulfed the living room, and only Gordy's hollow footsteps sounded on the kitchen floor. His parents had taken the twins to their after-school activities: soccer for Isaac and gymnastics for Jessica.

Gordy poured himself a glass of juice and unsleeved a handful of fig cookies from the pantry. Then he heard footsteps on the second floor and almost spilled juice down the front of his shirt.

"Hello?" Gordy called out, replacing the glass of juice with a potion vial from his bag and abandoning the half-nibbled cookies on the counter. "Who's there?" His voice came out high-pitched, and he labored to keep it in check. A muffled giggling of female voices drifted down the stairs, and Gordy's blood ran cold. "If you jump out at me, I'm going to smash this bottle in your face!"

"In my face?"

Gordy spun around and almost launched his Vintreet Trap at Max, who stood in the open doorway.

"Whoa!" Max held up both hands to shield his face. "What's gotten into you?"

"Were you the one running around upstairs?" Gordy's heart threatened to burst from his chest. He knew it couldn't have been Max—the giggling had definitely been from a girl—but he was hoping for an easy explanation.

Max knitted his eyebrows. "I just got here. Why are you whispering?"

Gordy responded by pressing his Vintreet Trap into Max's fingers, the potion bubbling. "Make sure you throw it at their feet, okay?"

"Who's feet?" Max regarded the greenish liquid as if it were a school textbook. "Why are you acting like a spaz? I thought we were going to play video games."

"Someone's upstairs!"

Finally, Max seemed to understand.

Gordy attacked the front pocket of his backpack and pulled out another vial, this one a pipette with orange fluid and streaks of blue crisscrosses. Aunt Priss's Funnel Formula was guaranteed to make a mess and stop any intruder dead in their tracks.

Max gripped the back of Gordy's shirt as though holding on to the reins of a horse as the two boys crept up the first couple of stairs.

"Just don't hit me with that," Gordy said. "Throw past me, okay? You have to arc it."

"I know what I'm doing!" Max said.

At the top of the stairs, Gordy noticed the door to the lab standing wide open. The Sequester Strap lay on the ground like a coiled snakeskin. The soft giggling was coming from inside the lab. Gordy approached the door, held his breath, and peered around the corner.

Adilene stood behind the table, a row of marked flasks and vials spread out in front of her. Behind her, a blonde-haired girl riffled through one of the recipe manuals.

"How did you get in here, Adilene?" Gordy demanded, lowering the pipette of Funnel Formula to his side.

Adilene looked up and smiled. "We snuck in," she said. "We walked right past you while you were drinking your juice."

That couldn't have happened. Gordy would have seen them enter the house. Maybe she was lying. Maybe Adilene and the other girl had broken into the house earlier and had hidden upstairs until his parents had left. But even then, how could she have done that? The home wards would never have allowed the both of them to just walk right in.

Max unleashed a cry and hurled himself at the opening. He lost his grip on his Vintreet Trap, and it smashed on the floor, coiling vines sprouting up.

Adilene gasped in surprise, and the girl with her glanced up from reading as the writhing vines harmlessly entangled the legs of a folding chair.

"Rivera?" Max asked in surprise.

"Did you mean to do that?" Adilene asked, snickering.

"That was just a warning shot!" Max's upper lip twitched. "Next one wraps you up for good." He held out his hand for Gordy to supply him with another round of ammo, but Gordy shook his head.

"You snuck into my house without permission?" Gordy was relieved to see that it was only his friend, but at the same time enraged that she had scared him. What if he had thrown his potion? A Vintreet Trap could be painful, but the Funnel Formula would have transformed Adilene into a mini tornado. She could have demolished the lab, or worse.

Adilene held her smile for a moment but then looked away, embarrassed. "I knew it was a bad idea. I told you we shouldn't have done this," she said to the girl behind her.

"Who are you?" Max asked, pointing his finger at the stranger.

"For being her supposed best friend, you don't treat her very well," the girl replied. "I'm Cadence. Nice to meet you." She snapped the recipe manual closed and laid it on the table.

Gordy noticed that the bottles of potions weren't the only items out of place. Several drawers in the apothecary table had been pulled open, their contents disheveled. In fact, every cabinet door stood ajar as though Adilene and Cadence had been looking for something.

"Aren't you going to give us the grand tour?" Cadence batted her eyes innocently.

Gordy didn't move. He couldn't move. He wanted to rush in, grab Cadence by her arm, and escort her out of the lab, but that was impossible. Even though the Sequester Strap had somehow been untied from the doorknob—and how had Adilene done *that*, Gordy wondered—it made no difference. Gordy felt an invisible force preventing him from entering.

"Get out," Gordy said. "Get out now!"

"It was just a joke." Adilene gathered a few of the bottles and started tidying up the workstation.

"Don't touch anything else," Gordy demanded. "I asked you to leave."

"Okay, we'll go." Adilene carefully placed the bottles back on the table. "I'm sorry."

"No, not you. You can stay. You need to explain yourself." He pointed at Cadence. "Just her."

"I'm going with Cadence," Adilene said. "We both made the decision to come here. It's not just her fault."

"It's all right," Cadence said. "Besides, I believe Carlisle is waiting for me. You should stay and have a nice chat." She strolled past Gordy, staring into his eyes and smiling. She looked at Max, and he puffed out his cheeks, his face reddening. Then Cadence skipped down the stairs and out the door. Gordy hurried after her and made sure the door was closed. He watched as the girl climbed into the passenger side of a pickup truck and drove away.

W ho was that?" Max stood in the doorway of the lab as Gordy returned upstairs. "She was like . . . uh, really strange."

"Everyone out. We're not supposed to be in here." Gordy tried once again to step across the threshold into the lab, testing the strength of the still-lingering ward that hadn't dispersed despite the absence of the Sequester Strap, but his feet wouldn't move forward. It was taking all of his will not to scream. Adilene and Max and even that weird girl, Cadence, could walk around freely in *his* lab without any restrictions. But he couldn't. It wasn't fair.

"Adilene, stop," Gordy said, annoyed. "My mom will clean the mess up later."

Adilene looked up from closing drawers and tucking away baggies of ingredients. Several test tubes clinked together as she moved them. "Please don't tell her what I did, Gordy."

She and Cadence had done a number on the room.

A whole bundle of Bolivian achocha cucumbers lay precariously close to a vial of Antarctic glacial water. Both were highly combustible substances generally used for explosive potions.

As the three friends headed downstairs, Max seemed caught up in a daydream. Gordy brushed past him and sat on the couch while Adilene nervously shuffled over to the recliner. Gordy didn't want to be mad at her, but after all that had happened this past year with Esmeralda and Yeltzin and B.R.E.W., pulling a stunt like that was beyond foolish.

"I'm so sorry, Gordy," Adilene said. She held her hands in her lap, staring at the floor. "I should have never agreed to come here."

"So it was Cadence's idea?" Gordy asked.

"Yes." Her meek voice quivered. "But it wasn't like that. We waited outside in the yard, and when Bolter dropped you off, we followed you inside. I thought you would have noticed—I was sure of it. But you didn't see either one of us. And then Cadence suggested we hide upstairs to scare you. She thought it would cheer me up."

"What a troublemaker." Max cracked a smile. "This Cadence girl's feisty and mischievous." He stuck his feet on the coffee table and reclined on the couch. "Does she have a boyfriend?"

"Cheer you up?" Gordy asked, ignoring Max. "From what?"

"Because of what Sasha said about you Projecting your ability onto me." Gordy started to object, but Adilene's breath hitched in her throat. "I know it's true, so you don't have to pretend just to make me feel better."

"Why were you looking through all of my stuff?" Gordy finally asked. That wasn't the only question on his mind, though. He needed to know how the two girls had slipped past the wards.

"Cadence said she had never seen inside a real lab. She was curious, and I should've stopped her."

"But she's a Dram," Gordy said.

Adilene shook her head. "She's not. She just knows a lot about potion making. And she gave me this." She held up a vial containing a dark-blue substance. "I was going to show you during lunch, but then Sasha sat down, and things became complicated."

Gordy narrowed his eyes as Adilene passed the bottle to him. He removed the wax and waved the vial under his nose. Inhaling, Gordy caught only a flavor of something grainy and thick, but he couldn't sense any other ingredient. Much like the Eternity Elixir had failed to give off a substantial scent, this potion was equally mysterious.

"It's just ink." Gordy squinted at the vial. Normal, basic ink. Nothing spectacular, and certainly nothing to get excited about.

"It's more than that," Adilene said. "It's very powerful."

"Yeah, right," Max scoffed. "How is it powerful?"

She glared at Max. "It got me in here, didn't it? Without Gordy seeing me. And it allowed me to untie the Sequester Strap simply enough."

Gordy studied the vial more closely. "You drank this?"

"Not at first. Cadence told me I had to build up to that. I rubbed some on my skin and blended in with everyone else at school." She smiled at Gordy. "I sat behind you in geometry, and you didn't even notice me. I called your name too, but you thought it was Brittany Lister."

"That was you?" Gordy remembered turning around when he'd heard someone whispering his name, but Brittany had only glared at him and told him to mind his own business. Gordy had assumed she had been trying to sneak a peek over his shoulder at his quiz.

Adilene rose up from the recliner and crossed the room. "It's really neat. I'll show you."

Gordy pulled back the vial. "I don't think you should be fooling around with this type of potion."

"She's just messing with us," Max said. "None of that is true."

Adilene pursed her lips, but she kept her focus on Gordy, as if he were the only one whose opinion mattered. "I wouldn't lie to you."

"But you did sneak into Gordy's house," Max reasoned.

Adilene held out her hand and waited.

Gordy knew drinking strange substances was a bad idea, but he gave it to her anyway.

"You'll see." She pressed the opening of the vial to her lips and sipped the inky liquid.

"Not too much," Gordy warned. He reached out to

pull her hand away from her mouth, just as Adilene vanished.

She didn't fade from view. One moment she was standing by the coffee table; the next moment, she was gone. It took Gordy a couple of blinks to register what had happened. He stared at Max and then back to where Adilene had stood.

Max shot up from the couch as though ejected from the cockpit of a fighter jet. "What happened to Rivera?" he shouted.

Something invisible ruffled through his hair, making it stand up like a reddish mohawk.

"Right here, Maxwell," Adilene's disembodied voice taunted from behind the couch.

Max unleashed an unnerving squeal as he and Gordy scrambled to their feet, watching as items began to float up from their resting places and dance about the room. It was awesome and surreal and more than a little creepy all at the same time. Max squawked as several magazines drifted from the coffee table, their pages fluttering. Gordy's half-full glass of orange juice flew into the room from the kitchen and circled about Max like a curious hummingbird.

"Make her stop!" Max demanded, swatting at the glass.

Gordy had taken plenty of stabs at trying to brew an invisibility potion over the years, but the most he had ever been able to do was make his teeth disappear for a short while. Not only had Adilene's potion rendered her

completely invisible, but it had also worked instanta-
neously. Was this how the girls had gotten into Gordy's
house? But the wards should've still recognized the intrusion and turned the two girls away—invisible or not.

"How long does it last?" Max asked.

"I only took a sip," Adilene said from over by the fireplace, "so about thirty minutes, I think. Cadence explained
it all to me. She said that a typical vial will last several
hours. But I've taken a few sips today."

Gordy found his voice. "That's not safe. You could get
sick from drinking too much of a potion you're not used to."

"I did get sick." Adilene was now across the room by
the stairs. "But not anymore."

"Stop moving around, Rivera!" Max demanded, falling
back onto the couch and covering his eyes with his hands.
"You're making me dizzy!"

"Where did Cadence get this potion?" Gordy asked,
suddenly alarmed.

"She didn't tell me," Adilene said, now back in the recliner.

"This girl just showed up one day completely out of the
blue?" Max asked, digging in his pocket. "Seems suspicious
to me."

"Max is right," Gordy agreed. "To suddenly appear
out of nowhere and then give you a potion like that—it's
weird. Maybe she's up to something."

Adilene giggled. "She's not up to anything."

"You let her into your house without questioning it,"

Max said, pulling something out of his pocket and tossing it in his hand. "What kind of moron takes a weird potion from a complete stranger and starts drinking it?"

"You do that all the time!" Adilene protested. "Gordy always tests his potions out on you, and you don't ever question it."

"But we're friends," Gordy said. "We've known each other forever."

"Cadence is my friend!" Adilene shouted. "She understands what it's like to know Elixirists and not be able to join them! She knows what's it like to see your friends working together but excluding you. I know you want Max as your lab partner. You don't even have to say a word and I know it already," Adilene said. "You'll act like it's a tough decision, but you'll eventually choose him."

Max opened his mouth, probably to say something sarcastic, but Gordy swatted his arm with the back of his hand.

"Adilene, stop." Gordy held out his hands to calm the invisible girl.

"And I just bought all my own brewing equipment. What a waste!" she yelled. "I might as well toss everything into the garbage."

Suddenly, the upper half of Adilene's body appeared in the recliner, her face momentarily enveloped with bluish light. She pawed at her glittering eyes in surprise, staring down at her forearms and wrists as they flickered within a strange beam of light. She was not quite transparent, but faded enough so that Gordy could see the outline of

the recliner behind her. Gordy followed the beam to the source, which originated from Max's fingers.

Max moved his hand, and the light transferred to the ceiling. Adilene vanished again, and Max guffawed.

"Did you see that?" Max asked, shooting up from the couch and staring at the object in his hand. He was holding the odd-shaped rock he'd found at B.R.E.W. Headquarters. The one he was supposed to return. It was glowing in his fingers. The crisp blue beam seemed otherworldly, and Gordy noticed it possessed a thick consistency, as though it had more substance than natural light. He wondered if he passed his hand through it, would he be able to feel the particles radiating from the stone?

Gordy snatched the rock from Max and redirected the beam to the spot where Adilene had been sitting, but she was gone. The front door flung open with a crash, and Gordy could hear the sound of her footsteps racing away.

He thought about going after her, but how would he find her? He stared down at the glowing rock in his hand. He rubbed its surface and felt the center section depress beneath his thumb.

All at once the light extinguished.

It was like some primitive flashlight. Gordy's thoughts whirled in his brain. Where had the rock come from? And how had it ended up on the floor near the Vessel room?

CHAPTER

30

Mrs. Stister stood in the lab, studying Max's rock with a magnifying glass, while Gordy and Max waited in the hallway. A pewter cauldron filled with quicksilver and a few ingredients simmered on the counter next to her. Max paced back and forth, checking through the doorway every few seconds, as though waiting for his pet dog to come out of the operating room at the veterinarian clinic.

"Just don't smash it, okay?" Max pleaded. "It's special to me."

Gordy's mom glanced up from her inspection and fixed Max with an incredulous gaze. "Tell me again where you found this."

"On the floor in the hallway at B.R.E.W.," Max said.

"And you just decided to bring it to me today?" she asked.

"I forgot all about it," Gordy answered. So much had happened since their first field trip to B.R.E.W.

Gordy's mom tapped a finger on her chin. Then she tossed the stone into the cauldron, where it produced a soft, chittering splash.

"What?" Max clamped his hands on either side of his face and squeezed until a deep fissure formed on his forehead. "You're boiling it? Great. Just great. I never even had a chance to test out all its features."

"It's a rock," Gordy said.

"Yeah, one that glows!"

"I hate to break it to you, pal, but whatever this is, it's not going home with you," Gordy's mom said. "From my initial scan, it doesn't contain any known minerals or elements, and"—she gazed into the cauldron as tendrils of smoke drifted from the bowl—"it's not registering on any Scrute level either."

"What could that mean?" Gordy wanted so badly to join his mom at the counter. His Deciphering skills were top-notch. If the stone contained any traces of a potion, Gordy would be able to detect it immediately. The stupid Sequester Strap was ruining his life.

"I'm not sure," she muttered. She didn't, however, seem that concerned. Or maybe she wasn't worried about B.R.E.W.'s affairs anymore. It had only been a couple of days since her termination, and she hadn't said much of anything since the weekend.

"It's alien!" Max's eyes widened. "I've made contact with an extraterrestrial."

Sometimes Max's enthusiasm bordered on insanity. But to Gordy's surprise, his mom nodded.

"He may be right," she replied.

"Are you serious?" Gordy asked.

Max started to squeal, and he thudded Gordy's shoulder with his fist.

"Easy, boy," Gordy's mom said wryly. "'Alien' doesn't mean it's from another planet. It's just not something recognizable within our databases. We're constantly discovering new species every day, on *our* world. So I wouldn't get my hopes up." She exhaled, watching the cauldron bubble aggressively. "Although, I don't know how such a thing ended up downstairs near the Vessel room," she said quietly. "I suppose someone might have accidentally transferred it there by mistake. I'll have Bolter ask the guard that was on duty that day and check his logs. I'd do it myself, but the wards won't let me near the property until they've completely disconnected me from the Vessel."

Gordy frowned. "Disconnected from the Vessel?"

"Yeah, it's complicated to explain." She killed the heat to the cauldron and fished Max's stone from the quicksilver with a pair of cast-iron tongs.

"Mom?" Gordy asked as she ran water over the stone in the sink, unleashing a barrage of fizzling steam. "Did you ever find out what set off the alarm at B.R.E.W.?"

She shook her head. "It's a mystery I'll never understand, I suppose."

"Could it have been . . . someone invisible?" The

question sounded crazy, but the idea had been gnawing on his insides ever since Adilene's demonstration.

"What do you mean?" She transferred the stone to a pocket in her satchel. Max stared after it longingly, which made her crack a slight smile.

Gordy coughed into his fist and cleared his throat. "I mean, could somebody have snuck into the Vessel room without being seen by anyone else, not even the wards?"

His mom looked weary, as though she weren't interested in entertaining bizarre notions. "No one can become completely invisible."

Gordy gave Max a sideways glance. "Adilene can."

Gordy told his mom everything that had happened that afternoon. He told her about Cadence and the weird inky potion. He told her how the two girls had snuck into the house without engaging the home wards and how Adilene had magically disappeared in the living room. Then Gordy told her how Max's mysterious object had revealed Adilene in a beam of bluish light. After the incident at the Brexils' house, Gordy had promised to never keep secrets from his mom again. When he finished his story, Gordy's mom leaned against the wall in the hallway, her head tilted slightly to one side.

"It's absolutely true," Gordy said, feeling sick to his stomach.

"I don't know, pal," Gordy's mom replied. "Sounds far-fetched."

"I would agree with you, Mrs. Stits," Max said, his tone

businesslike, "if I hadn't seen Rivera turn into a poltergeist myself."

"She didn't turn into a poltergeist." Gordy's mom paused. "I don't doubt you witnessed something extraordinary, but there's not a potion I know of that could do what you just described. It sounds to me as though Adilene might be pulling a clever prank on you. She's made a new friend, who happens to be a Dram—there are plenty of them in town who aren't registered with B.R.E.W. or don't go to public schools—and she probably made a potion that plays tricks on your mind."

"But, Mom . . ." Gordy started.

She held up a hand to silence him. "You've pulled your own share of stunts since you've starting practicing potion making. Cadence might just be a girl after your own heart."

"Yeah, but I called dibs," Max muttered.

"If it makes you feel better, I'll ask around about Adilene's invisibility potion," she said. "I'm meeting with your aunt this Friday morning to discuss a few things. Now that I'm unemployed, I suppose I had better find some work."

Gordy raised an eyebrow inquisitively. Meeting with Aunt Priss? She wasn't suddenly turning into a criminal now, was she?

"Don't give me that look, Gordy," she said, squeezing his shoulder. "I haven't fallen off the deep end yet."

School wasn't the same without Adilene. It had been almost a week since they'd spoken, and still she kept away from him. Gordy saw Adilene shouldering through the throngs of students in the hallway, but she wouldn't stop to talk.

At least he *could* see her.

Each day, he tried to get her attention in geometry, but that provoked more insults from Brittany Lister. Why did the most popular girl have to sit between him and his best friend? Then, right after school on Friday, Gordy attempted to catch up with Adilene outside the main doors. But she was too fast, and though she didn't drink any more of the potion, Adilene vanished just the same. This time it was onto the bus that would take her back to Gordy's old neighborhood.

Max moved up next to Gordy by the curb. "Are you ready to have a wonderful time at your B.R.E.W. training today?" he asked with mock sophistication.

Gordy shrugged. "You're sure your mom's okay to drive us?"

"Are you kidding?" Max cocked an eyebrow. "My mom loves all that Somnium garbage. She uses the facial stuff every night while she watches *Jeopardy*." Max's mom believed she was dropping the boys off for an after-school field trip to the Somnium building, which was really the cover for B.R.E.W.

"Yeah, but she's not going to be able to hang around," Gordy said. The wards surrounding the headquarters were so powerful Max's mom wouldn't be able to stay any longer than B.R.E.W. wanted her to before she'd have to drive away in a dizzying blur.

"Well, they better not have a sale going on inside. No wards will keep my mom out if she catches wind of that."

Normally, Bolter would have picked Gordy up from school, but he had canceled over the phone. Something about having to make a few extra modifications to Estelle. Gordy had heard the car screeching in the background like an enraged barn owl. Bolter had informed Gordy that Max's mom had agreed to drive them. When Gordy had asked how Mrs. Pinkerman would be able to make it past the security posts out front, Bolter insisted they would have no trouble whatsoever.

B.R.E.W. Headquarters looked like a cross between a typical office building and a high-security prison. There were bright neon lights showcasing SOMNIUM FINE CREAMS AND OILS above the front entryway, but also razor-wire fences around the perimeter of the property. Men and women in business attire and work badges entered the lobby while armed security guards patrolled at several checkpoints. This was the first time Gordy would be visiting B.R.E.W. without his mom working there. He didn't like the way it felt, and he busied himself taking a silent inventory of his potion ingredients.

Bolter had been right though. Max's mom was issued a temporary visitor's badge at the first security checkpoint, and she wove her way through the parking lot without a care in the world.

Madame Brexil greeted Gordy and Max in the lobby. She looked much like she had the night of Sasha's party. Elegant, powerful, and with a pleasant smile.

"Gordy Stitser. It's a pleasure to see you again." She held out her hand, and Gordy wanted to smack it away, but he would never do that. His mom would ground him for a century for that. "I trust you understand I was forced to make a difficult decision with the Sequester Strap. It was for the betterment of the Community." Madame Brexil leaned in close, speaking in a hushed voice. "No hard feelings?"

Gordy refused to make eye contact. "Nope. I'm good."

No hard feelings? That woman had fired his mom, had kicked Gordy out of his own lab, and was forcing him to be trained by a complete stranger. Which, by the way, if he didn't perform perfectly, could mean that Gordy would never be able to brew again. Why would he ever have any hard feelings?

Max turned and waved to his mom sitting out in the SUV. "Get out of here, Mom!" he shouted. "I'll text you when we're done!"

Gordy didn't actually think Mrs. Pinkerman could hear him, despite the deafening volume of his voice, but still the SUV pulled away from the curb.

Gordy gripped his satchel—the one Sasha had given him after her party. He had planned on burning it, but his mom had talked him out of it. Such a nice gift needed to be used, she had insisted. Still, Gordy missed his backpack. He also missed Adilene. He had texted her during the car ride over, but unsurprisingly, she hadn't responded.

Instead of the room they had used during Gordy's first training session on the main level, Madame Brexil led the two boys to a much bigger room on the second level. The one labeled in the directory as the Military floor. Gordy had passed through this zone when he had gone on his first tour with his mom and Bolter last year.

"Sasha and Pedro are already waiting inside for you," Madame Brexil explained, as she came to a stop by a closed door. "Pedro's agreed to be Sasha's lab partner. Good luck to the both of you. I will be watching." Then she strode off, her heels noisily clopping on the tiled floor.

"Good riddance," Max said under his breath.

Gordy watched Mrs. Brexil step onto the elevator and

vanish from sight. Then he turned back to the door and read the name on the placard: ZELDA MORPHATA.

"Zelda?" Gordy gaped in shock. The very same Zelda who drank milkweed nectar in his living room? Gordy pushed the door open, and there she was, an oversized garden gnome, standing barefoot on the table.

"How do you do, Gordy?" Zelda chirped. "Oh my, and you brought a friend."

"You're going to be my trainer?" Gordy stared at Zelda in disbelief.

She giggled. "And Sasha Brexil's too!"

Gordy saw Sasha frowning from behind one of the tables. She glared at Gordy, and he snorted, covering his mouth and passing it off as a sneeze.

Zelda's office was the polar opposite of Bolter's. Where Bolter had junk and automotive parts crammed into every available inch, Zelda had few possessions. Aside from a normal Elixirist workstation of Bunsen burners, vials, and ingredients, she owned an eyewash station and what Gordy guessed was a brick oven, like the kind used to bake pizzas. Zelda also had a weapons rack attached to the wall instead of a chalkboard. There were several weapons dangling from hooks. Jade-colored grenades, bright-yellow mortars, and a flamethrower with a dual-sectioned glass hopper containing both black and white liquids. Gordy had seen that potion before, though on a much smaller scale. Zelda had used the same one to set the stairwell in Gordy's previous home ablaze.

"Come in; let's get started," Zelda said. "Boys, please take your shoes and socks off."

Max's eyes bulged. "What? Why?"

"Because brewing is always better with bare feet!"

Gordy looked at Zelda and then back over to Sasha, this time noticing the girl's toes wiggling freely beneath her chair.

"Yeah," Sasha said, with a slight frown. "Brilliant, huh?"

Sasha's lab partner, Pedro Rodriguez, was busy setting up the workstation with a small cauldron, a Bunsen burner, and a spice rack with a variety of colorful ingredients. His black-and-white sneakers and wadded-up sweaty socks lay in a heap under the table.

Max gawked at Gordy. "What are we going to do? Walk across a bed of hot coals?"

Gordy didn't care what Zelda had them do. Yes, she was one of the most bizarre people he had ever met, even more so than Bolter, but she was a family friend. He didn't know how Zelda had landed herself the job of conducting his formal training, but it just might save his potion-making career. This changed everything.

Gordy slid out of his sneakers and pulled his socks off, kicking them aside. The floor felt chilly beneath his toes, but he took up his position at the table opposite Sasha and began setting up his workstation.

"Now, for your first lesson," Zelda squeaked. "You need to escape this room, but the door has been locked from the outside, and the windows are off-limits." She stood on the counter, which made her a foot taller than Gordy, and she had her chubby fingers clasped together in front of her waist. "What do you do?"

Both Gordy and Sasha immediately selected a brass cauldron from the table's offering. Gordy didn't know if this lesson was meant to be a race, but he intended on solving the problem first regardless. Unlocking a door was simple. There were at least a dozen different draughts Gordy could concoct. Indonesian Kunci Cream would work nicely. All he needed were five ingredients and a medium-heated Bunsen burner. Gordy gestured to Max, who hurriedly unzipped the satchel.

"Coneflower petals. Grab three of them, but don't touch the stems," he whispered to Max.

Beads of sweat had already started dribbling down Max's forehead, but he followed the instructions, uncorking the vial, and with semi-fumbling fingers passed Gordy the petals.

"I should have a small container of grated anoa horns, down in the center compartment," Gordy said next. "Hand me those and the bottle of honeybee wings as well."

"Check!" Max blinked into the bag, his face scrunching in concentration as he searched for the ingredients.

Maybe now his best friend would get a true taste of what it was like to be an actual lab partner. It wasn't just passing vials under noses or keeping track of an ingredient inventory. A qualified partner could easily cut Gordy's brewing time in half. That is, of course, until they graduated to

Dual Mixing, when Gordy would need a trained Dram to help him. But Gordy didn't want to think about that right now.

He glanced over at Sasha and noticed that she had already tossed a cube of yak butter into her cauldron while Pedro julienned stalks of lauku tea on a cutting board. They had opted to make a Latvian Certe Syrup, which would pick the lock, but it would take at least ten minutes to brew. Gordy almost laughed. He and Max had this competition in the bag.

Zelda cleared her throat. "Excuse me, young Drams," she said. "I don't believe I've told either one of you to begin."

Gordy looked up and frowned. Max was ready to hand him a pinch of grated anoa horns from a Tupperware dish, but Zelda waved him away.

"Unfortunately, neither one of you will be able to use your ingredient stores for this challenge." Zelda hopped down from the counter and placed six small containers in front of both Gordy and Sasha. "You will be using these."

Gordy squinted at one of the containers. "What's this stuff?"

"Pencil shavings, dirt, grass clippings, lint, an old chewing gum wrapper, and tap water. Ingredients you might encounter anywhere in the world at any given moment. When will things line up perfectly?" she inquired rhetorically, staring at the ceiling. "I propose they won't. Therefore, this locked-door scenario is a test of what both of you might find yourself facing one day."

"None of those ingredients are used to open doors!" Sasha said derisively.

"Oh, really?" Zelda scrunched her nose and batted her eyelashes at Sasha. "Then perhaps you'll fail."

Gordy tried to clear his mind and think. As much as he would have loved to see Sasha fail, he had to admit she was right. Pencil shavings? Dirt? An old chewing gum wrapper? As far as he knew, they weren't used in any of the potions he could make. There were some South American rain forest grasses used in certain potions, but that's not what was in the container. Gordy sniffed the clippings. He smelled fescue.

"One day, you will find yourself in trouble," Zelda said. "You will be alone and without the use of your precious satchels. You may not even have access to a fire source."

"But potions need to be heated." Sasha glanced sideways at Pedro and folded her arms across her chest.

"And you learned that where?" Zelda asked.

"From my mother, the Chamber President. Remember her?" Sasha snickered.

Gordy wasn't sure how to react. What was Zelda trying to say? That you didn't need fire to brew a potion? Or even the right ingredients?

"You look confused, my dear boy." Zelda flicked something off Gordy's shoulder with her finger. "The only thing standing between you and the other side of that door is the notion that you don't have what you need at your disposal. False!" she chirped. "True, the right ingredients will result in the proper mixture, but all potions are comprised of the same components—liquid, mineral, chemical, herb. With the proper application of will and determination, your horizons will stretch and your limitations will cease. Am I making myself clear?"

"Are you saying I don't need yak butter to make Certe Syrup?" Sasha asked, staring at Zelda.

"I'm saying that until you widen your gaze, you'll never get through that barrier." Zelda turned and pointed at the door that now stood wide open. She squawked like a clucking chicken, and Gordy noticed Max standing by the door, beaming from ear to ear.

"No ingredients necessary," Max said, waggling his eyebrows. "You left the key on your desk."

Gordy and Pedro started laughing. It took Sasha a bit to warm up to the idea, but then she giggled as well. Zelda marched across the room, yanked the key from Max's hand, and relocked the door.

"No more interruptions from the help, Maxwell Pinkerman," she said, her voice pleasant but dangerous. Then she spun around, facing the two tables. "The conundrum remains. Using only those ingredients, you must find a way to leave this room through that locked door."

CHAPTER

32

Gordy sighed as his Bunsen burner fried a section of gum wrapper. It smoldered and smelled like burnt rubber. He scrubbed his hand through his hair in frustration. He was no closer to unlocking the door now than he was an hour ago, when Zelda's lesson had begun. Max was playing a game on his phone, and Pedro snored in the corner of the room, with his socks covering his eyes. How Pedro could stand the stench was quite an accomplishment.

With an angry groan, Sasha shoved her cauldron and glowered at Zelda. "You're wasting our time. My mom will hear about this."

Zelda's nose twitched. "Your mother's watching you right now." She gestured to the security camera nestled in the corner of the room near the ceiling, identical to the one Gordy had seen in the Brexils' home. "But it makes no difference. Unless I'm replaced as your instructor, which I don't think will happen, my rules are all that matters."

"I've never seen my mom brew anything with dirt!" Sasha's voice echoed in the room, bouncing off the walls. Pedro stirred on the floor, and one sweaty sock dropped from his eye.

"Are we finished? Did we do it?" Pedro mumbled.

"Zip it, Pedro!" Sasha snapped.

Zelda shuffled up behind Gordy and placed her hands on his shoulders. "Your time is almost up," she said. "If you fail this assignment, I will have to place it in my report, which could delay your training for weeks or months or . . ." She shivered and smiled forlornly at Gordy. "In your case, indefinitely."

A feeling of helplessness crept over Gordy. "This is impossible."

"It's not," she answered. "You have all the necessary ingredients here"—she pointed to the containers on the table— "and here." She poked Gordy in the temple with a fingernail. He recoiled and rubbed the side of his head with his palm. "Think about what you need. Think about the motions required. And make these ingredients work for you."

Gordy puffed out his cheeks. He couldn't just transform dirt into honeybee wings or lint into coneflower petals. And yet there had to be a way. Zelda had allowed this charade to go on far too long for it to be just some elaborate joke.

"Next time, Rivera can take my place," Max said, yawning.

And then Gordy had an idea, one he knew he shouldn't even consider entertaining. What if he Blind Batched his way out of the room? Is that what Zelda was trying to coax out of him? It hadn't gone so well for Gordy at the Brexils' house, but maybe this was different. Maybe while in the safe zone of the B.R.E.W. training room, Blind Batching could be an acceptable practice. However, Gordy had only ever created new potions. He didn't know how the process would work with something that already existed. Would he just be spinning in circles?

"Time's running out," Zelda said with a high-pitched trill in her voice.

Max blew a raspberry with his lips. "Thank goodness."

Sasha sighed exaggeratedly and tossed a test tube into Zelda's eyewash sink. They were finished, and she had no intention of playing this game anymore.

Gordy closed his eyes, and the sounds in the room dimmed, even Sasha's frustrated mumbling, but it was difficult not to think about everything that had happened recently. He had to push his mom's being fired from B.R.E.W. and Adilene's vanishing potion into some dark corner of his brain.

In order to leave, Gordy needed a way out.

Selecting the container of tap water, Gordy emptied half the contents into his cauldron. He turned the knob of his Bunsen burner up to a seven and sprinkled in some dirt, which he then stirred with his glass wand. The water and dirt turned to a mud, but Gordy kept the heat on high as he removed the wooden pieces from the pencil shavings with a knife and added only the graphite tips to the cauldron. Gordy imagined the doorknob to the room disassembling in his hands, the metal latch crumbling into pieces.

The graphite-mud mixture suddenly began to sparkle.

Gordy held the piece of lint under his nostrils and sensed faint traces of nickel and copper. The lint had once been in contact with coins. Gordy clasped the lint with his tongs and redirected the flame of the Bunsen burner away from his cauldron. With deft hands moving almost of their own accord, he disconnected the fuel line of the burner and doused the fuzzy substance with butane. Gordy heard Zelda cluck her tongue, which could have meant she disapproved of his technique, but he continued regardless.

Gordy then scraped the waxy coating from the gum wrapper with his fingernail and kneaded it together with the oiled piece of lint until it rolled into a tiny ball. Next, he pinched a few pieces of the grass clippings and stuck them into his mouth.

"Dude!" Max exclaimed from somewhere close by, though to Gordy it sounded as if he were several rooms away. "That probably came from a yard with a dog."

Gordy ignored him.

With the grass gnashed to a pulp, Gordy combined the ingredients in the cauldron. Lastly, he took the knife and pricked his finger, adding a single drop of his blood to the potion.

And then he exhaled.

Gordy wasn't entirely sure he had breathed at all during the brewing phase, but he felt winded, and his chest ached.

Wordlessly, Gordy scooped out the sparkling mixture onto a sheet of parchment paper and then moved to the door. Careful not to spill a single drop, Gordy applied the entire Blind Batched potion to the doorknob and stepped back.

He sensed the others behind him, waiting for something to happen. Even Sasha was crowding close, her whispers doubtful. But it didn't matter what they said or thought. Gordy knew what would happen. He could feel it in his heart and see it in his mind as though it had already worked.

The knob produced a deafening pop as the potion dislodged it from the door, and it clattered to the ground. Gordy looked over his shoulder at Zelda, who stood in silence, a baffled look etching her features. He glanced at the others, who had huddled together, looking equally shocked and surprised. Then their mouths all dropped open, but they weren't applauding. Gordy frowned and turned back to see what was wrong.

The muddy mixture had multiplied and now spread up the door, devouring wood, glass, and metal. Gordy leaped back, heart thudding in his chest as his potion traveled on, crumbling the lintel. The fluorescent lights above him shattered, and Zelda grabbed Gordy's shoulders, pulling him out of the way as a section of ceiling toppled to the floor.

Through the doorway, Gordy could see a commotion as Elixirists fled from their offices, scrambling, bumping into each other, and reaching for vials of potions.

"I . . . I didn't mean to—" Gordy tried to explain, but an overhead claxon unleashed a blaring emergency alarm, drowning out his voice. For the second time in one week, B.R.E.W. Headquarters was being evacuated. Only this time, it was entirely Gordy's fault. How could this have happened? Gordy had only used basic ingredients. Was he that powerful? Or worse—was he that dangerous?

A crack split the floor and gobbled up squares of tile, traveling from the hallway into the training room beneath Gordy's feet. He leaped to one side, grabbing Max by his collar to keep him from falling. The crack was wide enough that Gordy could see to the floor below, the main level where more Elixirists had gathered near the entryway of B.R.E.W. Headquarters.

"What did you do?" Sasha screamed. "Are you crazy?" Wires and rebar poked out from the floor, and water sprayed from busted pipes. Red lights flashed overhead as the alarm blared relentlessly.

"It was an accident!" Gordy shouted back. No way could he have done this. He had only meant to open the lock.

Through the widening crack in the floor, Gordy watched in horror as the far wall of the main entrance suddenly imploded. The Elixirists downstairs crowded together, clutching their weapons. Where would he be sent for his banishment? Antarctica? He would never survive on his own.

"Run, children!" Zelda commanded. "We are under attack."

Smoke rose up from the collapsed wall. Gordy could see shadows in the cloud. Forms of figures appeared from the outside as a barrage of glass and colorful potions showered through the opening. At least a dozen Elixirists dropped stiff and still to the floor, while another half dozen struggled in the grasp of vines.

Sasha leaped awkwardly over the crack and tore off down a side hallway, heading in the direction of the elevators, Pedro trailing close behind. Zelda had yet to move, but she nodded at Gordy and Max.

"Keep yourself hidden," she warned.

As Gordy grabbed Max by his sleeve and turned to leave, he saw something that made his blood run cold. There, stepping through the crater and across the threshold of B.R.E.W., was his grandfather, Mezzarix Rook.

The elevator door stood ajar, the light flickering in the ceiling, when Gordy and Max raced up to it. Gordy smashed the call button, but it didn't work.

"Which way did Sasha go?" Max demanded.

"Probably down the emergency stairs," Gordy suggested.

"The same stairs those lunatics are using to get up here?" Max spun around wildly in circles.

Gordy heard voices growing closer, echoing up through the opening in the floor his potion had made. That couldn't have been his grandfather, could it? He must have imagined seeing him. Although, he doubted there were too many Elixirists who bore any resemblance to Mezzarix.

Gordy looked down at his bare feet and silently cursed Zelda's unusual training tactic. He wished he'd thought to grab his shoes and, more importantly, his potion satchel. Both remained back in the room. The room Gordy had demolished. Try as he might, he couldn't wrap his brain around what had happened. Why were there Scourges attacking B.R.E.W. at that exact moment? How had they made it past the guards and the wards? Gordy had a sinking feeling that his Blind Batched potion had given them entry. He had unintentionally rolled out the red carpet.

Smoke rose up through the crevice in the floor like phantom fingers, and then there were heads and arms scrambling up to the second level. The corridor lit up with purple and gold light as more potions, thrown from below, smashed into the backs of several Scourges. Gordy heard shouts of anguish, but the potions only slowed them momentarily. With no time to escape through the emergency stairwell, Gordy and Max kicked open a door across the hall and slammed it shut behind them.

"What do we do?" Max shouted, digging his fingers into his hair. He jammed the back of a chair under the doorknob.

"We just need to calm down," Gordy said. "And I don't think that's going to help."

"This is what they do in movies!"

The chair swiveled free and clattered to the floor. Max shook both of his fists, the veins bulging in his neck.

Gordy looked around the room for something to use as a weapon, but they were in a regular office. There was a desk, stacks of papers, a stapler.

Max saw the stapler a second quicker than Gordy and snatched it up. He clacked off a couple of rounds of staples, which clinked silently to the floor.

"Great! You lure them in, and I'll whack them over the head with this." Max shook the stapler threateningly.

"They're not here for us," Gordy said, rushing to the window. They were on the second floor of the building, which would make it difficult to climb down to the lawn.

"What do they want?" Max asked.

Wasn't it obvious? Maybe not to Max, but Gordy knew without any doubt. "They're here for the Vessel." He tried to open the window, but the latch appeared to be welded shut. Down below, outside of B.R.E.W., men and women battled the Scourges. Though from where they stood, it was impossible to tell who was fighting for or against B.R.E.W. Gordy could see splashes of bright colors as potions exploded.

"How did they get in here?" Gordy wondered. It had to have been a carefully orchestrated attack, and yet they had entered the property without any resistance from the wards. Gordy hadn't seen any insects lapping up the protective potions.

"Gordy!" Max's voice rose anxiously.

Gordy looked around as the door to the office opened and a woman with curly hair and golden chains stormed in. She moved rapidly, almost blurring in Gordy's vision, and before he could react, he and Max were on the ground, entangled in vines.

"Hello, kiddos," the woman said in a gruff voice. "You haven't by chance seen a golfing trophy around here, have you?" She laughed like a horse, but then sputtered with recognition. "Gordy Stitser?" she asked in disbelief. "And in the first room I checked. Walsh!" she shouted over her shoulder. "Get in here!"

Gordy could hardly wiggle, and one of the vines had woven its way under his chin, clamping his mouth shut. He did, however, hear Max trying to staple the vines wrapped around his arms.

A man with grayish hair, and also decorated in gold jewelry, pushed through the door, but not before turning back to hurl an agitated bottle of Torpor Tonic at the attacker behind him. The man's red-and-white-striped pants smoldered just below his knees, and patches of his hairy legs had been seared, leaving behind painful-looking burns beginning to blister.

"What?" the man demanded, frowning at the woman. He pawed at his legs to extinguish the fire. "Did you find it?"

"Nope," the woman said. "But I did find a sweet consolation prize." She pointed a ringed finger at Gordy and snickered. "He'll be ecstatic, don't you think?"

Walsh's caterpillar-like eyebrows folded, and he nodded. "They're like two pigs in a blanket, aren't they?" He fished another vial, this one a dull-brown substance spotted with pink, out of his satchel and juked his head into the hallway. As he hauled back his arm to launch, a murky white bottle smashed into his chest, and a spiderweb wound tightly around his body. He flopped about on the floor, the web muffling his cries of frustration.

The woman unleashed a bellowing battle cry and flung

herself at the door, but she tripped over Walsh as a purple bottle shattered above her. When she fell, she sank shoulder-deep into the tiled floor. She struggled momentarily, trying to wade through quicksand, but then she froze, the sand having solidified around her, leaving her looking as though she had sprouted from the floor like a curly-headed daisy.

"That's what I'm talking about!" Max shouted. "That's Trapper Keeper!"

He was right, which could only mean one thing. Gordy freed his chin from the tightening vine enough to cheer as Aunt Priss raced into the room.

"Lolly Gittens!" Aunt Priss shook her head in disgust, staring down at the woman caught in the floor. "I'm guessing that's your husband, Walsh, I bagged just now."

"How long's it been, Priscilla?" Lolly asked. "Three years? Four? You still walking on the dark side?" She cackled disturbingly, and Gordy cringed at the sound.

In response, Priss spritzed Lolly in the face with a bottle from her satchel, and the burly woman fell completely silent. Then Gordy's aunt noticed the two boys flopping about on the floor like a couple of desperate fish.

"Looks like I arrived just in time," she gasped, hurrying over to help. Pulling a knife from her bag, she carefully cut Gordy free from the vines. "Are you okay?"

"Never better," Gordy answered breathlessly. Lolly's Vintreet Trap had felt like a boa constrictor around his midsection.

Max was shaking but wearing a goofy smile. "I named that," he said.

"You what?" Priss raised her eyebrows.

Max sat up and caught his breath. "Trapper Keeper. You have me to thank for that."

"Come on." Priss gave each of them a hand and hoisted them up from the floor. "This place is crawling with scum."

"How did you know we would be here?" Gordy asked.

"I didn't know the exact location, but your mom told me you were training. As for how I knew about the attack, well, let's just say there should be no more questions about the reliability of my source from Bolter or Zelda anymore."

"Is my mom here?" Gordy felt a wave of hope flood through him.

Priss shook her head. "She can't get near this place. Not until she has permission."

"*They* don't have permission!" Max pointed at Lolly's curly-haired head.

"Which is odd, I know," Priss said.

"We have to warn Madame Brexil!" Gordy urged. "We have to try to help her." He wasn't that concerned about Mrs. Brexil, but he felt a sense of responsibility to help Sasha and Pedro, who were probably hiding somewhere.

Priss held up a hand. "We're not taking you anywhere near that woman. The Chamber President thinks you're in on the invasion. You and your mom. Madame Brexil has already issued a warrant for your arrest."

"How did she do that so fast?" Max asked. "We just saw her an hour ago."

"That woman follows her own set of rules. Goodness knows why she blames you, Gordy, but until we can reason with the Chamber of Directors, getting you clear of head-quarters is our only option."

Gordy swallowed. He knew exactly why Madame Brexil had pinned this on him. She had been watching through the cameras and saw how his potion had opened the door to let the Scourges into B.R.E.W. If Gordy had been in her position, he would've come to the same con-clusion.

"They're after the Vessel, aren't they?" Gordy asked.

"They won't find it here. The Chamber moved it weeks ago." Priss shot a glance toward the door and selected a flask from her satchel. After instructing Gordy and Max to take cover behind the desk, she launched an amber-colored potion at the window. The glass instantly melted, dripping down like maple syrup. Then she uncorked a Vintreet Trap and hurriedly added a few ingredients for modification. Pressing her thumb against the mouth of the vial, she agi-tated the mixture and then poured out the green liquid. As soon as the Vintreet Trap made contact with the tile floor, it transformed into one long, pliable length of vine.

She handed Max one end of the vine. "Tie that around the leg of the desk," she instructed.

"That won't hold," Gordy said, as his aunt tossed the other end out the window. The vine unraveled to the ground below, becoming taut once it reached its limit and pulling the desk almost a foot toward the window.

"It'll be fine because I'll be guiding you down," she answered. "Now hurry up. There'll be plenty more Scourges where those two came from."

"And Grandpa too!" Gordy erupted. "He's here as well."

Priss fixed him with a confused expression. "Your Grandpa Stitser is at B.R.E.W.?"

Gordy shook his head. "Grandpa Rook."

Priss grimaced. "I don't think so." She nudged him toward the window and coached him on how to handle the vine on the way down. "It's sticky enough so you shouldn't fall, but watch your footing."

"I'm no good at rappelling." Max leaned cautiously out the window, his face contorted with concern. "I'll drop like a boulder."

"Would you rather tag along with me as I clear Scourges from the building?" Priss offered.

Max responded by grabbing the vine. "Just don't let go."

"What about Mezzarix?" Gordy caught Priss by the arm.

"You saw somebody else. Your grandfather is in Greenland," she said through gritted teeth. "He's been banished."

"And yet here I stand."

They turned to see Mezzarix standing in the doorway, looking mostly how Gordy remembered him when they had met nine months ago—an unruly mane of gray hair, a black tuxedo, gnarled bare feet—but there was something distinctly different about his appearance. Mezzarix looked older and frail, his lips were white, and dark circles shadowed his eyes.

"Hello, grandson." He winked at Gordy, his voice strained and quavering. "You've grown."

Priss caught her breath, flinching in astonishment. "You can't . . ." she started, but then she stopped and hurled a bottle at her father.

Bluish liquid splattered over Mezzarix's body. The potion should have sent him crashing to the floor, stiff as a board, but he remained standing, blinking away the liquid as though it had been nothing more than colored water. Then he gasped, clutching his stomach in pain. But that wasn't a result of Priss's potion. He was obviously feeling something else.

"Good to see you too," Mezzarix wheezed. "Torpor Tonic antidotes are easier to brew when I'm not trapped in my cave."

Priss dug in her bag and withdrew a Spinnerak Net, like the one she had used against Walsh. But instead of throwing it, she held out the bottle as a warning. "Stay back from us!" she wailed, her chest heaving.

"I'm not going to hurt my family," Mezzarix said, sweat dripping from his ragged face. "You know I live by that rule. But this is quite a mess we find ourselves in. Do you know where they've hidden it?"

Priss's eyes flashed toward Gordy. "Go! Now!"

Holding the vine, Gordy climbed onto the windowsill

and tested his weight against the slack. The desk moved another few inches but seemed to hold. With his eyes glued to his grandfather, Gordy stepped out through the melted window. Down below, on the lawn, amid the scores of battling Elixirists, good and bad, Gordy saw another familiar face emerge.

For the first time since Gordy had met Bolter, the man was wearing his goggles properly over his eyes. Bolter waved his fingerless hands at Gordy, motioning for him to hurry down.

Mezzarix leaned his shoulder against the doorjamb, puckering his lips to one side. "You're liable to seriously injure yourself, Gordy. Your aunt is choosing poorly on your behalf."

"Eat snot, you old turkey!" Max yelled.

Mezzarix scowled and raised an eyebrow at Max. "And you are?"

"None of your beeswax." Max grabbed the next section of vine. "You coming?" he asked Priss.

The appearance of her father had seemed to rattle Priss to the core. "You don't know what you've gotten yourself into," she muttered. "This new Chamber President is not like the ones in the past."

"I hear she's vicious." Mezzarix licked his lips, clamping his eyes shut for a moment.

Priss's eyes narrowed. "She ExSponges her prisoners. She's already passed judgment on dozens of people she's captured. Esmeralda Faustus. Cuffington Polark. That Willows fellow from Conrad. They've all suffered her wrath. You will too."

Mezzarix stepped into the room and produced a bauble of black potion. "Enough of this charade. I need to have a word with my grandson. I need his help, and you're going to get those boys killed."

Gordy tried to move as fast as he could down the vine ladder, but he knew that Mezzarix would be upon them in no time. He looked to his aunt for direction, but her shoulders sagged, and she released a labored breath. As Mezzarix's bottle hurtled through the air toward her, Priss yelled something out the window to Bolter and slashed the knife through the vine, sending the two boys falling to the ground below.

ordy hit the ground and bounced. He took in a gasping gulp of air, but it hadn't been a bone-breaking fall. He had expected to at least have the wind knocked out of him. Two floors down from that window was easily twenty feet, but from what he could tell, neither he nor Max had sustained any injuries.

Max bellowed, "She cut the vine on purpose! Your crazy aunt just tried to kill us!"

"No, she didn't." Gordy directed Max's attention down. "Look!"

They *had* hit the ground, but the grass, mulch, and a corner of the sidewalk had been changed into a springy surface, much like that of a trampoline.

"Ha! How was that?" Bolter exclaimed, rushing over to help them off the unusual wedge of ground. "Jondy Finau's a genius. That's his batch, you know. He calls it a Ke'oki Cordial. It's Hawaiian. Priss didn't give me much of a warning though. I almost overshot my throw. Up we go!"

Gordy was having trouble processing Bolter's words, but he more or less caught the gist of it. Following Priss's command, Bolter had thrown a potion that had prevented Gordy and Max from splattering on the ground. None of the rest of the conversation mattered.

Max grumbled as he checked his arms and knees for scrapes. "I could have whiplash," he said, massaging his neck. "I feel a kink."

Bolter giggled. "Such a funny boy, Maxwell. You should be a comedian."

Bodies of the unconscious lay everywhere, most of which were draped in security guard uniforms. They were still breathing, but no one moved.

"Should we help them?" Gordy asked, though he didn't know what they could do for either the fallen Elixirists or the guards.

"There's no time for that," Bolter said, his focus glued to the shattered wall that had once been the main entry-way into B.R.E.W. Bits of drywall and wood rained down from above. "I've been given specific instructions from your mother to ferry you two boys to safety, and that's what I intend to do. There's a warrant out for Gordy's arrest, I'm afraid."

"Yeah, we heard," Max grunted. "Tell us something we don't know."

"Okay." Bolter blinked. "Slovakian Bulva Torts can make you permanently cross-eyed," he said, raising an eyebrow.

"You've got to be kidding me." Max threw his arms up in exasperation. "I was joking."

"What about Aunt Priss?" Gordy asked. "She's still up there."

"Yeah, and that cookie crisp of a woman—Zelda?" Max added.

"They can handle themselves." Bolter dug in his satchel. "Believe me. Most of the Scourges you see lying about here are the result of Priss's masterful skill. And I'm almost disappointed that the building hasn't caught on fire yet, what with Zelda on the warpath."

"Mezzarix is up there," Gordy said. The words sounded strange on his lips. Mezzarix. Not *Grandpa*.

"Yes, and Mezzarix is up there— Wait . . . what?" Bolter dropped his satchel. "*The* Mezzarix? As in your grandfather, Mezzarix Rook?"

"And he's cornered Priss." Gordy nodded toward the second-floor window. The melted glass had left long streaks on the side of the building.

There was an awful cracking sound, followed by an explosion of colored light, orange and neon greens. Then the eastern wing of B.R.E.W. Headquarters dropped an entire level. Smoke billowed out from shattered windows, blotting out the sky. Gordy shielded his eyes and then hurtled himself toward the building.

"Aunt Priss!" he shouted. She and Mezzarix had been on the second floor just moments before the collapse.

Bolter grabbed Gordy, flinging his arms around his

chest and holding him back. "There's nothing that can be done! You'll just get yourself killed running in there now." Bolter puffed out his cheeks and forced air through his lips with a whistle. "I'm sure Priss will be fine. Like I said before, she can handle herself, trust me. This way."

Gordy didn't want to leave her, but like Bolter said, he knew she could handle herself. It was his grandfather who had him worried. Mezzarix was old and feeble and currently looked to be in a state of excruciating pain. Gordy fought against Bolter's arms, trying to run back to the building.

"You will only be helping the Scourges by getting yourself caught right now," Bolter said, his voice even and somber. "And I made a promise to your mom to get you out. Don't make me drag you."

"Come on, man, we've got to go!" Max pleaded.

Gordy's resistance fizzled, and he nodded. What other choice did he have?

Creeping low to the ground, Bolter beckoned Gordy and Max to follow him. "We just have to get to—"

Sinister laughter cut him off midsentence as a group of two men and two women, clutching an assortment of frothy vials, surrounded the three of them. More Scourges. Ones that Priss had failed to incapacitate. Gordy had never seen such unusual criminals. Under different circumstances, Esmeralda Faustus might have been a pleasant woman to be around, and at least Yeltzin had cared somewhat about personal hygiene. These four had ratted hair clumped with mud and rags for clothing. What rock had they crawled out from under?

"You're on the wrong side, sir," said a gnarly woman with blackened teeth and a patch covering her left eye. "We'll be taking that one with us." She pointed a curled, gunk-filled fingernail at Gordy.

"Blast these cave people!" Max demanded. "Hit them with something!"

Bolter tsked. "Unfortunately, I didn't come prepared with enough potions to battle any Scourges today. My job was search-and-rescue only."

Max's lower lip curled down in a pout. He looked at Gordy for help, but Gordy didn't know what to do. He had no potions in his pockets, and he had no shoes, which made running away a problem.

"However . . ." Bolter wiggled his nose and cleared his throat. "I did come prepared with Estelle."

Like a megaphoned trumpet blaring a single, earsplitting note, the orange Buick suddenly screamed onto the lawn, sending a spray of grass, dirt, and rocks from all four tires. Estelle performed an impressive donut, shattering several more windows on the first floor of B.R.E.W. with an onslaught of debris, and then she circled the Scourges, engine growling, horn blaring like a siren. All four of the dark Elixirists dropped to the ground, cowering in the wake of the car's violent majesty.

Gordy pumped his fist in the air, victorious. He never

thought he would live to see the day when he actually wanted to hitch a ride in Estelle.

"Impeccable timing, as always," Bolter proclaimed over the roaring automobile. "Fasten seat belts and . . . here, put these in." He tossed Gordy and Max each a pair of earplugs.

"What are these for?" Max asked.

"Um . . ." Bolter winced. "You'll see."

He swung the driver's-side door open, and pure nauseating noise vomited out. Like an amplified symphony of giant grasshoppers, the sound issuing from inside Estelle's cab made the Scourges lying on the ground wriggle in agony.

Gordy couldn't get his earplugs inserted quickly enough. Instant dizziness almost overtook him. Max ended up on his knees, tears pouring from his clamped-shut eyes, as he fumbled the spongy plugs in his pudgy fingers. Bolter appeared unfazed by the buffeting sound as he took up position behind the steering wheel and fastened his seat belt.

"Hurry up and get in!" Bolter shouted.

Gordy didn't actually hear the words, but he could read Bolter's lips. Fighting the sensation to pass out, Gordy grabbed Max's arm and helped him into the car.

"What's wrong with Estelle?" Gordy screamed once they were inside, the earplugs only slightly dulling the noise.

Bolter waved a hand by his ear and then snapped open the glove compartment before handing the two boys an Auditory Tablet. The pill would allow the three of them to carry on a conversation without having to raise their voices and despite the wild noise filling the car.

"I said, what's wrong with Estelle?" Gordy repeated after having swallowed the tablet. The effect instantly quieted the car's racket, though he could still hear the noises carrying on in the background.

"I don't know," Bolter said. "I was working on her earlier today when this happened. And now I can't get it to stop."

"Is it the radio?" Max still had both hands cupping his ears.

"Could be." Bolter shrugged. "But it could also be an endless array of other possibilities. This car is no longer what you would call a standard-issue automobile, if you know what I mean."

Just then, the engine revved, and the gearshift plunked from park into drive all on its own.

Bolter blinked. "I'll figure it out eventually. Just a hiccup."

The female Scourge with the eye patch sprung up from the ground, wobbling as she fought off the disorienting racket of the Buick. She succeeded in stabilizing her balance and pitched a potion at Estelle.

Gordy ducked as the glass vial shattered and splashed murky liquid across the hood. Two other Scourges also launched their weapons with surprising accuracy. Bolter gritted his teeth, cowering in anticipation of what might happen, but in response to the attack, Estelle only accelerated and plowed through a square of perimeter fence, leaving the grounds of B.R.E.W.

"Ah, well then," Bolter said, relaxing. "My ol' girl weathered that onslaught better than expected."

Gordy wasn't so sure. Flaring his nostrils, he inhaled the fumes of the various tinctures seeping through Estelle's hood and onto the engine. He sensed snakeroot and belladonna, but also a faint smidgeon of barium. Gordy glanced sidelong at Bolter, who stroked the steering wheel lovingly, the car purring in response.

Over the next few minutes, Estelle negotiated the busy streets while Bolter rummaged around in his satchel, never once glancing up to see the road they traveled upon. Gordy, on the other hand, *was* watching the road, cringing as drivers sped off to either side like matadors as Estelle bulled her way through.

"We're going the wrong way," he said, taking note of their northerly direction. "My house is back there."

"As will be the police and B.R.E.W.'s Lead Investigators—not to mention an army of Scourges, eventually," Bolter said. "No, my boy, that would be the wrong way. Your father and siblings are with Wanda driving north as we speak. They've packed some essentials and will meet us near the border."

"Border?" Max blurted out. "Of Canada?"

Bolter's head perked up from his rummaging, and he squinted at Max. "Don't be ridiculous. Why would we go there?"

Estelle took flight through an intersection. Two of her hubcaps dislodged and spiraled through the air, careening off the hood of a poor, unsuspecting minivan.

Gordy flinched. "Then where?"

"To the only place B.R.E.W. doesn't have any jurisdiction. To the Swigs, of course," Bolter said. "It's the only safe place to go, now that you're a member of a wanted family."

Max groaned and smeared his cheeks with his splayed fingers. "Why isn't any of this making sense?"

Bolter responded with a cackle.

The Swigs. They were heading to one of the most dangerous places in the country.

One hundred miles north of B.R.E.W., the excruciating symphony coming from Estelle came to a sudden stop.

Gordy opened his eyes. He had been trying to doze in the passenger seat, plugs still wedged in his ears. The effects of the Auditory Tablet had worn off half an hour earlier, ending any chance of a conversation, but sleep had been an impossibility with the persistent noise. Gordy looked at Bolter, who was also blinking open his eyes and lowering his feet from the dashboard. Bolter jiggled his right earplug free and looked around. Estelle tutted along a winding back road, flanked on either side by a heavily wooded forest.

Max bolted up from sleeping. He gasped and slapped at the air as though fighting an invisible foe. "What happened? Where are we?"

"It would seem we're close to Cheerbick, which would make *that* Harcourt Lake." Bolter gestured out the window to the large dark-green lake spreading out like a massive mirror. "Beautiful."

"How come your car's no longer blasting my ears off?" Max asked.

"'Tis a mystery, that's for certain, but what a pleasant surprise!" Bolter exclaimed.

Just then, Estelle's hood ejected. The square sheet of metal catapulted end over end like a gigantic Frisbee, glinting in the setting sunlight, as three tentacles uncoiled from around the engine.

Gordy and Max screamed.

Grasping the steering wheel, Bolter slammed both feet down on the brake pedal, but Estelle wouldn't respond. As the lower half of an enormous octopus struck violently against the windshield, the Buick suddenly veered off the road, slashing through trees and underbrush without any sign of stopping.

"We're going to have to evacuate!" Bolter shouted.

One of the tentacles, more than a foot in circumference, reared back and penetrated the glass. Gordy shielded his eyes as shards rained down upon him. The tentacle slapped around, trying to find something to grip with its suction-cup feelers.

"This has been the worst day of my life!" Max shouted.

"Out! Get out!" Bolter swatted the tentacle with a rolled-up automotive magazine over and over, but it simply snatched the periodical like an elephant's trunk and tossed it out the window.

Max tried to yank open the car door, but the latch wouldn't budge. "Do something! Hit it with a potion!"

Bolter blinked at Max for a second and then wrenched open his satchel in search of a weapon. Estelle, never slowing, continued her maddening descent through the trees, somehow managing to miss any massive trunks that would've ripped the Buick in half.

Gordy pulled open the glove compartment, but only an owner's manual and a tire gauge dropped out. For being an Elixirist's car, Bolter certainly hadn't equipped it with anything useful.

Estelle's radio kicked on again, screeching. Gordy clamped his hands over his ears, earplugs all but useless, trying to drown out the hideous sound, as another grotesque tentacle, smelling of brine and fish, punched a second hole through the windshield and latched onto the top of Bolter's head.

"Bolter!" Gordy exclaimed. He reached out, trying to pull the creature away from him, but it was like grabbing a grease-coated tube. Gordy's fingers simply slipped right off.

"Stop it!" Max shouted, kicking the back of the front seat with both feet. "Hey!" He jerked up in surprise. "I think your car just bit me!"

"She'll do that if she doesn't like how you're treating her," Bolter said, keeping his focus on his bag.

"Treating *her*?" Max said in shock.

As the tentacle pulled on Bolter's goggles, the Elixirist continued to dig in his satchel, tossing aside several vials, a bicycle pump, and an old license plate before shouting triumphantly.

"Aha!" He held up a bright-yellow balloon bulging with what looked like bronze powder, but before Bolter could douse the tentacle with his potion, he looked out the broken windshield, and his victorious expression withered and died. Tentacle slime dripped down his cheeks.

Gordy followed Bolter's gaze, and the wind whooshed right out of his lungs. "Oh, *sacapuntas!*" Gordy shouted as Estelle arrived at the end of the trees and plummeted off a cliff into Harcourt Lake.

The drop only took a moment, but it felt like an eternity. All three of them opened their mouths, but the sheer force of their downward thrust extinguished any screaming. As the lake rose up to greet them, a flood of water rushed in through the punctured windows, and the three-tentacled monstrosity nesting around Estelle's engine pulled free from the windshield.

"Now what?" Max demanded. "I can't get the—"

All four doors suddenly opened, and Estelle promptly ejected the three of them.

Estelle floated in the water for several minutes, and Gordy helped Max and Bolter onto the roof. The tentacles coiled around the front of the car, a gigantic kraken attempting to bury a shipwreck in the sea.

"How good can you swim?" Gordy asked Bolter. The only thing close by was a sheer rock cliff face that rose up at least thirty feet above the water. Gordy doubted they'd be able to climb it, and he pointed to the shore about a mile away.

"Swim? As in dog paddle or breaststroke?" Bolter shook his head vehemently, hugging his drenched satchel to his chest. "Nope. I can't swim. I'll try calling for help." He opened his bag and pulled out a heavy, ancient mobile phone with a rotary dial. Lake water drizzled from the receiver.

"You think that's going to work?" Max asked.

Bolter frowned. "Why wouldn't it?" He began rotating the dial of the phone.

"No one will get here in time to save us, and the shore is too far away to swim." Max's teeth chattered. "We won't make it."

The metal of Estelle's frame buckled beneath the pressure of the squeezing tentacles.

"We're going to have to try," Gordy said. "It's not like we have a boat."

His eyes caught on the thin silver ring around his pinkie finger. It was the Sloop Solution Aunt Priss had traded to him a week ago. Gordy had almost completely forgotten about it. "Scratch that," he said. "Maybe we do."

While Bolter finished dialing on his phone, Gordy dropped the ring into the water, and within seconds, it had dissolved into a shimmering liquid. The potion soon expanded, becoming triangular in shape and bobbing calmly next to Estelle. Gordy tested his weight on the board, and it held. Max hopped on next, and though it lapped up a few waves from the jarring motion, the Sloop didn't sink.

"I think I'll wait," Bolter said, pressing the receiver to his ear. "Help will be on the way shortly."

"And you'll be at the bottom of the lake," Gordy said.

"We don't know that for sure. Estelle seems perfectly capable of . . . Oh dear!"

The front end of the Buick dipped forward, shifting on a downward angle, and a slew of bubbles belched out from the engine.

"Okay then," Bolter said. "If you're positive it will hold."

Gordy felt sick for Bolter, whose smile had withered down until he sat straight-lipped on the raft, watching one of his most prized possessions sink to the bottom of the lake.

"I'm so sorry about your car," Gordy said, paddling the Sloop toward the shore. He wasn't sure whether or not he should pat Bolter on the back for encouragement or leave well enough alone.

"Yeah, she was a good ride." Max slugged Bolter on the arm. "She'll be missed." He dragged his hand through the water on the opposite side.

Gordy narrowed his eyes at Max's insensitivity. Max just shrugged.

"Yes, well, thank you," Bolter said. "Very kind. Very kind. This sort of thing will happen from time to time. Fortunately, I do have a little of Estelle left in a petri dish back home. Perhaps I can salvage something from that."

Gordy didn't know how to respond, and they rowed the Sloop the rest of the way to shore in silence.

36

Gordy, Max, and Bolter stood by the side of the road next to the forest, shivering and dripping wet as a dark-red SUV pulled up alongside them. Aunt Priss sat behind the wheel, and green-haired Zelda peered over Priss's arm from the passenger side. Priss's dirty-blonde hair was dirtier than usual, and she now owned several nicks and cuts on her neck and chin. She looked as though she had gotten into a fight with a cactus. Other than a few strands of hair poking out at odd angles, Zelda looked no worse for wear.

Priss rolled down the window. "Hitchhiking's dangerous," she said, then flicked her chin toward the back of the SUV. "Hop in."

"How did you make it out of B.R.E.W.?" Gordy climbed over the seat and strapped on his seat belt, the image of the building collapsing still filling his thoughts.

"I almost suffered a nasty fall," Priss answered. "That could have been bad. Something must have weakened the infrastructure, because a crack split the whole floor in two. Luckily, my dad was there. He tossed a bottle of Heliudrops through the hole just as I dropped, and Madame Brexil's office chair floated up to catch me."

"Mezzarix did that?" Max asked. "On purpose?"

Priss nodded. "I think so."

"But I thought he was like a total evil dude."

Priss sighed. "He has his moments." She glanced at Gordy in the rearview mirror, and Gordy caught himself smiling. Hearing that his grandfather had done a kind deed gave him hope. Maybe it didn't mean anything, but he liked to imagine Grandpa Rook as an all right guy from time to time.

"What was he doing there, anyway?" Gordy asked.

"That I don't know, but he didn't look well. Any thoughts on how he might have escaped the Forbidden Zone, Bolter?" Priss asked.

"I'm afraid that's beyond my expertise." Bolter pressed his palm against the window, sharing a silent goodbye with Estelle and blinking back what might have been tears. "So long, Estelle. You were not only a good car but also a good cat."

"Do you have any snacks?" Max leaned forward and pushed his head between Priss and Zelda in the front seat. "Bolter hasn't fed us. I'd eat just about anything right now."

Zelda dug in her bag and tossed Max a package of dried aloe vera leaves. "Eat as much as you'd like. They're barbecue flavor."

Max appeared to deflate, scowling as he opened the bag and dry-heaved at the smell. Gordy crinkled his nose as well. The weird chips smelled nothing like barbecue.

"I think I'm not hungry anymore," Max said, gagging.

"Suit yourself." Zelda blotted her lips on a napkin. "They provide an excellent source of selenium."

"Are you two missing your shoes right about now?" Priss asked.

"Are you kidding?" Max's head perked up.

She flicked her chin over her shoulder. "All your stuff's in the back. Zelda got everything before we evacuated."

Gordy's eyes lit up. He and Max crawled over the seat and grabbed their shoes. Max flicked gravel and seaweed from his toes and then wriggled his feet into his socks, sighing with satisfaction.

"Never thought I'd be so happy to see these again," Max said.

Gordy also found his satchel. He unclasped the buckles and moved a few of his vials around. The bag felt heavy and full, and everything appeared to be just as he had left it.

Priss drove north for another fifty miles, weaving on back roads past old ramshackle homes tucked away in the trees. It was a quiet ride. Bolter occasionally jotted notes on a pad of paper, a miniature pencil wedged in the nook of his hand where his thumb and forefinger would have been at one time. Max snored next to Gordy, his fingers smudged with red barbecue powder and the crumbs of dried aloe vera leaves scattered across his shirt. It hadn't taken long for him to give in to his hunger and devour the bag. Max said the chips tasted better than they smelled.

Gordy silently replayed the moments leading up to B.R.E.W.'s epic downfall over and over in his head. So many things just didn't add up. Last year, when Esmeralda had infiltrated the headquarters, she had still needed permission to enter. Without that, no one could enter the grounds. After that attack, B.R.E.W. had increased both their security and their protective potions shielding the building from all outsiders. Despite all that, an army of Scourges had waltzed right up to the doors and into the building.

And yet Gordy wasn't dwelling upon these facts. He kept thinking about what his grandpa had said.

"I need to have a word with my grandson. I need his help."

His help. What for? What could Mezzarix possibly need from Gordy that would make risking his life worth it?

"What do the Swigs look like?" Gordy asked. Max slumped next to him, his sweaty head resting on Gordy's shoulder. Gordy didn't have the heart to nudge him away.

"We're not going to any of the trading posts," Priss said. "Just to a safe house on the outskirts. We're almost there." Her expression changed to one of concern. "We need to talk about what you did back at the headquarters. Zelda told me you concocted a Blight Bomb."

"A what?" Gordy had never heard of such a thing.

"It's what took out the door and the floor and the wall

and"—Zelda tapped her lip—"the whole of B.R.E.W. Headquarters, for that matter."

"This is serious, Gordy," Priss continued. "Where did you learn how to make that? Who taught you?"

Gordy stared at his hands, noticing the prick in his finger that had supplied the blood for the potion. No one had taught him how to make a Blight Bomb. He hadn't known prior to that moment what he was going to do. Somehow, Gordy had taken basic ingredients and made them into something deadly. Zelda had instructed them to think outside the box. That's what he had done. And because of his actions, the Scourges had taken over B.R.E.W.

"I was just tyring to make a potion out of nothing," Gordy said.

"Not out of nothing," Zelda replied. "Each of the items I gave you was specially treated. The gum wrapper was laced with artichoke sap, and the tap water had recently been percolating in a rusted watering can. Had you the sense to Decipher their full ingredients initially, you would have discovered all the necessary elements of making a simple Danish Plyndring Poultice, which would have easily opened the door."

Gordy stared at the back of Zelda's head, his mouth slightly ajar. Apparently, the woman did have a point to her training exercise. If only Gordy hadn't gone straight to Blind Batching. None of this would have happened.

"I'm sorry, Priss. I didn't mean for that to happen."

She was silent for a moment. "I know you didn't. But

from now on, no more Blind Batching. And we keep this a secret from your mom until we settle this business, deal?"

"Deal." That was the best suggestion Priss could have offered. Gordy didn't want to have that conversation with his mom just yet. He needed time to prepare for whatever punishment she would dole out.

After what felt like hours of driving, Gordy spotted the family Subaru pulled off on a dirt side road. Gordy leaped from the SUV and embraced his mom and dad. It had only been half a day since they'd seen each other, but all of them were crying, including Isaac and Jessica.

"Aw, I love you Stitsers!" Max said, joining the group hug. "Please tell me you brought snacks."

CHAPTER

37

P er Priss's instruction, Gordy and the others started out
on the dirt trail by foot, leaving behind the two vehicles tucked off the road to stay hidden. For the moment, the Stitsers' list of enemies could easily include both
sides of the fight, Elixirists and Scourges. Priss took the
lead on the path, instructing the others to stay a good five
to ten feet behind her at all times. Gordy didn't understand
why, but she wasn't giving out much information. She did
take time to fill in Gordy's parents on what had happened
at B.R.E.W., conveniently excluding the part about Gordy's
Blight Bomb. As expected, Mrs. Stitser didn't immediately
believe the information about Mezzarix's role in the attack
on B.R.E.W.

"It could have been a ruse," his mom said, shaking her
head. "Just another thug wearing a cleverly designed disguise. You've made plenty of Disfarcar Gels in your day,
Priss. You know how easy those are to fake."

"Wanda, it was him," Priss answered coldly. "I know

Dad when I see him. I don't know how he did it, but he's out."

Out of Greenland, Gordy thought.

"And he just let you go without a fight?" Gordy's mom asked skeptically. "I find that hard to believe."

"There was a fight, and then the building collapsed." Priss glared sidelong at Gordy's mom.

"What did he want with Gordy?" his mom asked.

"He just wanted to talk to me," Gordy said. *And my help.*

His mom folded her arms and looked at her husband. "I'll go along with this for now, but I'm struggling to believe it. If my dad has indeed broken free, he won't leave us alone. We need to be prepared for whatever retaliation he has planned."

"What exactly does that mean?" Gordy's dad asked. Jessica's legs kicked out from around his chin as she rode on his shoulders. Max huffed along at the rear, griping as he gave Isaac a piggyback ride. "I thought you said a banishment was permanent until lifted by B.R.E.W. Could someone at headquarters have freed him?"

"Only if they had possession of the Vessel," Zelda answered. "And that doesn't seem likely." Her little legs had to take two steps for each one of Gordy's strides, but she kept excellent pace with the group.

"Maybe Madame Brexil let him out," Gordy suggested. The notion had been weighing on his mind for quite some time. Every bad thing that had happened to the Stitsers lately had come about with the sudden appearance of the new Chamber President.

"No, Gordy, she would never do that," his mom said, dismissing the suggestion with a flip of her hand.

"She fired you, Mom!" Gordy raised his voice. "And she punished me with that stupid Strap for no reason. She's a bad person." Madame Brexil had to be considered a suspect, and one they shouldn't immediately rule out.

"Gordy has a point," Priss added. "She's definitely shady. We know that she has a penchant for dealing out maximum-punishment sentences, including ExSpongement, and as the Chamber President, she would have access to the Vessel to perform the necessary releasing ceremony."

"Don't be ridiculous," his mom said. "She's no Scourge supporter."

"You're being ridiculous!" Priss whipped around, facing her sister. "Tell me this, how did a whole army of Scourges walk right through the front door? Not one of them was stopped by the wards—wards *you* helped strengthen over the past few months, might I add. No one is doubting your ability, Wanda, but how could they have done that without help?"

Gordy's mom massaged a spot on the back of her neck. "It doesn't make any sense, but I firmly believe Talia Brexil has nothing to do with this. That's not how she operates."

Priss groaned. "You're not a part of B.R.E.W. anymore! And now that she's issued that arrest warrant for you and

Gordy, you never will be again. Yet you're so blinded by your loyalty, you'll endanger your whole family out of principle!"

"Always so impetuous!" Gordy's mom fired back, jabbing her index finger. "Think about this for a moment. Why would our father storm headquarters in search of the Vessel? And if Mrs. Brexil was working with the Scourges, why would they go to all that trouble when they could have just set up an appointment with her at their leisure? I may be blinded by loyalty, but you're blinded by hatred for B.R.E.W.!"

Gordy opened his mouth and looked at his aunt, but his mom was right. His grandfather and the Scourges hadn't acted as though they were in cahoots with the Chamber President. If so, they wouldn't have needed to attack the building.

Bolter hadn't said much since floating across the lake on the Sloop Solution, but now he cleared his throat. "I apologize, but are we getting any closer to our destination? As much fun as this little stroll has been, listening to your riveting conversation, I believe we would be wise to sit down soon and plan out our next course of action. We are at war, in case you've forgotten. And as long as the Chamber of Directors is still in possession of the Vessel," he added, "B.R.E.W. will continue to stand. Headquarters was just a building. It's the potions and people that matter."

"Agreed," said Zelda. "Thank goodness they moved

it. The relocation of the Vessel was the only smart thing Madame Brexil has done since the start of her term."

"Whose property is this, anyway?" Gordy's dad asked.

"It belongs to Priss's source, but she's choosing to remain tight-lipped on the matter," his mom answered. "Don't you think it would be wise to fill us in?"

"What's the point?" Priss asked, tromping down the trail. "We're already here."

The dirt road emerged from the other side of the forest and opened onto a flat, lush meadow. Wildflowers dotted the landscape, like brilliantly colored lollipops. Gordy had never seen such a beautiful vista. The flowers were purple and blue and pink. Several of them were fluorescent yellow, while others had checkered patterns or polka dots.

At the end of the trail, about a quarter mile away, there was a house with a tin roof gleaming in the sun. Behind the house stood a silo, and beyond that was an enormous garden plot. A storm cloud floated lazily above the garden, dumping sheets of rain upon the plants. Gordy had to do a double take. Other than that single cloud, the sky was virtually clear, and the sun hung low on the horizon, inches away from setting behind the trees. It had to be some sort of weather anomaly.

Midway through the meadow, as the group neared the rustic brown fence circling the property, a peculiar cool mist appeared at their feet. The mist felt wet and sudsy, like bubble bath nearing the end of its life in a tub, and

Gordy knew it had to be something unnatural, something created in a lab, but he wasn't certain of its purpose.

"What is this slop?" Isaac demanded, scrambling down from Max's back and wading through the soapy substance. Jessica giggled, and her dad set her on the ground. The twins frolicked through the mist, scooping up handfuls of suds and blowing the bubbles at each other.

"Don't play in that!" Gordy's mom demanded.

"It's harmless," Priss said. "It's just a security measure, that's all. They'll be fine."

"Are those birds?" Max asked, jogging forward to join Gordy at his side. He pointed to a bright white mass high above the garden.

Gordy had initially mistaken the mass as part of the cloud, but as they got closer to the house, he could see hundreds, no, thousands of birds, cawing noisily above the low rumbling thunder.

"I've never seen anything like that in my life," Gordy's dad muttered. "What do you think they are doing?"

The birds circled madly above the cloud as though trapped in a funneling cyclone. The formation had to reach at least a mile or two above the ground, but not a single bird flew away.

"They're helping Tobias's garden grow," Priss answered matter-of-factly.

Gordy's mom suddenly looked up, infuriated, and snatched open her satchel. She tore into the pockets and produced a potion in each hand. "You brought us *here*?"

"I didn't have much choice, now did I?" Priss responded.

"I would stop right there if I were you!" an amplified voice bellowed over the squawking birds. "You have intruded on private property, and I have every right to defend myself, which I intend to do posthaste." The voice carried an Irish brogue. "Lower your weapons or I will be inclined to use deadly force!"

Gordy stood still, eyeing his mom and Zelda, who both clasped colorful bottles in their hands. Bolter stooped low, crouching next to Max, eyes darting around wildly.

"Where is that coming from?" Bolter asked. "Are we about to be ambushed?"

"Indeed you shall, kind sir, if you don't comply with my commands!" the voice answered, somehow having heard Bolter's hushed inquiry.

"Do as he says," Priss instructed. She nodded at the vials her sister held and patted the air in front of her. "Don't give him any reason to show off." Her eyes flickered toward the house with annoyance.

"Tobias McFarland is your source?" Gordy's mom asked in disbelief. She gawked at Priss as though she had magically sprouted wings. "After all this time, you've been putting Gordy's life in danger based on that madman's word?"

Priss's eyes narrowed. "Gordy's still breathing, isn't he? Thanks in part to him." She jabbed a thumb over her shoulder at the house.

"Priss!" Gordy's mom hissed. "We are not going in there!"

"That's right. You're not," Tobias's voice responded. "You're going to turn on your axles and hightail it out of here before I unleash the dogs."

"You don't have dogs," Priss said, rolling her eyes.

"I could have dogs, Priscilla!" Tobias shouted, his voice booming as though coming through a megaphone. "And I'll sic them on you first for allowing your nasty sister to sully my mist with her vindictive shoes. Now, if you don't want to find yourself smothering in my swamp, you best be on your way before I command my wards to drown you."

"Maybe we should go back?" Gordy's dad suggested. "He clearly has a problem with you." He looked at Wanda. She didn't respond, but gritted her teeth.

"I agree with Gordon," Bolter said, already facing the other direction. "We're not welcome here."

"If he wanted us gone, we would have never made it this close to his house. He's bluffing." Priss cupped her hands around her mouth to project her voice. "We both know you're not going to turn any of us away. Not until you hear what happened at B.R.E.W. So quit sniveling and hiding in your loft and come down to let us in."

A crackle of lightning erupted from the cloud, followed by a resonating clap of thunder. The birds continued their circling motion, unfazed by the disruption. Gordy braced himself as he waited to hear the sound of barking dogs racing around from the rear of the house, but there were no other noises, and Tobias's megaphone had gone unnervingly quiet.

After several tense seconds, the door leading into the small cottage creaked opened, and a man of no more than forty years of age, and with the brightest shock of red hair Gordy had ever seen, stepped onto the porch. In one hand, the man held a long wooden spoon about the size of his arm. In the other, he held a device he had used to amplify his voice, though it looked like a miniature phonograph horn connected to a handheld radio.

Tobias squinted at the group for a moment and then furiously attacked an itch on his upper lip with his finger. He puckered his lips to one side and huffed.

"Priscilla," he said, acknowledging Gordy's aunt with a modest nod.

"Tobias," she replied, shifting her weight to one side, and glaring at the man with disapproval.

"Well, don't just stand there like a bunch of vegetables." Tobias turned and waved his wooden spoon at the group. "I just put a pot on. Come inside before it gets dark."

38

Tobias McFarland's house carried the pungent aroma of manure and spoiled milk. Fortunately, the smell didn't linger; rather it occasionally wafted through the rooms as though caught upon a breeze. Pots brimming with leafy vegetation filled every inch of available space. Vines as thick as Gordy's leg dangled from the ceiling like garland, and honeybees the size of golf balls alighted on flowers that dripped with pollen.

"This is moss," Max whispered in Gordy's ear, pointing to the floor. They weren't walking upon carpet after all. "Who is this nut?"

Gordy held up his finger to shush Max as Tobias led them into the dining room opposite the kitchen. This wasn't the time to insult the host, especially one who lived in a house that hummed and buzzed as though it were alive.

"Have a seat." Tobias directed the group to a table with several chairs. "The wee ones can go play in the back. I have built a sandbox in the guest bedroom. Just don't bury yourself too deep."

"Uh, no, that's a bad idea," Gordy's mom said, when Isaac and Jessica were about to dash off down the hallway. "I want you close by."

Tobias chuckled mirthlessly. "Right, because all I need to do is make an enemy out of Wanda Stitser's children. Let them play, you mean hornet, and drink your tea." He slammed a saucer down in front of Wanda, splashing the brownish liquid onto the table, and glowered at her. Gordy's mom returned the expression, and Tobias turned up his nose before meandering back into the kitchen for more cups.

"I love sandboxes," Zelda said, beaming. "I'll keep an eye on them." She held out a hand to Isaac and Jessica and escorted them down the hallway.

"Okay, what did I miss?" Gordy's dad asked, his voice low. "Why does that man hate you so much?"

Gordy's mom sighed and stirred a spoonful of sugar into her teacup. "Because he's spiteful," she said, staring pointedly at Priss. "He holds grudges for far too long, and he's not someone to be trusted."

"That's not the reason." Priss raised her eyebrows. "Tobias hates Wanda because she had him fired from B.R.E.W."

"Really?" Gordy asked.

"Yes, well, he was breaking the rules." Gordy's mom

swallowed a sip of her tea and puckered her lips in satisfaction. "It's highly illegal to brew weather potions."

Weather potions? Gordy had never heard of such a practice, but it made sense. The rogue storm cloud, hovering above Tobias's garden. The strange mist. Admittedly, Gordy wasn't sure how the birds factored into the equation, but it probably had something to do with the weather as well.

"Get out!" Max slapped his knee. "That dude worked for B.R.E.W.? Here all this time I thought Bolter was the biggest kook to ever call himself an Elixirist."

Gordy looked over and saw Bolter spooning a dollop of mayonnaise into his tea from a half-empty jar in his satchel, oblivious to the conversation.

"I never meant for Tobias to lose his job, but he couldn't carry on doing what he was doing while living within the general public," Gordy's mom continued. "Weather potions are unstable and dangerous, and he put innocent people's lives at stake for selfish reasons."

"Obviously, he doesn't see it that way." Priss casually stirred her cup. "Lots of people take risks in the name of exploration."

"A miniature hurricane in a public swimming pool is not worth the risk!" Wanda snapped.

Max snickered in surprise and elbowed Gordy's ribs. Gordy started laughing as well. Tobias McFarland sounded like a genius.

"Don't laugh," Gordy's mom chided through a half

smile. "I did the right thing by reporting him to the Chamber, and he didn't handle the consequences with dignity or grace. Tobias could have applied for reinstatement after one year of his termination, but instead he went on the lam. Sounds like criminal behavior to me."

"A criminal who has helped us take down quite a few Scourges over the past months," Priss said. "All while in defiance of his father."

"Yes, that's the other thing." Wanda pounded the end of her spoon on the table. "His father is Ravian McFarland, who was once Mezzarix's right-hand man! And who's never been caught by B.R.E.W., by the way. I'd bet the contents of my entire potion satchel that Ravian was in on this attack."

"Aye, he was," Tobias said, returning from the kitchen carrying a large platter with what looked like a gigantic gourd steaming upon it. "Orchestrated the whole skirmish from the shadows. Been dreaming about it for years, trying to recruit me to his cause. But we'll not talk of that over supper." He carefully lowered the platter with his oven mitts and slid it to the center of the table. "Careful now. It's piping hot."

"Uh, what is it?" Max asked, cowering away from the platter.

"What is it?" Tobias gawked at the others in astonishment. "It's squash, you dolt! What do you think it is?"

With a sharp knife and spatula, Tobias served up slices of squash onto ten separate plates. The inside flesh of the gourd possessed a bright-pink hue, like the color of upset-stomach medicine, and there were yellow seeds peppering the vegetable.

"I'll set out some for the kiddies. They'll want to try it, believe me," Tobias said. Gordy could hear Isaac and Jessica's raucous squeals coming from the back room.

"I think I'll pass," Max said. "I had plenty of dried leaves earlier today. I'm good."

"Really now?" Tobias asked. "You don't want to sample my Bardoo McBoogal Squash? It's my own design, and it tastes just like fettuccini Alfredo and garlic breadsticks, but with only a fourth of the calories!"

Max folded his arms defiantly, but Gordy felt too hungry to resist. He cut a piece with his fork and took a bite. The squash tasted exactly how Tobias had described it. Salty and creamy and oh so garlicky. He did have to close his eyes while he chewed in order to not think about the weird pink-and-yellow vegetable, but after several bites, he no longer cared how it looked. Soon everyone at the table tucked into their pieces of Bardoo McBoogal Squash, savoring several helpings of Tobias's unusual creation.

After dinner, Tobias handed out garbage bags for each of them to wear over their clothes to keep them from getting soaked and took the group through his backyard for a tour of his garden.

"The rain lasts for three weeks, and then I have to rebrew the batter," Tobias said, stepping through a gate. "Takes a while though. Very tedious. And the birds provide an excellent source of nutrients for my plants." He pointed skyward, and Gordy realized why they needed to wear the garbage bags. Along with the rain, the birds supplied an endless onslaught of droppings.

"Don't look up for too long, and whatever you do, don't open your mouth," Tobias warned.

Max clamped his mouth shut, and Gordy suspected it would be the first time he kept silent.

"You've trapped those birds," Gordy's mom said.

Tobias shivered as though he had just stepped in something disgusting. "Yes, dear Wanda, I trap the birds, but I let them go from time to time. And I feed them well. Be sure to include that in your report to the Chamber when you rat me out for the second time."

Gordy wasn't sure what to expect beyond the gate, but nothing could have prepared him for what he saw. Pumpkins the size of small cars sprouted up along the path, pulsating as though the vegetables were enormous hearts. There were rows of strawberries and blueberries as big as basketballs and stalks of fat corn with plump kernels the size of Gordy's cellphone. But Tobias had a variety of other fruits and vegetables as well, ones that Gordy knew didn't exist outside of the garden. He called one species Doober McTuber, which could have been a potato had it not been bright blue and covered in hair. And yet another one Tobias had named Shiny McFiney; it was a long and thin fruit with a reflective surface that tasted oddly like carbonated raspberry Jell-O.

"And over here." Tobias directed Gordy's attention to a patch of ordinary earth that had been cordoned off with electric wire. "I call this Spikey McOuchy!"

"No offense," Max said from the rear of the group, finally opening his mouth, "but you've got the dumbest names I've ever heard."

"Who said that?" Tobias strained his neck to see to the back. "Ah, and your name? What would that be?"

Max frowned. "Max."

Tobias scoffed. "Max. What kind of dimwit name is that? I'll have you know, Max, that my names all have a certain important meaning. And if you pay close attention to that name, it might just save your life." He tossed a half-eaten wedge of squash onto the patch of ground, and sharp spikes suddenly shot up, impaling the vegetable. Juice splattered, and the spikes, like multiple pairs of scissors made of a spiny, scaly material, diced the squash into a pulpy mash. "I have planted this stuff on different parts of my land and have it marked very carefully with its name. So you remember Spikey McOuchy, Max," he said scornfully, "and you won't end up befooted. Lucky for you, Priscilla is a friend of mind. Even if her harpy sister isn't!"

Tobias's property was very impressive, and though he spat out venomous names at Gordy's mom whenever the opportunity presented itself, Gordy felt a strange appreciation for the man. He had saved Gordy's life. It had been his information that had led to Yeltzin and Esmeralda's capture. And without Tobias's helpful tip, Priss may have never found out about the attack on B.R.E.W., and Gordy and Max would have still been tied up in vines.

Back inside the house, Tobias laid out blankets on the floor and rounded up as many pillows as he could find. Max called his mom and explained why he hadn't texted earlier, but he left out the part about the Somnium building nearly exploding. Mrs. Pinkerman was mad for about ten seconds until Max told her he would be coming home with loads of Somnium samples the next day. And since it was the weekend, she didn't require any further persuasion to grant Max permission to stay the night with Gordy.

Had Gordy's mom not given each of them a sip of sleeping potion, it would have taken the twins hours to settle down after having played in the sandbox, which remarkably took up the entire spare bedroom. Even after digging for two solid hours, Isaac, with Zelda's help, had yet to reach the bottom. Gordy's dad had to jump down in the hole to help them both out.

Gordy had hoped to have a discussion with his mom and the others about what had happened at B.R.E.W., but when the night truly took hold outside, everyone's fatigue caught up with them. It had been an exhausting day, after all.

~⁀⁀~

Gordy must have fallen asleep sometime in the early hours of morning, because, try as he might, he couldn't remember the events that happened next.

Stumbling through the kitchen, Gordy took up his

satchel and removed every potion vial from the various compartments. He laid them all in a row on the kitchen counter and ignited a flame on one of the oven's burners. Blue fire licked the bowl of his porcelain cauldron, and he began absentmindedly tossing in ingredients. He emptied a bottle of ogon oil into the mixture and sprinkled in Icelandic volcanic sand from a salt shaker. Then Gordy yanked several strands of his own hair from the top of his head and added that to the mixture. The potion began to thrash and collapse upon itself, steam whistling as it drifted out of the bowl.

Gordy rummaged deeper into his bag, lifting up a flap of leather at the bottom and revealing a hidden compartment. From this, he removed a small glass jar containing a murky gray liquid and a roughly hewn piece of rock clinking against the glass. The jar did not belong in his satchel, and Gordy hadn't known about the secret compartment prior to that moment. With the lid removed, he took up the jar in his hands and readied to pour it into his cauldron.

The light flickered on in the kitchen, and Gordy blinked, shaking his head and waking, his hand and the jar of strange liquid still hovering above the stove. Tobias stood with his arms folded at his chest, leaning against the refrigerator, watching Gordy brew.

"Having fun, are we?" Tobias chewed on his lip, his eyes unreadable, his expression cold.

"Uh . . . I . . ." Gordy stammered and looked down at the cauldron in astonishment. What was he doing? How had he gotten there? "I have no idea what's going on."

CHAPTER

39

Once again, as Tobias's house sat cloaked in darkness with the exception of a single luminary potion glowing at the center of the table, Gordy found himself in the dining room, only this time under less-than-favorable circumstances. Everyone, except for Gordy's dad, Max, and the twins, was awake and seated around him. Their eyes were puffy and red from sleep deprivation, but Gordy's mom had never looked more worried. Gordy felt as though his chair might catch fire beneath him, just by the way she watched him.

"I've seen one of these before." Tobias studied the peculiar gray jar. "I helped my father make one several years ago to spring my grandmother from her exile on her ninetieth birthday. We had a celebration for her, complete with cake and ice cream. The potion lasted the whole of two hours before the banishment dragged her back to Inishmore. It's called a Clasping Cannikin, and it's highly complicated to concoct."

"Ah, yes," Zelda chimed in. "I thought I recognized it. Haven't seen one in quite some time. A Clasping Cannikin can also be used to temporarily free someone from a Binding."

"Why would you even try to make that, Gordy?" Gordy's mom demanded. "You've crossed the line this time."

"Oh, you doof!" Tobias shook his head and chuckled scornfully. "He didn't make this. But he *was* about to add to it."

"Why?" Priss leaned across the table, one hand held out in front of her. "What were you trying to do?"

"I wasn't trying to do anything," Gordy reasoned, feeling his pulse race. "I was asleep, and then I woke up. And now everyone's mad at me again." This had become a common occurrence.

"Brewing in your sleep?" Bolter's head perked up from where he had been resting upon his forearms. "That's probably not the safest practice."

Gordy dragged his hands through his hair. "I didn't do it on purpose." He was in hot water, that much was for certain, but this wasn't his fault. He had been lying down on Tobias's mossy floor, covered in blankets, then everything went haywire.

"Do you know how a Clasping Cannikin works?" Tobias held out the jar, the dull gray liquid looking like old mud. Priss took it from him and squinted at the strange potion, swirling it in her hand. The gloppy substance bubbled and clung to the side of the jar.

"It forms a temporary Blood Link between the prisoner and a close relative," Zelda answered. "Their actions can be mimicked from time to time because of their connection."

"Bravo, Ms. Morphata," Tobias said, nodding at Zelda. "In this case, I would say the 'close relative' is Mr. Gordy here, which would make the Blood Linked prisoner—"

"Mezzarix!" Gordy blurted.

"Bingo." Tobias snapped his fingers. "The potion binds them together so that it can extend beyond the Forbidden Zone. My guess is that piece of rock came from Mezzarix's cave, but there's also some of Gordy folded in as well. Mezzarix is still technically in exile, but now he has the freedom to go anywhere within range of Gordy. That would explain the sudden appearance of your grandfather at B.R.E.W."

"And my Blind Batching episodes," Gordy said, suddenly realizing the gravity of this news. "When I made that Mangle potion in the lab." He looked at his mom. "That wasn't me, was it?" And what had happened just now in Tobias's kitchen wasn't his fault either. Somehow the potion was causing Gordy to mimic his grandfather's brewing techniques.

"I suppose we can also assume that the Blight Bomb Gordy made at headquarters during training was a manifestation of Mezzarix as well," Zelda offered.

"His what?" Gordy's mom asked, alarmed.

So much for keeping that a secret. Gordy had known Zelda was bound to spill the beans eventually.

"He Blind Batched a Blight Bomb," Zelda said and then snickered. "Say that five times fast."

"It was an accident," Gordy said. "I was just trying to open the lock."

"That's why there's a warrant for Gordy," Bolter said. "Madame Brexil believes his potion was what let the Scourges into B.R.E.W."

Priss glowered at the table, flashing her teeth as though blaming herself for not piecing together the puzzle sooner. "But he couldn't help what he was doing. We have to remember that."

"I know," his mom said. "I can't believe Dad knowingly put my son at risk!"

"But how would he have formed this link?" Bolter inquired. "He lives in Greenland. Gordy is here. That's quite a distance."

Tobias held the jar to the light. "He would need an item of the boy to connect them. Blood is best, but it's not entirely necessary. And he wouldn't need much. My father used a fingernail from my grandmother to brew their Clasping Cannikin. And she was old and feeble at the time. Died shortly after, rest her soul."

"When you brought Gordy with you to see Dad last year." Aunt Priss eyed Gordy's mom. "He must have taken something then."

Gordy's mom covered her mouth with her hand. "This is my fault. I did this to you," she said to Gordy. "I should have never taken you to see him." Tears fell from her eyes, dampening her cheeks.

"It's okay, Mom. You didn't know." Gordy was relieved to discover he wasn't going crazy. All the Blind Batching that had gone awry had been the result of the connection with his grandfather. Maybe they could find a way to explain that to Madame Brexil. She then could lift the Sequester Strap from off their lab.

"In order to last this long, Mezzarix would have needed to add upon the potion from time to time to keep the spell active," Tobias said. "As soon as it weakens, he will have no choice but to return to his cave. And quickly too."

"What happens if he doesn't go?" Priss asked.

"He'll die, I think," Tobias answered grimly. "I can still remember my grandmother's screaming on the flight back to her cottage. She kept clutching her stomach as though her insides were about to burst. My dad swears it's what caused her eventual death."

Gordy remembered his grandfather's behavior back at B.R.E.W. He had looked emaciated and desperate for help. Gordy's help. That's what he wanted! Mezzarix needed Gordy to strengthen the potion to keep him from suffering. Despite knowing how evil Mezzarix's intentions had been trying to overthrow B.R.E.W., Gordy couldn't help but feel guilty for his grandfather's condition.

"You said my father has to stay in range in order for the Cannikin to work," Gordy's mom said. "What sort of range?"

"A few miles, thirty at most, but it's not just that. He would need to be in close proximity of the Cannikin as well." Tobias tapped the jar. "I suppose he could have made another to extend the distance, but even then, I figure he was counting on Gordy supplying the potion with some hair or blood to keep the Blood Link strong."

"What's going to happen to him now?" Gordy asked.

"We're over a hundred and fifty miles from B.R.E.W. and Mezzarix's last-known whereabouts. It's not as though he can track you easily," Bolter answered. "My guess is that he is in pretty poor shape right now."

"If he doesn't get back to his Forbidden Zone soon . . . Well, perhaps that would put a proper end to this predicament once and for all." Zelda squeaked with laughter, her head bobbing from side to side as though she had shared something hilarious.

There was nothing funny about it. Gordy looked at his mom, panic rising in his throat. They couldn't just let his grandfather die, suffering in the worst possible way. From the expressions on their faces, he could tell his mom and Priss were thinking the same thing.

"That doesn't explain how that jar ended up in Gordy's possession," Bolter said. "Someone would have had to plant it on him."

"Someone close," Zelda suggested.

Everyone at the table turned and stared at Gordy's satchel. It was such a lovely bag. Expensive and made of the finest leather. How long had the Clasping Cannikin been hidden within that secret compartment?

"Sasha and Mrs. Brexil gave me that bag." Gordy turned to his mom.

Priss's upper lip curled into a snarl. "That hideous woman! I'm going to poison her!"

Gordy's mom palmed her chin. "I know it seems obvious, but there are too many holes to the story. Why would she fight back at headquarters? Why didn't she just hand over the Vessel immediately? The Chamber moved it to keep it safe, and no one knows where it's hidden. That doesn't sound much like guilt to me."

"She's just trying to keep up appearances for the public," Priss said. "Wake up and smell the corruption!"

"Maybe she was Blotched," Bolter suggested.

Priss scoffed. "The Chamber President Blotched? Oh, come off it!"

"It could happen," Zelda chimed in, her voice chirping like a bird. "Someone as powerful as Mezzarix could do that."

"Blotching still doesn't explain Talia Brexil's behavior. She's not exactly cooperating with the Scourges!" Gordy's mom smacked the table emphatically. "If she had been Blotched, Dad would already have the Vessel in his hands. The fact that B.R.E.W. is still standing at all is a testament of her innocence."

"Here we go again!" Priss shouted.

"We're not going to solve any of this by fighting with

each other," Gordy said, interrupting what promised to be another thunderous argument. "Right now it doesn't matter who planted the potion in my bag. The Scourges were able to attack B.R.E.W. and would've stolen the Vessel had it been there. They'll do it again unless we stop them."

"Gordy's right," Tobias said, starting to whittle a piece of wood with his knife. "We need to solve this mystery first. How many Scourges did you say there were?" he asked Priss.

"I didn't say," Priss answered. "But there had to be several dozen."

"At least," Bolter added. "My count would be closer to eighty."

"Eighty?" Tobias looked bewildered. "Can't be that many. My father has plenty of followers, I'll give him that, but there's no way a group of Scourges that large could have made it onto the grounds of B.R.E.W. One or two, sure. Even a dozen, maybe. But eighty?" He shook his head and nicked a sliver of wood off from his whittling block. "What did they use? Bugs? Mice?"

"They didn't use any Wardbreakers." Zelda had removed her knitting from her satchel and teased threads through what Gordy had decided would one day be a sweater for an octopus.

"That's what we need to understand," Gordy's mom said. "What have you heard Ravian talking about? What do you know?"

Tobias clicked his knife closed and leaned forward,

but instead of erupting with a series of insults and "how-dare-yous" to Wanda, he simply shrugged his shoulders. "I haven't the foggiest. He's a tough one to crack, my pop, but this he's kept close to the chest. Is there any way you could gain access to the security footage outside of head-quarters?"

This time Bolter answered. "I'm afraid not. The only one here who had access to the cameras was Wanda, and, well . . ."

"Got herself sacked, didn't she now?" Tobias clapped. "Best news I've heard all year."

"Can we stay focused, please?" Gordy's mom pleaded.

Max appeared in the kitchen doorway, yawning, a blanket wrapped around him like a tortilla. "Is it breakfast already?"

"It's like four o'clock in the morning," Gordy said, laughing at Max's unruly hairdo.

"You geeks," Max grumbled. "You woke me up for nothing." He scooched a chair over to the table and wedged himself between Gordy and Zelda.

"What good would the security footage do anyway?" Gordy's mom asked.

Tobias cleared his throat. "Well, it might show how they did it. Perhaps you missed a species of Wardbreaker going to work. I've known some folks to use gnats, and they don't get very plump, drinking up potions."

"Bolter was out on the lawn the whole time, and he didn't see any creature at all," Zelda chirped. "And I doubt

Madame Brexil was paying too much attention to the out-side security cameras. She had her hands full, proclaim-ing Gordy's outlaw status after watching him tear a hole through the training room."

"She does have it all on video," Bolter said. "Cameras can be very convincing."

"Yeah, but they can also be modified." Max had some-how found more dried aloe vera chips, and his mouth was filled with Zelda's snack. "People are always uploading fake videos of ghosts and magic tricks. The video never shows the whole story of what's really going on."

Gordy heard Tobias's voice chime in with something else, but he wasn't listening to him anymore. Right now, Max's words had triggered a thought in Gordy's mind.

"Mom, do you have your tablet?" he blurted out, inter-rupting the conversation. "The one with the security foot-age from the first breach of the Vessel room?"

"Yes, but—"

"Get it out, please, and also, do you still have Max's rock?"

"My rock?" Max asked. "What's that have to do with anything?"

After taking the glowing rock from his mom and wait-ing for her to cue up the footage from the breach exactly one week earlier, Gordy stared at the tablet, his heart rac-ing. The entire clip had a running time of fifteen minutes, start to finish, and his mom had insisted they would see no evidence of anything out of the ordinary on the screen.

Gordy fiddled with the stone until he felt the section depress beneath his thumb and the dark dining room lit up with a bright, bluish light.

"Stifle that, will you?" Tobias complained.

"Replay it, Mom. From the beginning," Gordy commanded. His mom didn't argue, and together they watched the footage once more, only this time with the rock light shining directly at the screen.

"There!" Gordy shouted, feeling as though he might jump right out of his skin. "Do you see her?" He gestured excitedly at the screen, his whole body tingling with goose bumps. A sensation of nausea almost overtook him from the harrowing pit forming in his stomach.

There, entering the Vessel room corridor, peering through the window of the empty room and hiding in the corner, until she plowed into Max trying to make her escape onto the elevator, was Adilene's new friend, Cadence.

40

Adilene clenched her jaw, steadied her finger, and pressed the doorbell to the Stitsers' home. She felt horrible for having ignored Gordy all week. He was her best friend, and she couldn't stay mad at him. Max, on the other hand, would get over it. She ignored him at least once or twice a day anyway. It was almost nine o'clock on a Saturday morning, and Gordy was probably eating breakfast, so Adilene didn't plan on staying long. Just long enough to apologize and become friends again and put the whole nonsense behind them.

She watched a few cars drive by as she waited for someone to answer the door. Then she noticed a blue pickup truck parked at the edge of the cul-de-sac. Somehow she had missed it on her way in. Adilene's eyes narrowed in suspicion. Was it weird Uncle Carlisle's vehicle? She glanced back and thought about pressing the bell again, but then she saw that the door was open a crack, and she heard rummaging noises coming from inside.

"Gordy?" Adilene called out, pushing open the door and gazing into the foyer. "Mr. and Mrs. Stitser?"

No one answered, and Adilene's eyes drifted up the stairs to where the door to the Stitsers' lab stood open. The rummaging noises were coming from there.

Adilene stepped into the foyer, forearms prickling. Oh, how she hoped Gordy's dad would suddenly appear in the kitchen, a steaming platter of pancakes clutched in his hands as he called the rest of the family down for breakfast. Maybe Gordy and his mom were just busy brewing in the lab and couldn't hear Adilene calling. That seemed like a possible reason, except that Gordy couldn't enter the lab. Not with that Sequester Strap still in place.

Slipping the vial of vanishing potion from her pocket, she uncorked the lid and took a sip. Disappearing didn't feel strange. No tingling sensation. Adilene didn't feel hot or cold or even warm, and the liquid, which had the consistency of cough syrup, only slightly reminded her of black licorice as it flowed down her throat.

When Adilene looked at her arms and hands, however, that's how she knew it was working. The shape of her body, the outline of her fingers, and the scuffed, worn-out patches on the knees of her blue jeans remained visible, but her skin and clothing had turned translucent. Almost half the bottle Cadence had given her was gone. Adilene liked being invisible. She enjoyed having an ability that others could only dream of having.

Tiptoeing softly up the stairs, Adilene supported her

weight with the handrail to keep from making any extra sounds. She was invisible, not weightless. As she approached the lab, Adilene knew instantly there was a problem. Not that she had heard any voices to give her a warning, but she could see a hunched shadow on the carpet and recognized it as belonging to Carlisle. Adilene froze in her tracks.

"Have you checked all the bedrooms?" Cadence's voice whispered from inside the lab. She sounded desperate. Frantic. What was she doing in Gordy's house uninvited? "And the parents' bedroom?" Cadence pressed. "Did you check their closet? Under the bed?" No one answered, and Cadence growled in frustration. "Go check them again, and don't come back until I call you! We have to hurry!"

Carlisle huffed into the hallway, almost bowling over Adilene, who only managed to leap out of the way as he blundered past, heading toward the back bedrooms. She hadn't noticed before, but Cadence's uncle walked with a limp, his back crooked and stooped.

Adilene tried to keep her breath from gusting forth from her lungs. She had held it all the way up the stairs and just now narrowly gave away her position when Carlisle suddenly appeared. But the old man hadn't even looked in her direction as he hurried off to obey his niece's wishes.

Peering around the corner, Adilene saw Cadence on all fours in the lab, scouring the dusty floor, her face almost pressed against the wooden boards. Cadence was wearing what looked like a maroon pantsuit with high-heeled shoes. Her hair had been pulled back into a bun, with a pair of glasses resting on top of her head. Adilene had never seen Cadence wear glasses before, but maybe they were more for show or a fancy accessory to complete her strangely businesslike outfit.

As she had done the last time they had snuck into the lab together, Cadence had opened every drawer and cabinet and piled up the ingredients, potions, and containers onto the countertop, the items grouped together in small clusters. Adilene realized Cadence wasn't just exploring Gordy's lab. She was searching for something.

"Blast!" Cadence sat up, pressing her hands against her knees. "It's not here." Then she checked the time on her wristwatch, one that sparkled with glittering gems.

Adilene kept dead silent, watching tremulously as her friend dusted off her knees and turned her attention to the counter and the array of items upon it. One by one, she began returning glass vials into drawers, careful not to spill a drop of any potion.

What was she looking for? What gave her the right to break into Gordy's home? Adilene pulled back, ashamed of herself because she had done the same thing. This time, though, she would handle things differently. She knew she needed to tell Gordy what was happening, but she couldn't do anything right there without alerting Cadence of her presence.

Once back in the hallway, Adilene pulled out her cell phone. With trembling hands, she began texting Gordy a message, but before she'd finished, Carlisle reappeared from Mr. and Mrs. Stitser's bedroom, and Adilene dropped her phone in surprise.

The moment the phone left her fingers, it regained its visibility. The transparent object solidified in midair, and Carlisle's eyes instantly honed in on the phone as it struck the carpeted floor with a muted thud.

Carlisle glowered, staring as though he couldn't quite tell what the object was, but as he began to understand, he suddenly barreled toward Adilene. She barely had time to snatch up her phone and turn for the stairs. In her haste, Adilene tripped and nearly rolled to the bottom. She felt her ankle twist awkwardly, and she skidded her knee on the rough carpet, but she didn't cry out.

"What are you doing?" Cadence shouted from inside the lab.

Quietly scooting back on the carpet, Adilene hid in the corner as Carlisle snatched at handfuls of air, searching for her.

At the top of the stairs, Cadence emerged, staring down at her uncle, annoyed. "What is it?"

Carlisle looked up but didn't say anything. A queer expression formed in Cadence's eyes as she gazed down to the main level, scanning the floor.

"Your friend took something of mine," Cadence spoke out, eyes narrowing. "I don't think he meant to take it, but it's very dear to me, and I need it back." She stepped onto the stairs, gripping the handrail. "I have to leave soon. I'm going home, but I can't without my keystone."

Keystone? Adilene didn't know what she was talking about. And when would Gordy have taken something from Cadence? They had hardly ever spoken to each other.

Cadence descended a few more steps, and Adilene pulled her legs close to her chest. How was she going to get out of this?

"You don't understand what's going on here," Cadence said. "I'm not like you. Any of you. Surely, you've figured that out by now, but there's more to it than just that."

Outside the house, Adilene heard a car door slam. Carlisle stiffened. He sniffed the air, nostrils flaring, and then he looked at Cadence. She nodded at him, and Carlisle turned and ran. The old man's footsteps thundered upon the floor; he moved surprisingly fast for his age. Then to Adilene's astonishment, Carlisle began smashing things. He started with the plates and glasses from the cupboards and dumped out the silverware drawers onto the floor. He turned over chairs and heaved the kitchen table onto its side. Had he gone mad?

The front door kicked open, and Wanda Stitser and Priscilla Rook stormed in, each holding bottles of potions and wearing determined, no-nonsense expressions.

Adilene turned to see what Cadence would do, but the girl had vanished.

Wanda and Priss raced past the stairs as Carlisle continued to rampage through the kitchen. Adilene heard a whoosh and a shatter of glass, followed by a heavy thud as Carlisle dropped, stiff as a board, to the ground.

"Do you know this guy?" Wanda shouted from the kitchen.

"No," Priss responded. "Maybe he's from B.R.E.W."

"He's not from B.R.E.W.," Wanda said. "That much I'm sure of."

"Then how did he get past your wards?" Priss asked.

"We need to take him somewhere for questioning. How long will he be out?"

"Twelve to fifteen minutes, I believe. It was a mild dose."

Adilene leaned forward, slowly stretching out her legs. She could see the soles of Carlisle's boots, his toes pointed upward as he lay on his back, unmoving. The two women stood on either side of his body. Adilene wasn't sure how much longer her invisibility would last, but she knew she needed to get out of the house as soon as possible before they discovered her. What would they do if they found Adilene hiding there? Gordy may have given her permanent access to visit the home whenever she wanted, but considering the circumstances—her sudden appearance alongside Carlisle when Gordy was nowhere in sight—Mrs. Stitser and Gordy's aunt Priss might be less forgiving of the uninvited intrusion.

Pressing her back against the wall, Adilene eased her weight off the floor, sliding up until she stood upright next to the door. She kept her eyes glued to the two Elixirists as she reached for the doorknob, but then remembered something that concerned her.

Was Cadence still in the house, or had she left? Adilene assumed Carlisle's sudden rage had been a way to distract Wanda and Priss so that Cadence could escape, but why was that necessary? Cadence could simply disappear whenever she wanted. Why would she need a diversion? Unless . . .

Too late.

Adilene came to the realization of what was happening just as something else shattered in the kitchen. She heard Wanda and Priss gasp, and then the two women collapsed on the floor next to Carlisle.

Gordy peered through the window of the Subaru, watching the house and waiting for his mom to give them the all-clear to come inside. Upon arriving in town, they had gone to the Riveras' house, only to discover that Adilene had left for Gordy's house twenty minutes before.

Max sat next to Gordy, munching on one of the *pupusas* that Mrs. Rivera had given them on her way to the farmers market. He hummed to himself as he used the rock to rewatch the security footage from a week ago.

"This is crazy!" he said, pointing at the screen.

Gordy wasn't positive, but he didn't think the only reason Max was watching the film was just to see Cadence disappear.

"She's like out of a movie!" Max said wistfully.

Gordy rolled his eyes.

Bolter and Zelda had gone to B.R.E.W. to assess the damage and see if they could uncover any other information on the mysterious girl from the video. They had taken Priss's SUV, and the plan was to meet back at the Stitsers' house in one hour. Tobias, who wanted to stay as uninvolved as possible, remained on his farm, along with Gordy's dad because somebody had to watch the twins. Until things calmed down with B.R.E.W., Tobias had opened his house to the Stitsers for as long as they needed to stay. Gordy was grateful for the former member of B.R.E.W., even if Tobias did hate his mom.

The group had had a long discussion earlier that morning on whether or not Gordy should stay behind as well. There could be plenty of trouble ahead, and Gordy was just a kid. In the end, it was Zelda who convinced Gordy's mom to let him come along. If they did find Mezzarix in time, Gordy might be the only way to save his life. Max probably should have stayed at Tobias's house, but he flat-out refused. Sometimes, Max's stubbornness was too much to handle.

"They've been in there for a while, don't you think?" Gordy asked Max.

Max shrugged. "Maybe, but your mom gave very strict instructions."

Mrs. Stitser had forbidden Gordy and Max to enter the house without permission. If they disobeyed, his mom had threatened severe punishment. The possibility existed that members of B.R.E.W., or even some of the Scourges, could have been hiding inside, and until Wanda and Priss secured the perimeter, Gordy and Max were to keep their behinds glued to their seats.

It had certainly seemed as though his mom and Priss had rushed inside all of a sudden, and there was still no sign of Adilene anywhere, despite her bike lying in the grass next to the driveway. How long did securing the perimeter take?

The front door moved, opening ever so slightly, and Gordy leaned out the window, eyes narrowed, trying to see. Soon after, the door closed again, and Gordy growled in frustration. The waiting was killing him.

"What's going on?" he demanded, glaring at Max. How could he just sit there watching the footage over and over? Cadence wasn't that cute.

"Just chill, dude," Max groaned. "There's no point in freaking out. You need to harness your chi and . . ." Max squinted, staring over Gordy's shoulder. "Why is that bike riding off by itself?"

"What?" Gordy whirled around just in time to see a driverless bicycle pedaling down the driveway.

"What's in these *pupusas*?" Max stared down at the doughy mass in his hand.

Gordy clawed at the door handle and swung it open.

"Adilene!" he shouted, watching the bike round the corner of the cul-de-sac. "Come back!"

The bicycle suddenly toppled over into the grass, and then Gordy heard footsteps hurrying toward him.

"Oh, my goodness! I didn't see you in the car," Adilene

said breathlessly. "I just came over to say that I'm sorry for acting like such a jerk all week. I would never have gone inside if I had known. I had nothing to do with it. I promise!"

"It's okay, calm down." Gordy reached out, patting the air until he found Adilene's shoulder. "Why are you invisible? What happened?"

"Your mom and Priss . . ." she wheezed breathlessly. "She hit them with something. One of the potions from your lab. It knocked them out. They're all in the kitchen." Adilene fired off information rapidly, increasing in volume as she spoke. Trying to listen to her while she was invisible made Gordy's head swim, but he did his best to stay focused.

"Who knocked them out? Cadence?" Gordy demanded. "Are they hurt?"

"I don't know. She set a trap, and they took out Carlisle."

"Who?" Max had emerged from the car and stood beside Gordy, blinking in bafflement as he searched for any signs of Adilene.

"Cadence's uncle!" Adilene gasped. "I'm sorry, I can't explain everything, but Cadence and Carlisle were looking for something in your lab. She said you took it from her. She said something about a keystone and that it's very important to her and that she's leaving."

"Is it that?" Gordy pointed at the small, round stone clutched in Max's hand.

"*¡Eso tiene que ser!*" Adilene exclaimed. "Yes, it has to be. She wants it very badly."

"Cadence was the one who broke into B.R.E.W. that night. We saw her on the video. She appeared when we used that stone," Gordy said.

"She did?" Adilene sounded confused. "You saw her?"

"Now do you believe us that your friend is bad?" Gordy asked, glaring at Max. Just a few moments earlier, Max may have been considering writing a love ballad to Cadence. Now he just stared at the ground, embarrassed.

"Okay, yeah, I believe it. I should have listened to you," Adilene said. "But we have to get out of here and call the police or someone."

"No, we have to help my mom." Gordy stared at the house and unclasped his satchel. He started to remove a Polish Fire Rocket but then thought better of it. The goal was to capture Cadence, not kill her. And there was no point in burning a second house to the ground if another potion would work just as well. Instead, Gordy pulled out a Vintreet Trap, a Torpor Tonic, and one of his newest creations.

"What is that?" Max asked, scrunching his nose with disgust.

"Gravity Gouda." Gordy unwrapped the dense substance from a waxy piece of cheesecloth.

"This is insane! We can't stop Cadence," Adilene said. "She can turn invisible whenever she wants, and she's so smart. I think there's something wrong with her."

"You're invisible!" Max fired back.

"Yes, but it's going to wear off soon, and I don't have much potion left."

"We have this." Max held up the keystone. "Let's see her try and disappear."

"We need help," Adilene repeated. "Where's Bolter? We should call someone from B.R.E.W. and let them know what's going on."

"B.R.E.W. will just arrest me, and we don't have time to waste." Gordy faced the house, weapons in his hands and satchel draped over his shoulder. He knew what he was about to do was crazy, but he had to try to help.

"You won't be able to get close to her without her knowing," Adilene warned. "Please, just think this through."

Gordy looked to the spot where he assumed Adilene was standing, and his eyes softened. Maybe she was right. If they just barged in, potions flying, bad things could happen. Cadence could get away, and Gordy's family could get hurt. There had to be a better way to do this. Patience had never been Gordy's strong suit, but then again, many of the mixtures he made in the lab required a calm and steady approach. Perhaps he just needed to treat this situation as if he were concocting another potion.

"Okay." Gordy held out his hand. After a moment, Adilene's invisible fingers squeezed around his. "Let's plan."

42

The front door to the Stitsers' home opened, and Adilene slipped through with hardly a sound. She allowed the door to close softly behind her, but she kept it from latching shut, partly because that was the plan but also in case she decided to abandon this ridiculous idea and needed a way to escape. Adilene had removed her socks and shoes just outside the door and stood on the hardwood entryway floor, barefoot and breathing as though she might hyperventilate.

"This is crazy!" Adilene whispered to herself. She couldn't do it. She would blow their cover, and then she would be knocked unconscious on the floor like the others.

As she was about to leave, Adilene remembered that most of this was her fault. She had shown Cadence where Gordy lived. They had snuck into the house together and had put Gordy's family in danger. If Adilene had used her brain and trusted her real friends, none of this would have happened. Clenching her hands into fists, Adilene steeled her nerves and moved toward the kitchen.

Carlisle had sat up from the floor, pawing at his eyes with his fingers, disoriented. On either side of him were two sticky cocoons molded around the bodies of Gordy's mom and Aunt Priss. They weren't moving, and for a moment, Adilene feared they weren't breathing either. But then she saw the gentle rise and fall of their chests and knew they were still alive.

"You acted foolishly," Cadence's voice rose from somewhere near the refrigerator. She was still invisible, and despite Adilene's frantic searching, she couldn't see any sign of the young girl. "Running downstairs like that. It left you no choice but to allow yourself to be caught. What have we talked about, Carlisle?" she demanded. "I took a chance bringing you here, and it almost cost us everything."

Why was she treating her uncle like a child?

Carlisle puffed out his cheeks and exhaled deeply, then he grabbed the edge of the overturned table and hoisted himself off the floor. He stood for a moment, wobbling, then staggered back and dropped into one of the available kitchen chairs.

"Yes, rest for a moment," Cadence instructed. "Then go get the truck and bring it close to the door. We need to move fast and take these two back with us. They will be valuable in our negotiations."

Carlisle looked sideways toward the refrigerator, still

breathing as though he might pass out again. He licked his lips and leaned forward, palms outstretched.

"That's not my fault," Cadence said. "I told you I wouldn't always have enough for you. It's been that way since our exile. You knew the risk, and you accepted it. What we are trying to do will not come without consequences."

Carlisle's eyes dropped to the floor. He looked ashamed.

Adilene's mind whirled with questions. How could they communicate with each other? What was Cadence talking about? She needed answers but knew they wouldn't happen right now. Not until later. Adilene squeezed the keystone in her hand and waited, knowing that at any moment her potion would wear off, leaving her standing in the kitchen, vulnerable and exposed.

Carlisle finally gained control of his faculties and stood up.

Adilene slid off to one side as he approached, but before he could step into the hallway, a blaring stereo kicked on upstairs.

Music blasted overhead, shaking the ceiling. Carlisle flinched, and he spun around, facing the refrigerator as the sound of Gordy and Max singing at the top of their lungs filled the house. It was awful and off-key—and oddly gave Adilene hope. She heard her friends leaping up and down on the floor, screaming and hollering as thunderous drums and shrill electric guitars threatened to shatter the windows.

"No, don't go upstairs," Cadence said. "It's clearly a trap. Go get the truck!"

As Carlisle headed for the hallway again, the sound of police sirens and the voices of officers rang out from behind the front door, and he nearly tripped backpedaling into the kitchen. More screaming arose as the music upstairs suddenly doubled in volume. Carlisle rushed over to the window above the sink and tried to pry it open.

"Now!" Gordy shouted, charging not down the stairs but through the front door at full speed.

Adilene fumbled with the keystone for a second before pressing her thumb on the correct spot, just where Gordy had shown her, and the blue light flashed on.

Cadence appeared by the stove, eyes wide and alarmed, as two vials of potion hurled into the room. She barely had time to speak as a Torpor Tonic struck her on the shoulder, rendering her unconscious.

Max's bottle sailed high over Carlisle's head, splattering the wall with a greenish liquid. The old man dropped to the floor as the potion dripped down on him, but not enough for the Vintreet Trap to be fully effective. The vines flopped about uselessly, missing their target.

"Keep the light on her!" Gordy shouted. He dove into his satchel, trying desperately to find another weapon. But Carlisle nimbly scrambled to his feet and was on Gordy before he could pull out a bottle. The man wrenched the bag free from Gordy's fingers and tossed it aside. The two struggled on the floor for a moment, but Carlisle was just too tall and wiry, and he had surprising strength.

"Eat it, Max!" Gordy demanded. "Just do it!"

Max looked hesitantly at the Gravity Gouda in his hand, then bit off a corner and chewed. "Yuck!" he gagged. "Oh, whoa. Do you guys feel that?"

"Grab him, Maxwell!" Adilene demanded.

And Max did.

Leaning down, Max wrapped his arms around Carlisle and the two of them fell over sideways. Carlisle tried to break free from Max's grip, but he couldn't. It was as though he were fighting a pointless battle against a marble statue.

Max laughed boisterously as Carlisle writhed about in his arms. "One, two, three, pin! One, two, three, pin!" he cheered. "Easiest wrestling match I've ever won."

Gordy got to his feet, pulled a spray bottle out of his satchel, and spritzed Carlisle in the face. The old man instantly fell limp. Gordy returned to the hallway and picked up what looked like a strawberry jam jar from the floor. As he screwed back on the lid to his Cacophonous Compound, the sounds of sirens and officers out on the lawn snuffed out, as did the rowdy music and Gordy and Max's earsplitting singing coming from upstairs. The house fell completely silent.

"We did it!" Adilene said as her invisibility potion wore off and she could see the outline of her arms and legs again.

"Yes, we did," Gordy said.

"Uh, when will this wear off?" Max asked, lying motionless on the floor.

"Could be a while, Max," Gordy answered. "You didn't have to eat that much."

After helping cut Gordy's mom and aunt free from their cocoons, the five of them tied the intruders to kitchen chairs with thick ropes. Eventually, a fully visible Cadence and a reawakened Carlisle found themselves bound and immobile. Cadence's usually pleasant expression had turned to pure hatred.

"How could you steal from me?" Cadence spat, glaring at Adilene, who stood back from the group, near the hallway. Cadence looked as though she might suddenly shoot lasers from her eyes. "After all I've done for you, this is how you treat me?"

"I didn't steal from you." Adilene looked away, folding her arms.

"Yeah, you're the one who dropped the keystone," Gordy said. "When you were snooping around B.R.E.W."

Cadence sneered at Gordy. "I see that you sent her in to do your dirty work." She nodded at Adilene. "You put her life at risk while you hid and waited for the right moment to strike. Some friend!"

"That was my idea," Adilene said.

"Putting my gift to good use then? Well done, Adilene. How quickly you turn on—"

"Enough," Gordy's mom interrupted. "Let the adults ask the questions, okay?" She looked at Gordy, Max, and Adilene. The three of them nodded. "We need some answers."

"You shall get none from me and certainly less from him." Cadence's eyes shifted to Carlisle, and she started laughing. The old man didn't struggle. He sat with his head bowed, eyes shifting to each of the others in the room.

"Then it's off to prison for you," Priss said. "I'm sure we can stick you in some juvenile correctional facility. Maybe there's a Forbidden Zone for kids somewhere."

"Sounds wonderful." Cadence grinned at Priss. "I propose you take me there right away."

"That won't do any good," Gordy said. "Wards and banishments don't work the same way on her. She'll just stay there for a few moments and then walk right out, and no one will stop her."

"That's a problem," Gordy's mom grumbled. "And if she can disappear whenever she wants, regular prisons aren't going to work either."

"Those ropes seem to be doing the trick," Max suggested. "Maybe we could just keep them tied up forever."

"We can't do that." Adilene stepped forward into the kitchen. "That wouldn't be right."

Gordy's mom sighed and rubbed her eyes. "Listen, kid, I don't know how you got mixed up with this, but believe me, it's not going to end well for the Scourges. In case you didn't hear, their attack on B.R.E.W. failed. If you cooperate with us, maybe we can cut a deal and your parents won't have to be banished for their involvement."

"Parents?" Cadence's forehead crinkled. "Oh, there's so little of what you understand."

"Well, help us understand!" Priss demanded.

A knock sounded at the front door, and everyone jumped.

"Easy, easy." Gordy's mom held out her hands to calm the group. "Bolter? Is that you?" she called out.

"In the flesh," Bolter replied.

Priss opened the door, and she and Bolter entered the kitchen. His boots clopped noisily on the hardwood floor as he stepped over the shattered plates and silverware. "This is an all-too familiar scene," he said, referring to the last time Gordy's house had been ransacked by enemies.

"Where's Zelda?" Gordy asked.

"She was right behind me," Bolter said.

"Coming!" Zelda's chirpy voice sounded in the hallway. "I stopped to search that old pickup truck outside, per Priss's request." She entered the room, toting a small handbag containing a thin vial of inky blue substance. "Does this belong to anyone here?"

Cadence stiffened, struggling against her bindings. "Be careful with that!"

Aunt Priss smiled. "Ah, I see we've hit a pressure point."

Gordy's mom took the vial from Zelda and dug out the wax with her index finger. She held the opened container over the sink, threatening to pour out what little potion remained. It couldn't have been more than four or five drops.

"Stop!" Cadence shouted. "You'll spill it!"

"What is this?" Gordy's mom asked. "Who are you?"

"That's mine, and I'm Cadence!" The girl craned her neck trying to see over the lip of the sink.

"Not good enough." Gordy's mom poured a drop out of the bottle. The liquid splattered, and Cadence screamed.

"Okay, okay!" She fought against her bindings again, but not only had the knots been tied especially tight, but Priss had also treated the rope with a special tonic. "It's called Silt. It's from my island."

"What are you doing with it here?" Gordy asked.

"I'm recruiting," Cadence answered.

"Scourges?" Priss asked.

"Sure, if that's what you want to call them. Scourges. Potion Masters. Anyone willing to help me return to my home."

Gordy was struggling to figure out Cadence. She talked differently from other kids their age, and she acted too brave and too resistant to her captors, who were adults, for crying out loud! His mom was an Elixirist who had taken down her share of nasty Scourges over the years, and yet Cadence addressed her as though she were a low-life criminal.

Carlisle simply sat wearing a passive expression of indifference, as though he had no desire to fight anymore. He just stared straight ahead, eyes crinkling with exhaustion.

Gordy's mom shook the vial of Silt at Cadence. "And in exchange, you helped Mezzarix Rook sneak into B.R.E.W. with *this?*"

Cadence fidgeted nervously against her ropes. "Careful!" she hissed. "But yes. Those were the terms of our agreement."

"Why go to him?" Priss asked. "How did you even find him? He was in Greenland, living out his days of banishment."

"I found someone who could track him. Because as you can see, I'm running low on my supply."

Gordy's mom glanced at Bolter and Zelda uncertainly. "You needed Mezzarix to Replicate your Silt?"

"He is the best, or so I've been told," Cadence said.

"And then what?" Bolter asked. "You Replicate this peculiar substance of yours, outfit an army of Scourges to claim the Vessel, and then . . . what? I'm sorry, I'm confused by your motives."

"Then I go home with them," Cadence said. "Then they help me take back my island, and I resume my place as leader of my people."

This girl had turned out to be so much more than

some annoying friend of Adilene's. Now she had people she wanted to lead?

"If you need to go home, why not go to someone at B.R.E.W.?" Bolter suggested. "They could have helped you."

"Oh, really?" Cadence raised an eyebrow. "Because B.R.E.W. enjoys helping people? I think not."

"It's not just that, is it?" Gordy's mom asked. "You're not wanted on your island anymore. Your people made you leave, and you want to go back against their wishes."

Cadence curled her lip, impressed. "Very good, Wanda. Would B.R.E.W. support a rebellion? I don't think so. From what I've heard, they would seize my supply of Silt and keep it for themselves. They'd lock me away and forget about me."

Priss sighed. "You don't think Mezzarix would do the same?"

"He wouldn't dare. He knows how powerful I am and what I could do to his life. I promised him wealth beyond measure. I'm willing to extend the offer to you, if you're interested. I can reward you with a king's ransom."

"My dad doesn't care about wealth. Neither do we," Gordy's mom said.

"Yes, what is it with your family? Spent too much time on the wrong side of the tracks? Determined to weasel your way through life driving that pathetic Subaru all the live-long day?"

"I saw that old truck of yours," Max said, snickering. "How much of the king's ransom did that set you back?"

"It's a front, you insolent little brat!" Cadence sneered at Max, and Gordy noticed that somehow her voice changed. Her words took on a different accent, and her voice sounded deeper now. Older.

"Who are you really?" Gordy asked.

"I told you, boy, I'm Cadence." She grinned. Her eyes grew darker, and her cheekbones became more sunken and pronounced in her face. "But my associates call me Ms. Bimini."

"Ms. Bimini?" Adilene stepped up next to Gordy and stared at Cadence in shock. "And is Carlisle really your uncle's name?"

"Why, yes, dear Adilene, it is." She puckered her lips as creases began to weave their way through her skin, transforming her young girl's face into a wrinkled mess. Her neck bowed, her hands and wrists twisting and curling as her knuckles and bones pressed against almost transparent skin.

"But he's not really my uncle," the elderly woman replied. The young Cadence was gone. "He's my son."

CHAPTER

44

Never in Gordy's thirteen years of existence had he seen anything as bizarre as what he had witnessed with Cadence and Carlisle. Sitting on the porch next to Max and Adilene, Gordy thought he might throw up. The image of Cadence's transformation from girl to ancient woman was too much to take in. But Max was handling it the worst.

"And to think I had a crush on that old hag!" Max grimaced, leaning against the outside wall of the house. "We almost kissed!"

"No, you didn't," Adilene said. "Stop making it worse than it already is!"

"Did you have any idea who she was when you guys were hanging out?" Gordy asked Adilene.

She shook her head and shivered.

The door opened, and Gordy's mom, Bolter, and Zelda joined the three of them on the porch. Aunt Priss remained inside the house to keep a watchful eye over their two prisoners.

"Pretty surreal, eh?" Bolter asked Gordy.

Gordy nodded. "Have you seen anything like that before?"

"Oh, of course. There are Disfarcar Gels that can disguise just about anyone for a decent amount of time," he answered.

"Yeah." Gordy remembered having brewed a similar potion with his mom the previous year, the effects of which generally lasted about twelve hours. "But Cadence is not an Elixirist, is she?"

"No, she's not," his mom replied.

"Then how did she make a Disfarcar Gel?"

"We don't think that's what this is." Gordy's mom stepped off the porch and onto the front lawn. "It may have a connection to her Silt, but it would seem that Ms. Bimini can alter her appearance as easily as she can vanish."

"Wow!" Max chimed in. "Maybe you all *should* replicate this Silt. We could make a fortune."

Bolter chuckled. "Something tells me that Priss might be doing business with Max in the Swigs one day."

Max gave Bolter the thumbs-up. "You better believe it!"

"So, now what?" Gordy asked. Now that Cadence and Carlisle were out of the way, what was their next course of action?

"We have to hunt down Mezzarix," Gordy's mom said. "But it might be almost impossible."

"Maybe not." Zelda glanced down at the tiny digital screen on her phone. "It would appear that I'm still patched into B.R.E.W.'s mainframe and receiving their bulletins."

"I should still be receiving bulletins too, then." Bolter peered over Zelda's shoulder, a look of concern crossing his features.

Zelda giggled. "How would you receive them? On that ridiculous brick phone of yours?"

"It has a messaging feature!" Bolter exclaimed.

"What's going on?" Gordy's mom demanded.

"Madame Brexil has issued a statement about the recent attack at headquarters." Zelda cleared her throat and read the message.

"'My fellow constituents. I am pleased to announce that the recent skirmish on the grounds of B.R.E.W. Headquarters has finally been contained. We have taken every measure to extinguish any evidence of this attack from the media and have used approved Memory Erasing Elixirs on the public in the general area to keep our existence from their knowledge.

"'Furthermore, we have captured the notorious Mezzarix Rook. Rest assured, my friends, the mystery behind Mr. Rook's escape from his Forbidden Zone shall be thoroughly investigated, and he shall be punished to the full extent of B.R.E.W.'s law.

"'Cheers,' etc."

Bolter's nose twitched as though he had suddenly sprouted whiskers.

Gordy looked at his mom, who was shaking her head in disbelief. It didn't seem possible. From what he had learned about his grandfather over the past few months, Mezzarix had always been too elusive to be captured. That is, until his own daughters had betrayed him. But now he had escaped the Forbidden Zone and gained access to a powerful vanishing potion. Hearing the Chamber President's statement was, in a way, anticlimactic.

"What if he was too sick to fight back?" Gordy asked. "What if the effects of the Clasping Cannikin are finally wearing off?" He remembered his grandfather's sickly appearance back at headquarters. Gordy's mom looked down at him, and he knew she was fearing the same possibility.

"Madame Brexil probably intends to ExSponge him," Zelda said. "ExSpongement while being so far removed from his Forbidden Zone?" She clicked her tongue. "That would certainly be the end of Mezzarix Rook."

"We have to help him." Gordy leaped up from the porch.

"You mean help the dude who was trying to destroy B.R.E.W.?" Max asked.

"Just help him . . . not die," Gordy reasoned. "We give him what he needs to feel better, and then we send him back to Greenland."

"But to do that, you would have to talk with Sasha's mom," Adilene said. "And she wants to arrest you."

"And she won't be at B.R.E.W. Headquarters," Gordy's mom added. "She'll be with the Vessel, but we don't have any idea where that is."

"It'll have to be somewhere highly guarded," Zelda said. "With more protective wards than you can count."

Max started chuckling. He had slouched down on the porch, his hands folded across his stomach.

"What are you laughing about?" Adilene asked.

"I was just thinking about when Sasha's wards sent me fishing," Max said. "That was awesome. I wish I could remember how it felt."

Gordy's eyes widened. "Mom, Sasha told me that the wards protecting her house were even stronger than the ones protecting B.R.E.W." At the time, Gordy had thought Sasha was trying to show off, but now he wasn't so sure. "And Max did end up in the middle of Swinton Lake when he tried to sneak into Sasha's party uninvited."

His mom stopped and cocked an eyebrow. "That would be a bold move, keeping the Vessel at her own house, but I wouldn't put it past that woman."

"None of us will be allowed to get close to the house without permission," Zelda said. "And I don't think Talia's going to just open the door for us. Not while she's performing an ExSpongement on your father."

"Maybe we could sneak in," Gordy suggested, the formulation of a crazy idea beginning to percolate in his mind.

Max scoffed. "You just reminded everyone about Sasha's wards, remember? There's no sneaking in the front door."

"That may be true." Gordy grinned and looked at Adilene. "But I'm pretty sure my best friend here has something that could help."

CHAPTER

45

Harper Hood Lane gave off an unsettling vibe. Most of the mansions had their outside lights extinguished, save for one motion-detecting bulb above the garages, the windows reflecting moonlight like square-shaped eyes gazing down upon the SUV.

Priss pulled off to the side of the road a few houses away from the Brexils and shut off the engine. Gordy's mom tucked vials into various belt loops and the pockets of her blue jeans. Her satchel was too big and bulky for a stealth operation, and she intended to go in as quietly and discreetly as possible. Zelda sat next to Gordy, arming herself, only the potions she selected were the type that could blast bricks from the walls.

"Okay, kiddo," Gordy's mom said, peering over the top of her seat. "We're going to form a circle, and you'll stay in the middle, right?"

"Right," Gordy said. "How will I see you?"

"Just follow our voices," Aunt Priss instructed. "We'll

try to stick together, and if we need to, we have Cadence's keystone that we can use to see each other."

"Perhaps I should take that," Zelda suggested. "That way you can keep hold on each other without worrying about me."

Gordy's mom nodded and handed Zelda the rock. She then reached back and squeezed Gordy's hand. "You won't throw any potions unless you have to, deal?"

"How will I know when I have to?" he asked.

"When all of us are either dead or disabled," Zelda answered. "That would be the perfect opportunity for you."

While he had plenty of potions at his disposal, Gordy, like his mother, wasn't going to take his satchel. He equipped himself with some Purista Powder, another Torpor Tonic, and a mini bottle of Detection Spray. Should he chance to come upon a Dire Substance inside the Brexils' home, which was a definite possibility, the spray could come in handy. Gordy also held on to Adilene's vial of Silt, though only a couple of drops remained. His mom had Cadence's bottle, and between the two of them, they had just enough potion to get onto the property and past the wards. Gordy had no idea how long they would remain invisible, but a single drop of Silt couldn't amount to much.

After taking Max and Adilene home, even though they fiercely protested not being there, Bolter took the Subaru and transported Cadence and Carlisle—still securely tied up—to Tobias's farm, where they would remain until Bolter got word from Gordy's mom that all was well. If they were successful in finding Mezzarix, Gordy needed to be there along with his Clasping Cannikin to help his grandfather survive. That is, if they found him in time.

"Do we drink this, then?" Priss asked, eyeing the vial of Silt.

Gordy nodded. "There needs to be enough for all of us."

Gordy's aunt dabbed a drop of the liquid onto her tongue. When she closed her mouth, Priss disappeared. It was as though someone had turned off a light and blinked Priss out of existence. The same thing happened with his mom and Zelda and finally with Gordy. The four of them exited the car, quietly shutting the doors behind them.

Being invisible was weird. He didn't feel different, but Gordy could see right through his hands as though he were a phantom come back from the dead. Staying between his mom and Priss without actually seeing them was almost impossible. Then he felt a hand reach out and latch on to his arm, and he breathed a sigh of relief.

"It's going to be all right," he heard his mom whisper. "We're going to get in, save your grandpa, and get out."

"I know, Mom," he said, though he thought his heart might explode.

The front door to the Brexils' home opened without a hitch. It hadn't even been locked, and Gordy didn't feel the tug or pull of protective wards trying to push him away. Entering the grand hallway, he peered into an adjoining living room just off the stairs. Empty. The kitchen was empty too, and so was the study, the dining room, and both of the main-level bathrooms. There was a bedroom at the end of the hallway, and bluish light glowed from the slit beneath the door.

Gordy held his breath, remembering that was the master bedroom, but as they approached the door, the bluish light flashed, and the sound of a television drifted out from the room. Principal Brexil was probably watching his evening shows. So where were the others? Where were Sasha and Madame Brexil?

Gordy's mom suggested going upstairs, but Priss adamantly refused.

"They're not like you," Priss whispered. "They wouldn't keep a lab upstairs."

"She's right," Gordy chimed in, remembering his conversation with Sasha. "The Brexils' lab is in the basement." If Madame Brexil had hidden the Vessel down there, it was no wonder they hadn't been allowed to brew in the lab. "But there are more wards surrounding it. Powerful ones." Earlier, Adilene had explained what she understood about the Silt and how once they passed beneath the shield of the protective wards, they could remain there even after the Silt's spell wore off. "We have to hurry."

Gordy felt his mom draw close to his ear. "Stay here, and we'll come get you if you're needed. I don't know what to expect down there, and until we clear the room, I need you to stay put and out of sight. I don't care that you're invisible. Don't enter any rooms or touch anything. Understood?"

Gordy nodded, but of course his mom couldn't see the action. "I'll stay put," he replied.

He heard them softly walk away, leaving him alone in the hallway. After a few moments, a door opened upon a flight of stairs leading down into the basement. For a faint moment, Gordy could hear footsteps on the stairs, but then the door closed, snuffing out all other sounds.

The Brexils' home was big enough that the stairs might have stretched deep into the ground. Gordy wandered over to look at the row of fancy family pictures lining the hall that he had noticed the night of the party. He looked at the images of Sasha gradually aging with each passing portrait. She *was* kind of cute, Gordy thought. But mean and snobby and full of herself. One of the family portraits leaned crookedly on the wall. Gordy considered straightening it but talked himself out of it. He wasn't supposed to touch anything or go into any room.

But that picture wasn't the only one that was crooked. Several of them were tilting on their hooks, and beneath the picture closest to the Brexils' bedroom was a dark, black scuff on the wall, like the kind left by dress shoes on a gymnasium floor. Gordy knelt down and rubbed his thumb against the mark. A rubbery substance came off onto his skin, and he frowned. It looked like that scuff had happened only recently.

Then Gordy heard something that made the invisible hairs of his invisible arms stand on end. It was the muffled sound of someone trying to call out, and it was coming from the other side of the bedroom door. Gordy straightened and looked toward the door leading to the basement. He didn't know if he should go get his mom or just leave well enough alone. They were about to take down the Chamber President, at least temporarily, but the muffled sounds had grown louder, more desperate. Perhaps it was just coming from the television, but Gordy didn't think so. By the way the portraits hung, crooked on the wall, it looked as though there had been a struggle in the hallway.

Unable to resist any longer, Gordy crept forward and slowly twisted the bedroom door open.

Principal Brexil and Sasha both lay on the floor, along with two other men wearing suits. All of them were bound and gagged. The two men in suits appeared to be unconscious. Sasha had tears in her eyes as she tried to wriggle free from the ropes. Neither of the Brexils had noticed the door open.

Gordy almost ran over to help them. Then he remembered he was invisible, and he didn't think that would go over too well with the Brexils. As quietly as he had entered the room, Gordy stepped back out into the hallway.

Why are they tied up? He shook his head in confusion. Madame Brexil had brought Mezzarix to her home. She had the Vessel. She was in charge! Why would she tie up her own husband and daughter? And who were those other two men? If they were Elixirists from B.R.E.W., there to assist the Chamber President with the ExSpongement, then why were they unconscious? Then it dawned on Gordy.

"Someone else is here!" he whispered.

No longer worrying about keeping quiet, Gordy raced down the hall and saw to his horror that the door to the basement was standing wide open. He remembered his mom and Aunt Priss had closed it behind them when they had gone down. Without any hesitation, and sick with anxiety, Gordy bounded down the steps toward the lab. A thick white mist gathered at his feet and swirled along the floor, lapping at Gordy's legs as he passed through it. Bright blue light shone from beyond the opened door at the end of the corridor, but Gordy kept running, straight through the mist and right into the room. He didn't stop until hands closed around his arms.

"Last one to the party, but the one everyone came to see!" a man announced from behind Gordy.

Before Gordy could react, the man with white, fluffy hair pried the potions from his fingers and forced him into the room. Gordy's mom, Aunt Priss, and Zelda, no longer invisible, all sat in wooden chairs, their hands tied behind them, no sign of their potions anywhere. Beside them, also tied up, was Madame Brexil, her head bowed in defeat.

In the center of the room was a pedestal, but instead of the Vessel, the keystone had been placed there, casting magnified blue light and revealing everyone in the room.

And lying on the floor, curled into a ball and surrounded by frothy mist, was Gordy's grandpa, Mezzarix.

46

Hang on, old friend," the pudgy man with the white hair said to Mezzarix. "Help is on the way. Come now, boy, don't be a stranger." His Irish accent sounded oddly familiar, and Gordy figured out at once that this man had to be Ravian McFarland, Tobias's father.

Ravian forced Gordy to his knees next to his mom's chair.

"I ran out of seats, I'm afraid," Ravian said. "I hope you don't mind playing the gentleman for now."

Strewn about the floor were pieces of glass and a slurry of spilled potions from busted vials. Gordy wasn't sure how it all had gone down, but there was proof of a skirmish before Ravian had somehow subdued his mom and the others.

The Brexils' lab looked like something straight out of an epic fantasy movie. Mossy walls, ancient oak fixtures, and a bejeweled sarcophagus lying in one corner of the room. Gordy wondered if that box contained any mummified remains; memories of his last encounter with Bawdry made him shudder. Resting on the table were two identical jars of gray, gloppy liquid. The Clasping Cannikins, one belonging to Gordy, the other to his grandfather.

"Where did this stuff come from?" Gordy asked, raising his hands above the floor as tendrils of mist reached for him like ghostly fingers.

"Like that, do you?" Ravian asked. "Ancient family recipe. I've found that while you may be invisible to my eyes, you can't hide from the mist."

Having Cadence's keystone rigged up like a spotlight had definitely helped as well, but how had Ravian taken possession of it?

"We were ambushed," Gordy's mom muttered. "I don't know how he knew we'd be here, but Ravian was waiting for us."

Aunt Priss spat on the floor. "Our mistake was trying to help Mezzarix. We should have never come here."

"Oh, don't be so hard on yourselves." Ravian pressed a hand to his chest. "You did the right thing. Your dear old dad is about to kick the bucket, and he would have, too, had you not arrived in the nick of time."

Mezzarix groaned from the floor.

Gordy's mom leaned toward Madame Brexil. "Is your family all right?"

Madame Brexil glanced up, her jaw clenched. "How would I know?"

"They're okay," Gordy said. "They're tied up in the bedroom, but they're not hurt."

Relief filled Madame Brexil's face, but followed closely by a sudden burst of anger. "Why are you in my home?" she demanded. "You've endangered my daughter, and you are interfering with my duty as Chamber President!"

"You don't understand the extent of Mezzarix's condition," Gordy's mom said. "We came here to make sure he made it back to his Forbidden Zone. An ExSpongement would kill him."

"One less Scourge to worry about," she muttered. "One less problem for the Chamber. And how did you even know my intentions? B.R.E.W. must have spies on every floor."

"We read your announcement," Priss said. "If you wanted to keep that a secret, you should've never sent an email."

"What email? What announcement?"

"Are we finished with the banter?" Ravian asked. He turned to Gordy. "Now, son, stick out your hand and be brave."

Gordy winced in surprise. "What are you going to do?"

"I'm going to give your grandfather a boost of energy so he can survive the next while. And then it's nighty-night for all of you—after Madame Brexil leads us to the Vessel, of course."

"I'll never show you," she said. "That much I can guarantee."

Ravian grinned. "We'll see." He picked up one of the Clasping Cannikins from the table and brought it toward Gordy. "This will be tedious and painful, but it is necessary."

"Keep your hands off my son!" Gordy's mom threatened.

Mezzarix groaned again, his body jerking, his gray hair sopping wet with sweat.

"Wait any longer and we'll all be attending a funeral. Is that what you want?" Ravian asked. "I don't suspect so. Now, hand please."

Gordy looked at his mom and then down at Mezzarix. He extended his hand toward Ravian. In one fluid motion, Ravian grasped Gordy's wrist and punctured his index finger with the end of a sharp blade. Gordy recoiled from the instant twinge of pain. A few drops of blood dripped from his finger into the jar.

Ravian returned to the table, where a small metal cauldron had been set up next to a Bunsen burner. As Ravian went to work concocting a potion, throwing in ingredients that made the cauldron whistle and steam, Gordy looked up at his mom. She was crying, her cheeks streaked with tears.

"It's okay." Gordy held up his finger. The blood had already started to congeal. "It doesn't hurt."

"This was not how I wanted it to go," she said. "Not with Ravian, and not at such a heavy cost."

Madame Brexil leaned forward, glaring at Gordy. "You

came here to set Mezzarix free. One of the most dangerous Scourges to have ever lived will walk out of here because of you."

Why did she have to be so difficult? Wouldn't she have done the same thing for a member of her own family? Gordy looked away from her, his focus drifting over to where Zelda knelt quietly, her eyes closed as if in tranquil meditation. No one had any satchels or potions. Never had Gordy seen his mom so vulnerable. And then, like a whisper in his ears, Gordy heard Zelda's high-pitched voice squeaking instructions from his previous training session.

One day, you will find yourself in trouble. You will be alone and without the use of your precious satchels.

Gordy's eyes flashed toward the bits of potions scattered about the floor. Orange and blue liquids, smashed pieces of cork, powders, tinctures, and tonics all blending together. Their ingredients, having been spent in battle, were useless. Gordy looked to his right and saw an herb-drying rack nearby and several clusters of sneezewort and honeysuckle stems. A thought struck him.

Could he Blind Batch something out of all these spoiled substances?

He had done it before, when the situation needed it. Once, out of desperation, Gordy had mixed together Blogu and Oighear Ointment and made an Ice Ball that took out Bawdry the mummy. If only he had access to a cauldron. Potions needed fire to blend and mix. Without it, the magic wouldn't take.

Zelda's words of instruction once more entered his mind. *You may not even have access to a fire source. The only thing standing between you and your freedom is the notion that you don't have what you need at your disposal.*

Ravian had neglected to tie Gordy up, whether on purpose or by accident; it made no difference. Gordy could use his hands. He could make something that might work.

Ravian finished bustling around the workstation, and he turned and knelt beside Mezzarix, who lay dormant on the floor, hardly breathing. Ravian drew blood from Mezzarix's finger and added it to the second jar of now-agitated liquid.

Mezzarix gasped, taking in a deep, raspy breath. Then he began to move, slowly at first.

"There we go, Master Rook." Ravian coaxed Mezzarix up into a sitting position. "Take all the time you need."

While Ravian rubbed Mezzarix's shoulders, Gordy closed his eyes and reached out his hands. Raking them across the floor, he encountered an oily substance, hot and acidic. His fingers tingled. *Coral snake venom.* That was one of the key ingredients in a Latvian Dunka Draft, one of Priss's specialties. Gordy dragged his fingers toward him and absentmindedly broke off a sprig of sneezewort from the drying rack. He spat into his hands and rubbed the venom and herb together. Nostrils flaring, taking in the scents and smells of the lab, he reached out again. Sharp pieces of sticky glass scratched his skin, and he found traces of black rat tail and clubmoss, both used in brewing a Funnel Formula. As he added the two new ingredients, the greasy mixture began to fizzle.

From somewhere outside his consciousness, Gordy could hear his mom whispering, trying to get his attention. She would make him stop in fear of hurting himself or others in the lab, but Gordy could see it all in his mind. He didn't know exactly what he was making but knew it would work.

The five ingredients stuck to his hand, and he could feel the mixture trying to change. He needed one more critical component for his potion. He had liquid and herb, and chemicals from the caustic clubmoss, but he needed a mineral to combine with the other elements.

One last time, Gordy reached out and felt along the floor, discovering the granular substance mortaring the stones together. He sensed limestone and sand, which should do the trick, and added it to his potion.

Suddenly, his fingers blazed with light.

Gordy opened his eyes and looked around. The women were staring at him, wearing expressions of confusion and worry, except for Madame Brexil, who looked outraged. None of them were talking.

Mezzarix sat hunched over on the floor, mumbling incoherently to Ravian. And then the Irishman finally noticed what Gordy had been up to.

"Have something to say to me, do you, boy?" Ravian's voice purred like a cat.

Heart racing, as it had been doing throughout the

entire bizarre brewing process, Gordy leveled his eyes on Ravian and stuck out his hand.

"Just this," Gordy said as a bright orange chain shot from his fingers.

Ravian tried to scream, but the chain coiled around him, constricting like a python. It wove under his arms and around his legs, wrapping him to where he could no longer move a muscle. Gordy sprang to his feet, fearing that the chain might be molten hot. He hadn't intended to kill Ravian. But then the coils momentarily flashed brighter before settling and becoming charcoal in color, hardening into an unbreakable metal.

"I didn't see that coming," Ravian grunted, steam wafting up from the cooling coils.

"How on earth did you do that?" Gordy's mom asked as he cut away the ropes from her wrists.

Gordy was still buzzing from his concoction. He stared down at his hand, a faint reddish glow lingering on his fingernails. Had he really just shot a blazing chain from his fingertips? Did that mean, completed training course or not, Gordy was a full-blown Elixirist?

"I don't know," he said. "I just threw something together."

His mom pulled him into an enormous hug, and Aunt Priss joined in.

Zelda stood away from the group, shaking her head. "That was impressive," she said. "You used your body heat instead of a cauldron to supply the necessary fire element."

"I guess." Gordy hadn't done any of it on purpose. It had been instinct. Like magic.

As the ropes fell from Madame Brexil's chair, the Chamber President sprang to her feet and hurried over to the brewing table. After collecting a couple of potion vials, Gordy heard the high-pitched chirp of electronic buttons being mashed on a security pad, followed by a pneumatic hiss. A section of the table began to separate and rise up. Silvery light poured out, revealing the Vessel.

Wordlessly, Madame Brexil grasped the handles of the powerful potion and moved around to face Mezzarix.

"What do you intend to do with that?" Aunt Priss demanded.

"Stay where you are!" Madame Brexil held out a bottle threateningly. "No more impeding my business. I intend to do what I brought him here for in the first place. He will be ExSponged and then banished to a new location. Upper Siberia sounds cold enough, don't you think? And you will have zero access to his whereabouts. No more leniency from the Chamber."

"You can't just change his Forbidden Zone." Gordy's mom raised her voice. "You have to follow the proper procedures. And if he has no way of brewing simple potions to keep him warm, he'll never survive in those frigid temperatures."

"Well, then, perhaps he should've made better life choices." The Chamber President's eyes flashed. "If there are any further disruptions, I will extend the same punishment to all of you!"

Aunt Priss froze in her attempt to reach for her satchel perched on top of one of the apothecary tables.

"You don't have the authority to ExSponge any of us,"

Gordy's mom said. "You will be breaking our laws. There aren't witnesses or documentation."

"There are witnesses," she spat. "They're upstairs, tied up, I'm assuming. Documentation is just a formality and something I can attain easily enough once work resumes at B.R.E.W. I will have no trouble convincing the Chamber of your involvement with the Scourges, so don't test me! I'm in no mood for games. All of you will be arrested. I'll personally see to it that you're punished to the full extent of the law. It's over, Wanda. You've dragged your whole family through the muck, and now you'll pay the consequences. And I do have the authority. I'm the Chamber President!"

Madame Brexil produced a long glass cylinder, etched with golden symbols, from inside her suit coat. Mezzarix still had his hands pressed against his knees, his head somewhat bowed, but he managed to lift his chin high enough to gaze at Madame Brexil.

"Get on with it, then," he said, his voice weak. "This has been a waste of a perfectly lovely Saturday evening."

Madame Brexil offered Mezzarix a thin smile and then nodded curtly. "By the power vested in me as Chamber President of B.R.E.W.—"

"Mom!" Gordy stared at his mother, wondering when she would do something to stop this. He didn't have time to whip up another Blind Batched potion to help. Gordy's mom and aunt both bore expressions of defeat. They didn't have their potions either, and they knew they couldn't defy the Chamber President. Not while she had command of the Vessel.

"Don't interrupt!" Madame Brexil hissed at Gordy. "In front of these witnesses, I hereby declare you, Mezzarix Rook, ExSponged." She dipped one end of the cylinder into the Vessel, squeezing up a portion of the seething liquid through a yellow sponge. Then she carefully placed the Vessel on the counter and stepped toward Mezzarix.

Gordy's grandfather lifted his head all the way up and closed his eyes. He wore a faint smile of contentment as the Chamber President approached him with the dropper.

Suddenly, Madame Brexil reared back as a small bottle shattered against her chest and dark-green vines wrapped tightly around her midsection. She grunted with discomfort and surprise, her enraged eyes darting around the room, searching for the source of the potion. They settled upon Zelda, who stood near the back of the room, her hand still extended from having thrown the Vintreet Trap.

"What have you done?" Madame Brexil demanded. "You will be banished. You will be ExSponged. You will be—" But the vines cut her off, nestling between her lips and stopping her from saying anything more.

"I think we've all heard enough from you," Zelda squeaked, shaking her index finger down at the wrapped-up Chamber President.

Gordy's mouth dropped open. He didn't know all the rules and statutes of B.R.E.W., but attacking the Chamber President had to be a bad idea!

"You shouldn't have done that," Gordy's mom told Zelda, gesturing down at Madame Brexil.

Zelda giggled and pinched Mrs. Stitser's cheek. "I take full responsibility for my actions. And although I will no doubt be on the run, I don't believe Mrs. Brexil will pose much of a problem."

"Thank you for helping our father, but you haven't thought this through, Zelda," Aunt Priss said. "All of B.R.E.W. will be notified of your actions. They'll come after you."

"B.R.E.W." Zelda sighed and looked at the ceiling. "I don't think so."

There seemed to be no getting through to the quirky Elixirist. Zelda acted as though she had just smashed a Vintreet Trap on a practice dummy.

"I'll take Dad to the airport and escort him to Greenland," Gordy's mom said. "Priss, you stay here and keep Ravian secured."

"What about me?" Gordy asked.

"You shouldn't be hanging around here any longer than you have to. I'll call you a cab," Priss said. "They can take you out of town, and Bolter can meet you at the rendezvous point."

Madame Brexil grunted, trying to bite through the section of vine muffling her voice.

Gordy's mom glowered down at her. "Zelda will call the members of the Chamber tonight and tell them what

Talia was doing. We'll testify against her, and we'll get the support of every faction of B.R.E.W."

Zelda casually cleared her throat. "I'm sorry, Wanda, but I don't think I'm going to be doing any of that."

"Yeah, that's a bad idea," Priss agreed. "She just attacked the Chamber President. She won't have much opportunity to speak here. We'll need to make the call from a safe location."

"I don't think you understand," Zelda said. "I'm not going anywhere with any of you."

"What are you talking about?" Gordy's mom asked.

Zelda sighed. "Oh dear. This next part might be difficult for the three of you to take. Perhaps you should sit down." She pulled a spray bottle from her satchel and spritzed Gordy's mom right between the eyes. Mrs. Stitser stiffened and then fell backwards into her chair. Gordy barely had time to get out of the way before his Aunt Priss suddenly toppled next to them, collapsing into her seat, her legs rigid.

"This shouldn't even pinch." Zelda batted her eyelids at Gordy before firing off a jet of ice-cold potion into his face as well.

The padded chair smacked against his rear end and his arms dangled uselessly at his side. Unable to move, but still conscious, he watched as Zelda helped Mezzarix to his feet.

"I was beginning to worry you had forgotten," Mezzarix

said, leaning on the short woman's shoulders for support. "Always one for the dramatic."

"I would've acted sooner, had Gordy not confuzzled me so," Zelda replied.

Mezzarix turned and beamed down at Gordy. "You're quite the skilled artisan, my boy. You've grown in leaps and bounds and have made me very proud." He glanced over at Gordy's mom and Priss, both of whom sat gawking at him. "Don't give me that. You've known me your whole lives. You must have known I'd have one last trick up my sleeve. Oh, but don't come down too hard on Zelda." He clicked his tongue and squeezed Zelda's shoulders. "She's been a good friend to you and a faithful companion. You can't blame her for seeing the inevitable fall of B.R.E.W."

Gordy blinked, dumbfounded. All this time, Zelda had been working with Mezzarix? As he tried to process this, the pieces of the puzzle started fitting together. Zelda had been Gordy's trainer at B.R.E.W., and she had been the one to bring him back his satchel after the attack at headquarters. Gordy knew that the Clasping Cannikin had not been in his possession prior to that. Zelda had planted it on him.

She had also convinced Gordy's parents to let him come along in the hopes of finding and helping Mezzarix in time. Gordy remembered how confused the Chamber President had been about the mention of her email. Zelda must have fabricated the entire announcement. Gordy's eyes moved to the keystone casting the blue light. Zelda had been holding that when the fight began. She had betrayed all of them.

"I think we've worn out our welcome," Mezzarix said, winking at Gordy. "I expect great things from you, Gordy. And as for you two, my daughters"—he stared down at them—"I think it's high time you take some fatherly advice from me. I will refrain from executing my plan for a while, but I can't promise much more than that. Get out of town. Get as far away from B.R.E.W. as you can, and take your family into hiding. Don't try to save the day. I'll know if you follow me, and I won't be as forgiving next time. This will be my only warning to you. I'm proud of all that you have become, but I never want to see your charming faces ever again. Understood?" He grinned. "Good." Mezzarix then turned to Ravian McFarland, who was still wound up tightly in chains.

"Well done, old friend. I can safely say that worked better than I could have hoped," Ravian said. "Do you mind? I find myself in a bit of a bind."

Mezzarix fixed him with a pouty expression. "I'm afraid I don't have much time to tinker with this newfangled potion my grandson has so expertly concocted. You understand, don't you?"

"What? But . . ." Ravian stammered. "You can't just leave me here like some doltish diggory dock. I saved your life!"

"And I thank you from the bottom of my heart." Mezzarix bowed reverently. "But time is of the essence. You know this cause of ours is far greater than either one of our singular wishes. We have to look past our own inconveniences and think about the bigger picture."

"Bigger picture?" Ravian blurted. "I've been captured! I'll be banished!"

Mezzarix raised his eyebrows. "Ah, now perhaps I can help with that. Banishments are hereby outlawed by my decree. You feel better already, don't you?"

Ravian's eyes looked as though they might pop from their sockets.

"I'm only kidding, you numbskull." Mezzarix glanced at Zelda. "Do you have something to break this poor soul free from his current state of entrapment?"

Zelda brandished her belt and wiggled her fingers over a couple of vials teeming with volatile substances. Ravian looked relieved until he recognized one or two of the potions at her fingertips. For a moment, it appeared as though he might have preferred remaining chained.

Mezzarix moved toward the counter and collected the Vessel while Zelda squatted down and pried the Ex-Spongement cylinder from Madame Brexil's fingers.

The Chamber President tried to yell, but the vines had nestled too tightly in her mouth.

"Now, where were we?" Mezzarix gnawed on his lip and then extended one long finger. "Oh, yes, that's right. Talia Yasmine Brexil, by the power vested in me as sole possessor of the Vessel, I hereby proclaim you"— Mezzarix leaned forward and pressed the spongy end of the glass cylinder against her forehead—"ExSponged."

Madame Brexil, the former Chamber President of B.R.E.W., stiffened beneath the sizzling drops of the potion, and then she lay perfectly still.

48

The sunrise blazed bright gold and vibrant pink, and if Gordy hadn't known any better, he would've suspected Tobias had launched a specially prepared potion into the stratosphere. The circling birds had all flown away during the night, and the rain over the garden had finally stopped. From a distance, the farm looked perfectly normal.

It was early, well before six in the morning, but sleeping in at Tobias McFarland's residence was nearly impossible. Before long, the house bustled with the sound of Isaac and Jessica trying to dig their way to China through the sandbox. Priss and Bolter busied themselves with Tobias in the kitchen, brewing a variety of potions and lining the countertop with bottles and vials of every size and color.

Four days had passed since Mezzarix, Ravian, and Zelda had stolen the Vessel and vanished into the night, and so far, not a soul had appeared on Tobias's property asking about any of the Stitsers. After freeing Principal

Brexil and Sasha from their vines, Gordy, his mom, and Priss sped out of town. It had been too dangerous for them to even stop by the house to gather supplies.

Gordy's dad took the twins out back but stayed close to the house. Tobias had warned everyone that his booby traps were still active and that until he could go over the map of the property, no one was to leave the yard.

Gordy's mom sat at the dining room table, Bolter's brick mobile phone clamped to her ear, as she carried on an urgent conversation with one of her contacts.

"I understand that, Paulina, but you would be doing me a favor," Gordy's mom said into the phone, her voice heated. "I believe you owe me dozens of favors for saving your life more times than you can count. No. No, this would not be sanctioned by B.R.E.W. I no longer work for them, remember?" She sighed and glanced up, noticing Gordy standing in the dining room doorway. She offered him an exhausted smile and then closed her eyes. "Thank you, Paulina. Just those three, that's all. Of course. You know I'll keep my end of the bargain." She hung up.

"That wasn't Paulina Hasselbeck, was it?" Tobias asked, entering the room and removing a pair of rubber gloves from his hands. Sudsy liquid dripped from the fingertips of the gloves as though he had been washing dishes and not brewing a deadly effusion of Estonian Rebenemine Rub.

"How did you find her?" Priss asked, sliding into the room next to Tobias. "I didn't think her number was listed."

"It's not," Gordy's mom answered. "But we've kept in touch over the years, and Bolter's phone is surprisingly untraceable."

"Unbelievable!" Tobias shook his head, rubbing his eyes in feigned amazement. "In just one week, the woman I had always known to fly straight as an arrow has gone all crooked and rotten."

"Give me a break, will you? Paulina is sending agents to check on the Antipodes, Motuo, and McMurdo Station," Gordy's mom said, raising her eyebrows at Priss. "Her agents will remain there for the time being, just in case."

"Just in case what?" Gordy asked. Normally, he wouldn't have been able to be part of the conversation, but the situation had changed. Now, instead of talking in hushed voices whenever he walked by, Gordy's mom invited him to participate in all their meetings.

"Those are Forbidden Zones," Priss explained, "for some of the worst criminals your mother has ever exiled."

"Worse than Mezzarix?" Gordy looked at his mom.

"Worse for us, yes," she answered. "Your grandfather has had many opportunities to cause us harm, but he has chosen not to. I'm not sure if that's because he's run into trouble during his escape or if he's simply biding his time. I believe there's still hope to turn things around for him and for B.R.E.W."

She glanced down at the pages of notes she had scribbled during her phone call. Gordy could see numbers and dashes and knew they were coordinates, though he wasn't sure where they led.

"However, the moment he begins to tinker with the Vessel, we could all be in danger, and not just because he could reverse all that B.R.E.W. has established and managed over the years. I've made too many enemies as a Lead Investigator. Enemies who would stop at nothing to pay me back for the years I've taken from them."

Gordy didn't want to think about an army of evil Scourges trying to hunt down his family, but it was a real possibility now that Mezzarix had control of the Vessel.

"So that lady on the phone just now," Gordy said. "She's going to make sure the criminals don't escape?"

"Paulina. Yes, I believe she will. She was a former partner of mine. We spent seven years together on the force. And she'll also provide us with any information she discovers on the whereabouts of Mezzarix."

Gordy scratched his head, trying to understand. "If we're on the B.R.E.W. Most Wanted List, won't she get in trouble for helping us?"

His mom smiled. "Paulina Hasselbeck doesn't work for B.R.E.W."

"But you said she was your partner, and she has agents."

"There is more than one organization in the world that monitors potion making," Tobias said, suppressing a chuckle. "Honestly, Wanda, I never thought I'd live to see the day you teamed up with the Stained Squad."

Stained Squad? Gordy felt a tingle of excitement.

"I'm not teaming up with anyone." Gordy's mom fixed Tobias with a stern gaze. "I'm just keeping our options open. And unless you want us spending the next year crowding you out of your home, you're going to want their help as well. We have to take back the Vessel from Mezzarix and resume control of B.R.E.W., and we don't have the luxury of taking our time."

Gordy's mind whirled with the information that his mom's former partner now led a secret team of mercenaries.

As his dad and siblings came into the kitchen for break-fast, the conversation took a less serious tone, and Gordy took a break to go make a phone call.

"What up, bro?" Max's freckled face appeared too close to the phone. Gordy could hear the rumbling sound of the school bus and the noisy chatter of kids laughing and talking. "You haven't died yet, have you?"

"Yep, I'm dead," Gordy answered. "You're talking to my ghost."

"Well, your ghost looks way worse than you did when you were alive. Hey!" Max shouted as someone yanked the phone away. "That's my phone, Rivera!"

Adilene's face appeared, and she whispered something to Max. Max bellowed, but Adilene moved out of reach of his grabbing hands.

"Hi, Gordy," she said.

"You're riding the bus now?" Gordy asked.

"Yeah, it's the only time I get to talk with Max in pri-vate. There are too many people at school who could listen in. Plus, I don't know for sure, but I believe my house has been bugged."

Max laughed in the background. "It's not bugged. You're so paranoid!"

"No, that's a good idea. You guys need to be careful." Gordy wasn't sure if B.R.E.W. would go so far as to set up listening devices inside Adilene and Max's houses, but it was better that his friends stayed cautious.

After Gordy had filled them in on all that had happened back at the Brexils' house, they had agreed to become Gordy's spies at Kipland. Adilene was taking the mission seriously. Max—not so much.

"What have you heard so far?"

The image shook as Adilene and Max grappled with the phone. Gordy heard Max say a few words in Spanish; they may have been inappropriate words, but they also might have been random, everyday sayings as well. Instead of struggling, Adilene compromised, extending the phone out as far as she could to allow Max into the picture.

Gordy laughed, but he missed his friends. Four days didn't seem like much time to be away—family vacations had lasted longer—but Gordy had no idea when he would be able to hang out with them again. As long as he and his mom were fugitives from B.R.E.W., they wouldn't be dropping by the old neighborhood anytime in the near future.

"Sasha came back to school yesterday for the first time all week," Max said. "She's been asking about you."

"I bet." She probably wanted to douse Gordy with her

Ragaszto Ragout and permanently glue him to a wall. Not that he could blame her. If something like that had happened to his mom, he'd be angry too. "What does she want?"

"She told me to tell you that she has information that might be helpful if you decide to go looking for Mezzarix," Max said. "She believes you did the right thing back at her house and that her mom was way out of line."

Gordy scoffed. "You don't actually believe her, do you?" Madame Brexil had probably sent Sasha out looking for him. "I think you guys should stay away from her. Don't talk to her at all."

"That's not going to be easy, dude." Max smirked. "She came to my house last night and brought cookies as a peace offering."

"You didn't eat them, did you?"

"Of course not!" Max grinned awkwardly. "Why? What would happen if I ate them?"

"Maybe she's trying to feed you a potion to get you to reveal our hiding place." Gordy had always known that Max's stomach would end up being his worst enemy.

Max shook his head. "Nice try. There's not a potion she could make that would work. I slept the whole way there and the whole way back. My mind is like a dry-erase board wiped clean."

"Gordy," Adilene chimed in, her brow furrowing with concern. "I think Sasha's telling the truth."

For Adilene to think that about Sasha meant it could

be significant. Then again, maybe Gordy's friends had been Blotched. Maybe he couldn't trust anyone anymore.

"How is she going to help us find my grandfather?" Gordy asked. "He could be anywhere in the world."

"She told Max that after Madame Brexil became the Chamber President, she added a potion to the Vessel that made it possible to track its location," Adilene said. "I have this feeling about Sasha. It might be a good idea to give her a call."

"What kind of potion?" Gordy felt his pulse speed up in his throat. Was this for real? Could Sasha be telling the truth?

"She wouldn't tell us," Max said, sounding serious. "But she said she'll tell you."

"Yeah, right! Now I know this is a trick." Gordy looked away from the phone. He didn't want to snap at his friends, but they were being so naïve. Sasha was playing them both. "If she really does have a way to track Mezzarix, why doesn't she just give the potion to B.R.E.W. and let them hunt him down?"

"We don't know. She says she has her reasons and that you would understand," Adilene said. "Look, we're almost at the school, so we should go. Think about it, Gordy, okay? It couldn't hurt giving Sasha a call, just to hear what she has to say."

"Yeah, okay. I'll think about it."

"When will we see you again?" she asked. "It's not the same without you, you know?"

"I know." Gordy felt a twinge of sadness. "Maybe we can meet up soon at, like, a secret spot."

"Ah yeah!" Max said, pumping his fist. "Some place that serves waffles twenty-four hours a day."

Adilene playfully shoved Max's arm, and then they said goodbye.

CHAPTER

49

G ordy waited until almost everyone had fallen asleep before he crept into one of the bedrooms and borrowed Bolter's special phone from his satchel. After checking his own phone for her number, Gordy called Sasha.

"Hello?" Sasha asked, picking up after only one ring. "Gordy, is that you?" She sounded hopeful.

"Maybe," he said, struggling to keep his voice from cracking.

"Oh, good! I'm glad you called. How . . . how are you?"

"I'm fine, I guess. I've dropped out of school, in case you hadn't heard. It's not safe for me right now." Gordy wasn't trying to sound bitter, but it happened naturally. Gordy knew it wasn't Sasha's fault that his family was in this mess, but it was hard not to place some of the blame at her feet.

"I'm sorry about that. I really am. I didn't want any of

this to happen to you, honest!" Sasha was speaking fast, but in a whisper.

"You expect me to believe you?" Gordy asked, trying hard not to shout. "Your mom would have ExSponged us all. She told us that."

"You're right. I wouldn't believe me either. I treated you and your friends like garbage."

Gordy could hear sniffling. Was she crying?

"But my mom's different now. She can't brew anymore, you know? And it's changed her. She's not herself. She's . . ." Her voice broke off, and the phone became muffled, as though Sasha had covered the receiver with her hand. It stayed like that for almost a minute before her voice returned. "Look, it's not really a good idea for me to be on the phone too long. There are people from B.R.E.W. here going through all of our things."

"Why?" Gordy asked.

"They're searching for evidence. Ways to track you down. They know you're hiding somewhere. They just don't know the exact location. But they're going to find it, Gordy."

"Yeah, probably." Gordy's mom was already one step ahead though. They were planning on leaving for a new hideout within the week. "So, what did you want to tell me?"

"Max and Adilene told you already, right? I know a way to track the Vessel. There's a potion my mom created—"

"They told me," Gordy interrupted. "Why wouldn't you just tell B.R.E.W. and have *them* hunt down Mezzarix?"

"Because part of the recipe is missing. I don't know what happened to it, but half the page has been ripped, and only my mom knew how to complete it. But she can't remember anymore. She can't remember anything about potion making." More sniffling. Sasha's breathing became strained and rapid.

Gordy rubbed his forehead in frustration. He felt bad for Sasha, but why was she wasting his time?

"I'm sorry about your mom, but it wasn't us who did that to her," he said.

"I know! I don't blame you at all!"

"But without the full recipe, the tracking spell is useless," Gordy continued. "No one could complete the potion."

"You could," she answered at once.

"Me?"

"I watched you Blind Batch in my kitchen, and I saw you make that amazing potion at B.R.E.W. I've never seen anything like it before. I also heard about what you did in our lab and how you stopped Ravian McFarland without a cauldron and nothing but your hands! You could finish the tracking recipe. You could Blind Batch the rest and then use it to find the Vessel."

Gordy was at a loss for words. Now he understood why Adilene had believed her. Sasha sounded truthful and desperate. He felt goose bumps rising on his skin. Sasha made him sound like a superhero.

"I . . . I don't think I could—"

"I know you could!" Her voice sobered, and her tone changed to the bossy one Gordy had grown accustomed to hearing. "Don't act all humble, Gordy. It doesn't suit you. I know you can complete this potion, and you know it too."

Gordy swallowed. He felt somewhat frightened of Sasha, even though she was at least a hundred miles away. "Okay, let's say for a second that I could. Why would you just help me?" Gordy asked. "And don't say because you want to help restore order to B.R.E.W."

"You think I care about B.R.E.W.?" Sasha snarled. "They're treating us like outcasts. They've boxed up all our things. Taken away all our ingredients. Our lab is destroyed, and my mom has already been replaced. B.R.E.W. doesn't care about us. They care about keeping up their appearance to the Community, and they started by wiping the slate clean."

"Geez, okay. So, what's in it for you, then?"

"There's a way to overturn any action taken by B.R.E.W.," Sasha said. "Whenever a criminal's sentence ends, the Chamber has to remove their banishment, which they do with the Vessel."

"You think you can reverse your mom's ExSpongement, don't you?"

"Yes, I do. If you find the Vessel and help me cure my mom, then I'll make sure she drops all the charges against you and your family once she resumes her role as Chamber President."

Sasha fell silent, and Gordy's mind raced with the

possibilities. It made sense. If anything could reverse the effects of an ExSpongement on an Elixirist, it would have to be the Vessel.

"Okay," he said. "Tell me the recipe."

"I'm not going to just give you it over the phone and watch you run off and forget about me and my mom!"

"We wouldn't do that!" Gordy fired back.

"We do this in person or not at all. I will meet you, and then we will talk about how to get the Vessel back *together*. Do we have a deal?" Sasha asked.

"Uh . . ." Gordy wasn't sure he was ready to answer. He didn't think he knew how. "I don't—"

"Don't think about it; just go with your instincts," she said. "That's what got you here in the first place. And that's what's going to get all of us out of this mess in the end."

Gordy held his breath and felt as though his back were pressed against the wall. Did he really want Sasha working with him? Would his mom even allow it? There was no way they'd be able to meet on Tobias's farm. Gordy would have to travel into town, or maybe Sasha could wait for him at some spot in the Swigs. But Gordy had yet to venture deeper into the Swigs. What were they really? What would he discover hiding in the secretive areas not governed by B.R.E.W.?

"Well?" Sasha demanded. Gordy imagined her anxiously tapping her toe against the floor.

"Okay," Gordy said, letting out a long, slow breath. "I'll do it."

CHAPTER

50

Down below the main level of Tobias's farmhouse, in a room with four musty walls and where thick roots hung down from the ceiling like scraggly whiskers, Cadence and Carlisle Bimini sat on the floor, chained to the wall by manacles clamped around their ankles. At first, it had seemed cruel to keep them shackled, but it didn't take Wanda long to realize that locked doors had zero effect on the Biminis. Cadence had apparently ingested such a large amount of Silt over the years, the doors simply unlocked whenever she approached them.

There was no way of knowing how old the Biminis were, but Wanda had her suspicions that Cadence might easily be over one hundred years. She wore it well, though, moving about the confines of the small cell with a sort of pep in her step. And, without any warning, Cadence could assume the form of the younger girl whenever she wanted to. It unnerved Wanda to be carrying on a conversation and watching Cadence suddenly change from an ancient lady to an eighth-grader in a blink of an eye.

Carlisle never spoke. He never made eye contact with anyone other than Cadence, his mother.

Thus far, Wanda hadn't had much success gathering information from Cadence. She danced around questions, threw out insults whenever the mood struck her, and alternately shouted and glared witheringly at Carlisle for his lack of gumption.

However, on the evening of the fifth day following Mezzarix's escape, Cadence Bimini's demeanor took a drastic change.

Wanda set down two trays of food on the table near the center of the room and then lowered herself into one of the folding chairs. After several minutes, Carlisle pushed himself off the floor and walked timidly over to collect his meal. He carried the food to the far corner, ignoring the plastic utensils and opting rather to scoop up the tossed salad and spaghetti with his fingers.

Cadence didn't make any movement toward the table. She sat shivering in the corner of the room, eyes unfocused, skin bearing more than the usual number of wrinkles. Wanda watched her for a couple of minutes in silence, the only sound being Carlisle's smacking lips as he slurped up tomato sauce.

"You don't look well," Wanda finally said. She folded her arms and sighed, wondering if the conditions of the dingy cell were contributing to Cadence's diminishing appearance. It was too dangerous to relocate the Biminis anywhere else, though. Too high a risk of them escaping.

"I can make you a tonic that might cure those shivers." Wanda leaned forward in her seat. "Perhaps you should take the form of your younger self. You seem to fare better that way." She had no idea how Cadence's Silt worked, how it allowed the woman to alter her appearance at will, but there was no sense in spending her days in confinement suffering in her elderly frame.

"Can't," Cadence muttered, her voice weak and trembling. "No longer able to."

"Why is that?" Wanda asked.

The woman's eyes blinked rapidly, returning to focus. "Why do you think?"

"You've run out of Silt," Wanda answered.

Cadence nodded solemnly. "And my age is finally catching up to me."

"How old are you?"

A faint smile cracked the surface of Cadence's fissured lips. "It had never mattered before. Not until they passed that death sentence upon me."

"Who?" Maybe Wanda could squeeze a few answers from the mysterious woman.

"My people," Cadence said. "My Atramenti."

"These Atramenti—they live on your island?" Wanda asked. "This invisible island?"

"Not invisible." A fit of violent coughing overtook Cadence, but she barely had the strength to cover her mouth. Carlisle glanced up from eating, staring with his emotionless eyes at his mother. "Just hidden. Hidden from all. Hidden now from me, thanks to your father," Cadence said. "He betrayed me. He should've come back and taken me home. That was the deal. That was his promise. I kept my end of the bargain."

"You don't know much about Mezzarix," Wanda said. "That's not how he operates."

"Clearly, I made a mistake. Our ways are not your ways and haven't been for hundreds and hundreds of years. I should not have trusted your father."

"What about him?" Wanda nodded at Carlisle, who had half a dinner roll crammed in his mouth. "Why isn't he sick?"

"Carlisle's just a boy. A wee pup. He shows his true age because he never drank too much Silt." Cadence's eyes drifted over to her son, but she wore a look that might have been resentment. "I wouldn't allow it. Forbade him from indulging in our practices." She sneered, her eyes turning cold and dark. "He's hated me for it all these years, but look at him now. Young and spry and full of life."

Full of life? Wanda would hardly label Carlisle as young or spry. He looked to be maybe seventy years old, with a crooked back and plagued by arthritis. Who were these people? Where had they come from?

"Look, Ms. Bimini, we have the means to help you. Potions. Elixirs that can perhaps heal your condition. I'll bring you something right away."

"It doesn't matter," she said, rasping.

"I need your cooperation," Wanda continued as Cadence broke out in another fit of harsh coughing. "Help me understand more about your island and where to find it on a map."

Cadence finally succeeded in pressing her fist to her lips and stifling her horrible hacking. Tears oozed from the corners of her eyes, but instead of sobbing uncontrollably, the woman began to laugh. "No map exists. There's nothing to understand. It's not written in books or scrolls or on stones. The fountain cannot be found, except by those who found it first."

Wanda wiped her face with her hand, growing frustrated with Cadence's cryptic conversation. "What are you talking about?" she demanded. "What fountain?"

Cadence cleared her throat and gazed up at Wanda, her eyes twinkling in the dimly lit room. "The Fountain of Youth."

EPILOGUE

Seventy-seven kilometers due east of the Miami shores, the puttering ship *San Cristóbal* began to slow its diesel-powered engines. Fishing nets lay in massive heaps on either side of the boat, unused and unwound. The once clear, star-studded sky had been smothered by a thick blanket of storm clouds churning ferociously overhead. The bow of the boat dipped into the Atlantic, sending a spray of salt water, as the captain of the three-man crew suddenly killed the propeller.

"*El Maestro*, we may have found something," the Puerto Rican captain announced into the cabin's intercom. The other two members of the crew gazed through the window, hands gripping the guardrail.

A few moments later, a door opened from below and footsteps arose as Mezzarix Rook ascended the steps. Ravian McFarland stumbled after, followed closely by Zelda, who was clutching her stomach and grimacing in pain. Her complexion almost matched the color of her green hair, and her lips were pale but not from her favorite white lipstick.

Mezzarix moved into the cabin and held his hand along the length of his forehead, staring out into the ocean. A hauntingly bluish light cut through the darkness, and Mezzarix had to strain his eyes as rain began to shower down upon the ship.

"I don't see anything, do you?" Mezzarix asked Zelda.

Zelda made a sound like a busted carburetor and leaned against the wall, trying not to vomit.

"There's nothing on the instruments," the captain said. "But something is out there. The stone—she showed me."

"Are you certain?" Mezzarix glanced sideways at the captain, his eyes narrowed. He had no reason not to trust him. Captain Davila and his crew had been thoroughly Blotched and would be for as long as needed. The potion hadn't taken any time to brew either. Not now that Mezzarix owned the Vessel. "Show me." He turned back to stare through the glass as Ms. Bimini's keystone lit up the night.

The captain gestured for Mezzarix to join him at his side. The two men gazed through the window for several silent moments.

"¡Allá!" The captain raised his voice with excitement. He pointed a finger to a spot almost completely hidden along the horizon. "You see it, no?"

Mezzarix pressed his nose against the glass, growing frustrated with the almost blinding rain.

"I don't—" But he stopped short.

In the bluish light, drifting in and out of view as the waves of the ocean continuously toppled, a distant island had suddenly appeared.

GLOSSARY OF POTIONS

A compendium of both approved and unapproved potions and ingredients, as well as common terms used throughout the potion-making community. Locations in italics pinpoint the exact source of where B.R.E.W.'s most-elite Elixirists have worked tirelessly to discover key ingredients to specific potions.

Auditory Tablet—*Costa Rica*. Concoction contained in a capsule that gives the user the ability to hear conversations and communicate without requiring cell phones, walkie-talkies, or other means of vocal transmission. Depending on dosage, the effects of the Auditory Tablet generally dissolve within ten to fifteen minutes of consumption.

Banishment (Exiled)—Term used by B.R.E.W. officials for sending a convicted Scourge to a Forbidden Zone for an extended period of time. Banishment prevents the need to build and staff prisons while also keeping the convicted safely away from the innocent population. Banished Scourges live out their term of punishment in a safe and almost entirely brewing-free environment.

Blight Bomb—*Chernobyl, Ukraine*. An explosive and unpredictable potion used for crumbling walls and destroying buildings. Increases in strength if left unchecked and will eventually demolish an entire structure before being rendered benign. (Key ingredients: plaited nickel; feather grass; radioactive water.)

Burning Rubber Reduction—*United States of America, Indiana.* Putty-like substance that, when applied to a vehicle's tires, propels the motorist forward, often at breakneck speeds, without requiring pedaling. Steering is still necessary and recommended. (Key ingredients: American cockroach intestines; peregrine falcon feathers.)

Cacophonous Compound—*United States of America, Michigan.* The purpose of this substance is to create utter discord and discombobulation by filling a general space with random and overlapping noise. Sounds that may surface from use of this potion include, but are not limited to, chattering children, off-putting music, and malfunctioning appliances. (Key ingredients: Magicicada wings; crinkled aluminum; strawberry preserves.)

Certe Syrup—*Latvia.* Replicating potion that, when poured into a locked device, such as a doorknob or a padlock, will produce an exact copy of the fastening mechanism. Perfect for making a spare key in a pinch. (Key ingredients: yak butter; lauku tea; puff adder venom.)

Chamber President—Leader of B.R.E.W.'s Chamber of Directors and presiding officer within the Community. This individual has the power and authority to govern the ongoing practice of potion making.

Clasping Cannikin—*Origin Unknown.* Highly illegal device used to form a modified Blood Link between two relatives. This potion allows a banished potion master the freedom of venturing beyond the borders of his or her area of exile. Most Clasping Cannikins have a short lifespan and can carry harmful, even fatal, consequences if the individual does not return immediately to his or her Forbidden Zone before the potion expires. (Key ingredients: proboscis monkey snout; spotted filefish spine; chipped ferrite.)

Copen Warner—A well-known and respected distributor of brewing equipment throughout the Community. Copen Warner offers high-end options of Bunsen burners, heating elements, and an assortment of handcrafted cauldrons for only the most seasoned Elixirists. The company slogan is "Why limit yourself with less when you can brew with the best?"

Decurdler—*United States of America, Wisconsin.* Acid-reducing potion that lines the stomach with a temporary layer of cooling gel, at which point the consumer may ingest any substance without upsetting the stomach. (Key ingredients: jack pine bark; carrion beetle shells.)

Dentadura Draught—*Peru.* Used by South American Elixirists for an array of dental remedies. Various applications of the draught may cause teeth to soften, help prevent teething babies from biting, or even strengthen the user's molars to the point of crushing stone. (Key ingredients: alpaca milk; ginseng; acorns.)

Distractor Potions—*Origin Varies.* A type of ward used by Elixirists to avert the curiosity of outside eyes. The concoction causes basic confusion and redirection to where intruders find themselves suddenly interested in some other location. (Key ingredients: dogfish scales; shattered pieces of a kaleidoscope.)

Dunka Draught—*Latvia.* Gritty potion that, when released within the general area of an opponent, will strike the intended target repeatedly with a series of hooks, jabs, and uppercuts. (Key ingredients: sessile barnacles, tapioca pudding, tow-truck axle grease.)

ExSpongement—Term used to describe the process of permanently removing an Elixirist's ability to brew. There have been forty-seven known ExSpongements carried out since the formation of B.R.E.W., and though sentencing may be reversed, it is an extremely difficult practice requiring highly trained Elixirists authorized to use the Vessel.

Fire Rocket—*Poland.* Dangerously explosive potion used primarily in long-range battles. As the name suggests, it propels a missile-like projectile across long distances and, upon impact, will envelop the intended target with a blanket of fire. (Key ingredients: barberry pulp; thorn apple seeds; Lebanese sika plant kernels.)

Funnel Formula—*United States of America, Oklahoma.* When squirted from a pipette, this potion transforms an intended target, either living or inanimate, into a mini tornado. (Key ingredients: black rat tail; clubmoss; pickled sycamore seeds.)

Fusion Potion—General term for a potion that aids in the melding of inanimate objects with the essence of a living creature. They are controversial concoctions that require full clearance from B.R.E.W. prior to use.

Ke'oki Cordial—*United States of America, Hawaii.* Spongy potion that can turn any solid ground into a trampoline. (Key ingredients: triggerfish lips; plumeria petals; seven-year-old Spam.)

Kunci Cream—*Indonesia.* Cleverly crafted potion that is used to pick the lock of a closed door. This concoction operates quickly and quietly, all while maintaining the integrity of the locking mechanism. (Key ingredients: grated anoa horns; honeybee wings; coneflower petals.)

Mangle Potions—*Origin Varies*. These potions can be brewed in a variety of ways and are used by Dark Elixirists in battle. Each Mangle potion yields a specific result to a particular body part—mainly arms, legs, fingers, and toes. (Key ingredients: Lonomia caterpillar husk; hemlock; oleander; pokeberry stalks.)

Ogon Oil—*Russia*. An instant liquid fire generally used for heating in cold, damp environments where dry tinder and a primary fuel source are not readily available. (Key ingredients: musk deer tongue; melic grass.)

Philtering Loofah—Instrument used by Philters to remove both the remnants of a potion and the resulting effects of an ingested liquid from a victim. Commonly combined with a deadening substance such as Cannonball Lead or Clove Oil.

Projecting—A term used for the rare practice of temporarily passing an Elixirist's ability to concoct onto someone else who would otherwise be unable to brew on his or her own.

Ragaszto Ragout—*Hungary*. A sticky substance that adheres an intended target's hands, feet, or other body part to any surface for an extended period of time. Commonly used by B.R.E.W. Investigators during arrests and questioning. (Key ingredients: shattered blue jeremejevite; stonefly blood; rusted knitting needles.)

Rebenemine Rub—*Estonia*. A rupture potion sold and traded within the Swigs and frequently used as a trigger for a variety of deadly booby traps. This rub is one of the primary potions included on B.R.E.W.'s List of Outlawed Concoctions. (Key ingredients: steeped narcissus bulbs; sand lizard fangs; lynx nostril lining.)

Replication—Unlike the Restorative skill of duplicating a known potion through a recipe, the rare Elixirist practice of

Replication uses modified substances to imitate the effect and result of a potion with unknown origins. Few Elixirists possess this ability as it is both dangerous and unproven. Several noted Scourge banishments have been the result of a Replication gone wrong. (Key ingredients: Portuguese man-of-war tentacles; Andean clover honey.)

Sequester Strap—*France*. A chemically treated belt, band, or strap used to create a preventative ward specific to an individual. Commonly used as a means of punishment for unruly Drams. B.R.E.W.'s Chamber of Directors are the only ones with the proper authority to initiate a Sequester Strap. (Key ingredients: cassava; coypu claws; scorched neoprene.)

Sessizlik Serum—*Turkey*. A minor exploding potion that transforms into a thin, fabric-like substance, which then can be used to silence an opponent for a short period of time. Primarily used by Scourge members of the Turkish mafia. (Key ingredients: gray wolf whiskers; crumbled bauxite.)

Sloop Solution—*Portugal*. Specially contained potion that, when dropped directly into a body of water, transforms into a malleable syrup, which will expand and solidify into a durable board. The Sloop may be used as a small raft for a short period of time. (Key ingredients: fig juice; balsa sawdust.)

Smelte Sludge—*Denmark*. Gloppy, amber-colored potion used for melting solid substances into a sticky sludge. Works best on glass, crystal, and some porous stones. (Key ingredients: flawed opals; juniper berries; tail fluff of a European hare.)

Sottusopra Serum—*Slovenia*. A concoction that gives clarity and balance by constantly rendering the environment right-side up, no matter what angle the user might be standing in. Great for tumbling and handstands. This potion is the only known Elixirist concoction publicly added to the banned substance list by the International Olympic Committee. (Key ingredients: pureed radishes, cuttlefish fins, pink peppercorns.)

Swigs—Term to describe locations all over the world that act as trading posts for unsanctioned potion exchanges. Dealings within the Swigs are often illegal and rarely governed by B.R.E.W.

Wardbreakers—A controversial method of disabling wards or eliminating distractor potions from a protected area by using chemically modified insects. Beetles are the most common form of Wardbreaker, but any manner of insect can be used in a pinch, including moths, caterpillars, and cockroaches.

Writ of ExSpongement—Formal document issued by the Chamber of Directors that grants permission to ExSponge an individual. Not to be taken lightly, such a writ is virtually a death sentence to one's potion-making ability and has been a heated topic of debate for many years.